For Christopher, the graduate.
Now and always, I am proud of you.

TRIAL ON MOUNT KOYA

ALSO BY SUSAN SPANN

Claws of the Cat

Blade of the Samurai

Flask of the Drunken Master

The Ninja's Daughter

Betrayal at Iga

TRIAL ON MOUNT KOYA

A HIRO HATTORI NOVEL

SUSAN SPANN

SEVENTH STREET BOOKS®

AN IMPRINT OF PROMETHEUS BOOKS

59 JOHN GLENN DRIVE • AMHERST, NY 14228

www.seventhstreetbooks.com

Published 2018 by Seventh Street Books®, an imprint of Prometheus Books

Cover image © Creative Market
Cover design by Nicole Sommer-Lecht
Cover design © Prometheus Books

Inquiries should be addressed to
Seventh Street Books
59 John Glenn Drive
Amherst, New York 14228
VOICE: 716–691–0133 • FAX: 716–691–0137
WWW.SEVENTHSTREETBOOKS.COM

22 21 20 19 18 • 5 4 3 2 1

Library of Congress Cataloging-in-Publication Data

Names: Spann, Susan, author.
Title: Trial on Mount Koya : a Hiro Hattori novel / Susan Spann.
Description: Amherst, NY : Seventh Street Books, an imprint of Prometheus Books,
    [2018] | Series: A Shinobi mystery ; 6
Identifiers: LCCN 2018006388 (print) | LCCN 2018009968 (ebook) |
    ISBN 9781633884168 (ebook) | ISBN 9781633884151 (softcover)
Subjects: LCSH: Ninja—Fiction. | Samurai—Fiction. | Murder—Investigation—
    Fiction. | BISAC: FICTION / Mystery & Detective / Historical. | FICTION /
    Mystery & Detective / Police Procedural. | GSAFD: Mystery fiction.
Classification: LCC PS3619.P3436 (ebook) | LCC PS3619.P3436 T75 2018 (print)
    | DDC 813/.6—dc23
LC record available at https://lccn.loc.gov/2018006388

Printed in the United States of America

AUTHOR'S NOTE

Although the characters in this book are fictitious (even when based on historical figures), I have tried to portray the time and its people as realistically as possible.

Mount Kōya has been the heart and center of Shingon practice in Japan for over 1,200 years. It is among the most beautiful, peaceful, and sacred places on earth. Myo-in and its priests are entirely fictitious, but aside from creating an annex off the worship hall to hold the dead—which might or might not have actually existed in a Shingon temple at the time when this book takes place—I have otherwise endeavored to remain faithful to Shingon Buddhist architecture, doctrine, life, and practice as it existed on Kōya during the sixteenth century.

Since Japanese names and terms can be tricky for readers unfamiliar with the time and culture, I've included a cast of characters—and a brief glossary—at the back of the book, as well as more information about the *jusanbutsu* (thirteen Buddhist deities that play an important role in this adventure). Where present, Japanese characters' surnames precede their given names, in the Japanese style. Western surnames follow the characters' given names, in accordance with Western conventions.

Thank you for reading—I hope you enjoy the adventure!

CHAPTER 1

WINTER 1565

"I question your judgment, Hiro." Father Mateo looked at the sky, which should have burned with the fiery colors of a mountain sunset.

Instead, a menacing wall of greenish thunderclouds churned overhead.

"We can beat the storm to the temple." Hiro Hattori increased his pace and tried to ignore the angry meow that issued from the basket in his arms.

"That's not what I meant, and you know it." The Jesuit glanced back over his shoulder at the building on the ridge, now almost hidden by the massive cedars that lined the earthen road. "I'm worried for Ana's safety, not for ours."

He gestured to Hiro's basket. "How can we trust women too superstitious to allow a cat beneath their roof?"

"The nuns' refusal to harbor the cat had nothing to do with superstition." The basket shifted in Hiro's arms as Gato moved inside. "The *nyonindo* has a resident cat. A fight between their cat and ours could be considered an omen of bad fortune."

"Superstition." The Jesuit made a derisive noise. "Bad fortune is not decided by a cat fight."

Hiro smiled. "It is for the losing cat."

Father Mateo frowned.

"You simply disapprove of leaving Ana at the nyonindo," Hiro observed. "I told you before we came that women are not allowed on Kōya's summit."

"A man can understand a thing and still not like it," the Jesuit said. "Besides, they *are* on the mountain's summit. The women's hall stands right at the top of the trail."

"Women can come to the edge of the summit valley, but no farther." Hiro increased his pace again as a frigid wind blew past, heavy with the smell of an impending thunderstorm.

Just ahead, a six-foot wall of wood and stone, crowned by a roof of mossy bark, ran along the north side of the road. Beyond the wall, the sloping roofs of a Buddhist temple rose among the trees.

Father Mateo looked at the rows of towering cedars that lined the south side of the road. Not even the winter wind could rock their massive trunks, but, high above, their branches flailed, warning foolish travelers off the road.

"I thought you said this place had many temples," the Jesuit said. "I see just one."

"Most of them sit farther along the *kōya*—the shallow valley between the peaks, from which the mountain takes its name." Hiro fixed his gaze on the gate set into the wall a hundred feet ahead. Its weathered wooden planks were bound with iron.

"Why force the women to stay alone in the nyonindo?" Disapproval weighted Father Mateo's voice.

Hiro shrugged. "Shingon priests believe a female presence would defile the temples."

"What kind of holy men leave women vulnerable to attack?"

Hiro gave the priest a disbelieving glance. "What kind of man spends eight long hours climbing narrow mountain trails to attack a group of aging nuns?"

"Not all the women in the nyonindo are nuns. I saw a samurai woman there, and Ana—"

"A man so inclined could find vulnerable women in any city, town, or village in Japan—without the treacherous climb."

Father Mateo changed the subject. "Did your cousin mention the name of the priest we came to see?"

"His name is Ringa." Hiro appreciated the Jesuit's use of "cousin" rather than the name, despite the empty road. Few people knew that Hiro was a *shinobi* assassin, or that his cousin was Hattori Hanzō, infamous leader of the Iga ninja *ryu*. Hiro and Father Mateo had come to Kōya on Hanzō's orders, to deliver a secret message to another Iga ninja hiding in a temple on the mountain—but the fewer people who learned that truth, the better.

When they reached the roofed double gates at the temple entrance, Hiro rang a small bronze bell beneath a wooden plaque with hand-carved characters that read "MYO-IN."

Footsteps approached the gate, and it swung inward, revealing a Buddhist priest.

The priest wore a dark blue robe that fell to his ankles and, over it, a hip-length surplice of pale cloth embroidered with a five-petaled flower, the crest of the Buddhist temples on Mount Kōya. His shaven head made it difficult to judge his age precisely, though the breadth of his shoulders and his lack of wrinkles indicated a man on the younger side of middle age. His right hand gripped a bamboo staff that looked more like a weapon than a walking aid.

The priest's gaze lingered on Father Mateo, though otherwise he did not react to the sight of a foreign face. "Good evening. Have you business at Myo-in?"

Father Mateo bowed. "Good evening. We are pilgrims, seeking shelter for the night."

The basket shifted in Hiro's arms as Gato gave another angry wail.

"You brought a cat on a pilgrimage?" The Buddhist shifted his weight to the balls of his feet, the movement subtle but indicative of a man prepared to fight.

"We mean no harm." Hiro spoke slowly, stalling for time to invent a reasonable explanation. "The cat—"

"Belongs to a friend of mine," Father Mateo finished. "I accepted responsibility for its safety and, thus, had to bring it with me."

"You are no Buddhist," the priest remarked, with a nod to the wooden cross that hung around the Jesuit's neck. "Do foreign priests take pilgrimages as we Buddhists do? And what kind of pilgrimage brings a priest of the foreign god to Kōya's summit?"

"I heard about your sacred mountain, and wished to see it for myself."

"In winter?" He looked pointedly at Hiro's basket. "With a cat?"

Father Mateo tipped his head in acknowledgment. "A man cannot always choose the timing or the circumstances of a pilgrimage."

Hiro wondered whether the Jesuit had overcome his aversion to lies, or merely become adept at partial truths. In either case, the shinobi admired the answer.

"My name is Father Mateo Ávila de Santos." The Jesuit gestured sideways. "This is Matsui Hiro, my translator—"

"And guide," Hiro finished, before the Buddhist could grow suspicious of the Jesuit's clearly functional Japanese. "We hoped to shelter here tonight, if you have rooms available."

"Had you made arrangements elsewhere?" The priest considered the darkening sky. "The storm approaches quickly, but I should have time to escort you to your original destination before the rain begins."

"We have no previous arrangements." Hiro took a chance. "My relatives in Iga Province recommended Myo-in by name."

The priest's eyes narrowed. "Iga?" He stepped to the side and gestured for them to enter. "Regrettably, you have arrived too late for the evening meal, but I am certain Gensho-*san* can manage something if you have not eaten. We have no standard fee for rooms, but always appreciate a small donation, if you have the coins to spare."

Father Mateo bowed. "We will gladly pay for room and board."

The priest returned the Jesuit's bow but directed his words to Hiro. "My name is Ringa. Welcome to Myo-in."

CHAPTER 2

Hiro followed Father Mateo through the gates and into the temple's graveled court.

Stone lamps positioned around the yard illuminated the space, their flickering light unusually pale and weak beneath the sickly sky. Directly across the yard to the north, an irregular pond designed to mimic a natural lake was surrounded on one side by stands of carefully manicured maple trees. Now barren of leaves, their branches stretched like questing fingers over the still, dark water. Landscaped hillocks on the opposite side of the pond created the illusion of a distant mountain range.

A single-story building bent around the pond. Its wide, roofed entry faced the gate, and although the shutters along the wide veranda that encircled the building were closed and dark, the doors at the entrance to the hall stood open, revealing the glow of lantern light inside. Based on its size and location, Hiro recognized it as the temple's residential hall.

To the left, on the western side of the yard, an enormous *hondō*, or worship hall, extended its curving, painted eaves like a falcon offering shelter to its young. Three long, wooden steps rose up to the entrance, whose sliding double doors were large enough to allow six men to enter the hall abreast.

On the right side of the gate, against the wall, an open scaffold-style tower with a curving roof supported the temple's large bronze bell. Beyond the tower, on the eastern side of the temple grounds, stood a smaller worship hall, most likely used for secondary services. The tiles on its roof were dull from age, the rafters blackened as if from soot and smoke.

A gust of wind blew through the yard, rustling loose a last dead leaf from the trees that stood around the pond. It swirled down to float upon the surface of the water, curled edges pointing skyward like the prow and stern of a miniature boat set sail on a darkened sea.

Ringa locked the temple gates. "Please follow me."

He led them across the packed-earth yard to the building that bent around the pond, and stopped in front of the wooden steps leading up to the covered entry.

"We ask all visitors to leave their shoes on the shelves inside this door." Ringa gestured to a weathered wooden rack upon which pairs of shoes sat resting like faithful dogs awaiting their owners' eventual return. At the moment, the rack was mostly empty. "If you need to leave the building by another door, you will find temple sandals near the exits. Please feel free to use them during your stay at Myo-in."

Father Mateo bowed. "Thank you. We will."

After leaving their sandals on the rack, Hiro and Father Mateo followed Ringa up a single, interior step and onto the wooden floor of a narrow passage that ran around the perimeter of the residence hall. To their left, a row of sliding wooden shutters sealed the building against the coming storm.

On the opposite side of the passage, lightweight *shoji* separated the passage from the residence hall's interior rooms. A pair of braziers lit the hall, their flickering light illuminating paintings on the sliding paper-paneled doors: scenes of animals, Buddhist priests, and gods engaged in prayer and pilgrimage. Despite their fanciful subject matter, the monochromatic scenes were unusually lifelike; the figures' eyes appeared to follow Hiro as he passed.

A chill went up his spine.

Ringa took a lantern from a hook nearby and started down the passageway, still carrying his staff.

A shoji on his right slid open.

Father Mateo jumped in surprise. Hiro instinctively shifted Gato's basket to his left hand as the right slipped down to the hilt of his katana.

A pair of priests appeared in the opening. The older one looked middle-aged, with slender fingers and a patient face. Behind him stood a teenaged priest whose face bore a disfiguring burn that puckered his cheek and pulled his left eye downward. Although the shadow of a beard was visible along his jaw, his body retained the gangly awkwardness of youth.

Ringa bowed to the older priest. "Good evening, Kenshin-*san*. These men have come to spend the night. Can you spare Shokai to prepare their welcome tea and bring it to the guest room around the corner, at the far end of the hall?"

"Of course." The older priest bowed to Father Mateo. "Forgive me, but are you a *Kirishitan*? A priest of the foreign god whose emissaries have built a temple in the capital?" He spoke with the hint of a Kyoto accent.

"I am! I am Father Mateo Ávila de Santos, a Christian priest, from Portugal." In his excitement, the Jesuit completely forgot to bow—or to introduce Hiro—though the shinobi did not mind.

"I am Kenshin, the temple physician. I have always wished to meet a Kirishitan. Perhaps, when you have rested, you will share a cup of tea with me and tell me more about your foreign god."

"I would be honored." Father Mateo's exhaustion disappeared. "Please come now, and share our welcome tea."

Kenshin raised his hands in protest. "I could not impose, after your arduous journey up the mountain."

"Please, it is no imposition. I—we"—Father Mateo's gesture included Hiro—"would be honored."

Although he felt distinctly less than honored by the thought of sitting through another dissertation on the Jesuit's foreign god, Hiro smiled benignly. He was used to it by now, and hopefully the talk would not last long.

"Then I accept." Kenshin clasped his palms together, fingers extended in a gesture like the one the Jesuit used in prayer. "I will prepare your welcome tea myself."

"Thank you, Kenshin-*san*." Ringa continued down the hall with Hiro and Father Mateo.

He paused at the end of the building, where the passage made a sharp left turn. "The rooms for guests are down this way, beyond the rooms belonging to the priests of Myo-in. We ask that visitors observe respectful silence, to help maintain a meditative atmosphere."

Without awaiting a response, he led them down the hall. The floorboards creaked so loudly Hiro doubted anyone could meditate when people passed, no matter how respectful their intentions.

At the far end of the passage, near a latticed door that led out to the temple yard, Ringa stopped in front of a sliding door that bore a painting of a temple perched atop a mountain peak. "This is our finest guest room." He hesitated, suddenly uncertain. "Unless you wish to stay in separate rooms?"

"One room is fine." Hiro had no intention of letting Father Mateo sleep alone and unprotected in an unfamiliar setting, even a Buddhist temple. Someone had hired the Iga ryu to provide the priest with a bodyguard, and Hiro had sworn an oath to keep the Jesuit alive on the unknown benefactor's behalf. He would not fail his duty—or the priest who had become his friend—for the sake of personal privacy.

The basket lurched in Hiro's arms, though thankfully Gato had stopped howling when they came inside.

"Very well." Ringa nodded acceptance. "The cat is welcome in your room, but, with apologies, perhaps you will not let it run around the hall unsupervised."

Behind them a door slid open, revealing yet another Buddhist priest, although this one wore a faded patchwork robe with a fraying hem. He looked about thirty, with the stubbly head and callused feet of an itinerant pilgrim, and an unremarkable face of the type that disappears into a crowd.

He bowed to Ringa, Hiro, and Father Mateo. "Good evening."

"Good evening." They returned the bow.

A bald, barefooted boy of eight or nine emerged from the room behind the monk, bowed quickly, and followed the older man down the passage, both hands holding up the skirts of his too-large saffron robe to prevent the hem from dragging on the floor.

Ringa opened the guest room door and used his lantern to ignite the brazier in the corner. As light filled the room, Hiro and Father Mateo followed him inside.

The six-mat room had *tatami* on the floor and a recessed *tokonoma* in the wall to the left of the entrance, with a built-in storage cabinet beside it. A knee-high wooden table sat in the center of the room. Across from the entrance, paper-paneled shoji suggested a veranda, though the doors were closed, obscuring the view.

Noting the fine calligraphy on the scroll that hung in the recessed alcove, Hiro crossed the room for a closer look.

Ringa followed. "The words of Kōbō Daishi." Turning to Father Mateo, he explained, "The master who brought Shingon Buddhism to Japan from China, and established Mount Kōya as a center for its practice and meditation."

Father Mateo stared at the scroll. "You hang his calligraphy in a guest room?"

"Forgive me." Ringa bowed apologetically. "This is a copy, not the original. We hang it here so visitors can meditate on Kōbō Daishi's words."

"May I enter?" called a voice from the hall. "I have brought your welcome tea."

Kenshin stepped into the room. He carried a tray with a teapot, a wooden canister, and three lacquered cups, along with a plate of delicate cakes. As he set the tray on the table, he asked, "You truly are not too tired for conversation?"

"Not at all." Father Mateo knelt by the table and gestured for Kenshin to do the same. "I am never too tired to talk about the Lord."

"Forgive me, but I cannot stay." Ringa began to leave but paused in the doorway. "Do you also follow the foreign god, Matsui-*san*?"

"No." The word came out more forcefully than Hiro intended, but no one appeared to notice.

"Perhaps I could show you our temple grounds, while your friend and Kenshin-*san* discuss religion?" Ringa offered. "I believe we still have time before the storm. Also, you can sign the temple register, to document your visit here."

"Of course." Hiro took the hint. "I would enjoy that very much."

CHAPTER 3

Ringa led Hiro back through the passage to the building's entrance, where they slipped on sandals and stepped out into the yard. A cold wind blew, and thunder rumbled overhead, but rain had not begun to fall.

With Ringa in the lead, they turned to the left and crossed the yard toward the smaller worship hall beyond the bell. Its doors were closed. The overhanging roof cast shadows over the recessed entrance. Despite the gathering darkness, Hiro noticed the heavy layer of soot along the underside of the building's eaves.

Ringa climbed the stairs and stopped in front of the wooden doors. Hiro followed cautiously. As he stood beside the priest, he noticed the shadows and the recess hid them from the view of anyone crossing the temple yard.

"With apologies for my directness," Ringa said softly, "what message do you bring to me from Iga? Also, when did Hattori-*sama* enlist the aid of foreign priests?"

Hiro ignored the second question. "What makes you think I have a message for you?"

"Hattori Hanzō does not send his relatives on idle journeys, and your resemblance to our leader is too great for mere coincidence."

Hiro saw no reason to deny the truth. "Oda Nobunaga has attacked the Iga ryu." As he said the words, unexpected anguish gripped his heart and choked his throat. He clenched his jaw and stared into the twilight, overwhelmed with emotion and furious that he lacked the strength to discuss the recent events in Iga without a physical reaction.

The recent events . . . including Neko's death—he pushed the thought away as quickly as it came.

Panic flashed in Ringa's eyes. "Successfully?"

Hiro shook his head and forced the painful memories away. "Hanzō lives." He drew a long, slow breath. "But not everyone in Iga was as fortunate. Hanzō wants you to deliver an urgent message to the Iga agents along the coastal travel road between Kyoto and Edo."

"Me?" Ringa asked. "Why not someone closer, someone already in Kyoto or on the travel road? What reason could I give for leaving Kōya? I am Myo-in's guardian, its only warrior-priest. Anan—the abbot—will not release me without cause."

"Surely he can find another priest to guard the temple," Hiro said.

"But—"

"Perhaps you did not hear me clearly," Hiro interrupted, speaking quietly but forcefully. "Hattori Hanzō ordered you to go."

Ringa bowed his head. "Of course. When Hanzō speaks, no one from Iga can refuse. I will talk to Anan tonight, and leave as soon as possible."

"Tomorrow, after the storm has passed, we can take a walk outside the temple." Hiro gestured toward the gates. "I will share the names of our agents, and their locations. You must memorize the information. Hanzō ordered it must not be written down."

"Of course." Ringa looked around, though the yard was empty. "We should return to the residence hall, before we draw attention."

Back in the guest room, Hiro let Gato out of the basket and poured himself a cup of tea while Father Mateo and Kenshin continued their conversation about the Christian faith. The Buddhist priest asked curious questions about everything from the Jesus god to the rite of Holy Communion and the other rituals of Christian worship.

Hiro had heard it all before. His thoughts began to stray. Despite his efforts, his mind returned yet again to Iga and the devastating loss the ryu—and he—had suffered just three weeks before. He tried to divert his mind, but the talk with Ringa had brought the events to the surface, where they were less easy to ignore. To avoid the memories of Neko, he forced himself to consider the cut on his arm, now almost fully healed, and the fight with his cousin Hanzō that could easily have cost him his life instead of merely adding another scar to the ones that already marked his body and his soul.

Gato pawed at Hiro's kimono and leaped onto his lap. She circled once and lay down, curling her body into a purring ball. He ran his hand across her black-and-orange fur. As always, he found her presence comforting, though he also found it strange that he cared so much about an animal's affection.

Eventually, Kenshin stood and bowed. "Thank you for a pleasant and informative discussion. Please forgive me, but the hour grows late and we should rest."

"I assure you, the pleasure and the honor were both mine." Father Mateo rose and bowed.

"May I impose upon you, one last time?" Before the Jesuit could answer, Kenshin asked, "Would you pray for the soul of the shogun, Ashikaga Yoshiteru, who was killed in Kyoto several months ago?"

Hiro kept his facial expression neutral, but found it curious that the physician characterized the death as a killing. Official reports declared the shogun's death a suicide. Only insiders knew the shogun had not taken his own life voluntarily.

Kenshin raised a hand to his chest. "I am one of the priests appointed to pray for the shogun during the time when his soul is being judged by the *jusanbutsu*—the thirteen Buddhas and *bodhisattvas* who determine the fate of our spirits after death. I ask all visitors to Myo-in to join me, and my fellow priests, in these important prayers."

Father Mateo's smile grew fixed. Hiro knew the Jesuit well enough to know his friend was struggling between the desire to avoid offense and the Christian's belief that prayers did not help the dead—at least, not anyone who died without professing faith in the Christian god.

"I will gladly pray with you, and for you," Father Mateo said.

Once again, Hiro admired his friend's newfound facility with truths that, although accurate, were also not entirely responsive to the questions asked.

"Thank you, I am in your debt." Kenshin took the tray and departed, closing the sliding door behind him.

In the silence that followed, Gato raised her head abruptly. When she saw the scroll in the tokonoma, her ears flicked forward. Her purring stopped.

"No!" Father Mateo lunged for the sacred object, startling the cat, who leaped from Hiro's lap and raced around the room.

The Jesuit unhooked the scroll from the wall as Hiro dove for Gato. She dodged. He hit the floor with a thump, but grabbed her just before she fled his reach. He held her close as Father Mateo rolled the scroll and tied it with the strip of fabric that had held it on the wall.

Only after the Jesuit placed the sacred scroll on the highest shelf of the cupboard did Hiro finally release the cat. She glared at him, whipped her tail around her feet, and licked her side with a vengeance born of anger and humiliation.

"Thank you," Hiro told the priest. "We'll have to explain why we put it away—"

"Still better than explaining why she ate it." Father Mateo reached into the cupboard and removed a pair of folded futons. "Did you deliver Hanz—that is, the message?"

Hiro slid the shoji open and inspected the veranda beyond. As he suspected, wooden shutters enclosed the narrow porch completely, creating a room about three feet deep and the same width as the guest room. In better weather, he would have opened the shutters to view the yard beyond, which lay on the opposite side of the building from the temple gates. Tonight, the shutters rattled ominously in the wind, and Hiro decided he preferred the warmth inside to a frigid view.

Satisfied that no one could overhear them, or enter the room through the veranda without him hearing the person's approach, Hiro slid the shoji closed and faced the Jesuit. "Yes, and he will leave as soon as possible."

Hiro helped the priest arrange the futons on the floor, removed his swords, and laid them on the tatami beside his mattress. "Sleep in your clothes. The mountain nights get cold."

"I remember Iga." Father Mateo lay down on his futon.

Hiro extinguished the brazier, stretched out on his own futon, and faced the wall, remembering Iga also . . . and wishing that he could forget.

CHAPTER 4

Hiro awoke to panicked shouts and pounding feet in the creaking passage just outside the guest room. He pushed Gato off his legs, grabbed his swords, and jumped to his feet, prepared to fight.

"Anan! He's dead!"

"Come quickly!"

The door at the end of the passage rattled open, then shut. The shouting ceased, though doors along the hall slid open. Floorboards squeaked at the far end of the passage. The footsteps seemed to move away from Hiro and Father Mateo's room. Soon, they also faded into silence.

A distant rumbling overhead suggested thunder.

"What's going on?" Father Mateo's sleepy question came from the darkness.

"Stay here. I'm going out to see." Hiro thrust both swords through his *obi* and slid the door open, revealing the darkened hall.

He paused on the threshold. The passage seemed too quiet.

"On second thought, you'd better come with me."

Father Mateo joined him just as the latticed door at the end of the hall slid open. A pair of priests entered the passage, along with a blast of frigid wind. The younger man, who walked in front, held a lantern that cast a flickering light across the burn that scarred his cheek. Behind him walked a slender, elderly man in purple robes.

The young priest—Hiro remembered him as Shokai—continued past them down the hall, but turned back when he realized the other man had stopped to bow. "Anan-*sama . . ."

24

The older priest completed his obeisance before responding. "Patience, Shokai. Respect for the living does not offend the dead."

"Has someone died?" Father Mateo asked.

The Jesuit's skill for stating the obvious remained as strong as ever.

"No," Shokai replied. "At least, he is not *only* dead. Ringa-*san* was murdered."

"Ringa!" Father Mateo repeated. "I thought someone said Anan was dead."

"Not yet." The old priest bowed. "I am Anan, the abbot of Myo-in."

"You must have heard me calling for the abbot." Shokai shifted his weight from one foot to the other. "After I discovered Ringa-*san*."

"With apologies for our brief introduction," Anan said, "I must go see what happened to Fudō."

"Fudō?" Father Mateo's forehead wrinkled. "You said Ringa . . ."

"Forgive me." Anan bowed again. "Ringa-*san* watched over Myo-in so fiercely that we called him *Fudō*—short for Fudō Myō-ō. Again, with apologies, I must go and see what Shokai found."

The abbot stepped around them and continued down the hall behind Shokai, who held the lantern high to light the way.

"Who is Fudō Myō-ō?" Father Mateo whispered.

"A Buddhist deity." Hiro followed the abbot and Shokai. "An angry one."

He spoke with a calmness he did not feel. The sudden death of any priest would have caused concern, but Ringa's death—so soon after their arrival and his delivery of Hanzō's message—made Hiro's pulse race with alarm.

They rounded the bend in the passage just in time to see Anan and Shokai meet another pair of priests near the building's covered entry at the far end of the hall. The priests conversed for a moment before stepping down into the entrance, where they disappeared from view.

Moments later, Anan cried out.

Hiro and Father Mateo hurried down the hall and into the crowded entry.

Anan and Shokai stood in the outer doorway, backlit by the flickering orange light of fire in the temple yard. Just behind them, two more priests stood facing the exit, frozen in horror and mouths agape. Hiro craned his neck to see over Anan's shoulder.

The yard resembled a scene from Buddhist hell.

Directly in front of the temple gates, three blazing wooden stakes sent tongues of fire into the freezing air. The flames burned wildly, flapping like banners in the frigid winds that swept the yard.

Ringa sat cross-legged on the ground, his upper body leaning back against the lower portion of the stakes so it appeared he wore a crown of living fire. One of his eyes was closed, the other open, staring lifelessly ahead. His right hand held a sword. The left one gripped a coil of rope.

"Fudō Myō-ō . . ." Anan whispered.

Father Mateo glanced at Hiro, clearly confused.

"His position resembles the deity," Hiro murmured in Portuguese, as his pulse continued racing. "Fudō is usually portrayed with a crown of fire, holding a rope and sword."

He switched to Japanese. "You found the body?"

"I did," Shokai confirmed. "I saw the light from the fire and came to investigate."

Thunder rumbled overhead. Another freezing wind swept through the yard. The flames blew sideways, but snapped upright instantly, like well-trained soldiers, when the wind abated.

"What happened?" Kenshin appeared in the passage doorway, carrying a lantern. "I heard shouting."

"Ringa is dead. He . . ." Shokai gestured to the yard, unable to complete the sentence.

"Make way!" A diminutive but burly priest pushed past them, carrying an enormous tub of water. His shaven head, which barely reached the middle of Hiro's chest, sported a lengthy growth of stubble.

Without stopping for sandals, the muscular priest hurried out across the yard.

He tossed the water on the stakes.

The fire died with a muted hiss, plunging the yard into darkness.

Shokai raised his lantern, though the light did not carry far enough to illuminate the body.

The stubble-headed priest returned to the entry. "Is everyone accounted for? Where are Doyu-*sama* and Bussho?" When no one answered, he set the bucket down beside the door and wiped his feet on the mat beside the entry. "I will find them."

"Thank you, Gensho-*san*," Anan replied.

Kenshin slipped on a pair of sandals. "Shokai and I will retrieve the body—"

"Not Shokai!" The objection came from a teenaged priest who stood directly behind Anan—one of the two who had met the abbot and Shokai at the entry. "I am Ringa-*san*'s disciple. He is not. It is my right—"

"I studied with him also, Myokan." Shokai blocked the path to the exit.

"He taught you only self-defense." Myokan squared his shoulders. "Ringa-*san* was my teacher in all things."

Anan raised his hands to end the argument. "You may both assist Kenshin-*san*: Myokan with moving the body, Shokai with the examination."

"Examination?" Hiro repeated. He had not expected Buddhist priests to show much interest in the dead, aside from performing the required rituals. Even in Kyoto, few deaths merited an investigation.

The decision made him wonder how much Anan knew about Ringa's true identity.

"We need to determine the cause of death." The abbot looked grim. "Clearly, he did not commit suicide."

"Speaking of which, how did you see the fire?" Myokan asked Shokai. "All the shutters that face the yard are closed."

"You accuse me of lying?" Shokai gripped the lantern tighter. Shadows flickered across his scar.

"Enough." Both young men turned at Kenshin's quiet command. "Do not shame Ringa-*san*'s spirit with petty quarrels."

Myokan clenched his jaw.

"He would want you to put aside your differences," Anan agreed. "Kenshin-*san*, please let me know when you identify what killed him."

"Immediately." The physician bowed and headed out into the yard. Myokan followed, pushing past Shokai.

"May I keep your lantern?" Anan asked Shokai, extending a hand. Shokai nodded, gave the light to the abbot, and left the hall.

"Jorin." Anan faced the remaining priest, a skeletal man with bony limbs and eyes set deep in his narrow face. "Would you please check on our other guests? The pilgrim and his son?"

Jorin bowed, his bald head shining in the lantern's glow. He stepped up into the passage and drew back quickly. "They are here already." He disappeared into the darkened passage, floorboards creaking under his narrow feet.

"Forgive us for remaining in the hallway." The tattered pilgrim's voice came from the passage. "I did not wish my son to see the dead."

Hiro realized, with concern, that he had not heard the man approach or noticed the light from the pilgrim's lantern, which glowed faintly in the hall beyond the door. He shifted position to place the man and child in his line of sight.

"A wise decision," Anan said. "Now, I recommend that you return to your room, for safety, and remain there for the balance of the night."

"You believe we are in danger?" The pilgrim rested a hand on the child's shoulder.

A flash of lightning lit the yard. A moment later, thunder split the air. The child startled.

"I do not know why anyone would kill my temple guardian," Anan said slowly. "Until we learn what happened here, I would advise all men to act with caution."

The tattered pilgrim bowed and departed with the silent child at his side. Their feet made very little noise, despite the squeaky floor.

"We should return to our room as well," Hiro murmured in Portuguese, wishing he had stopped to bring a lantern. Although he trusted his fighting skills, he would rather not encounter a killer in a narrow, pitch-dark temple hall.

Anan's expression suggested no understanding of Hiro's foreign words. "I apologize for my . . . for our . . . regrettable failure of hospitality."

"Please do not apologize," the Jesuit replied. "This incident does not reflect on you."

"Thank you, but I meant my failure to welcome you personally when you arrived this evening. I had already commenced my evening meditation. By the time I spoke with Ringa and learned of your presence, the hour had grown too late to greet you properly."

"You owe us no apology for that," Father Mateo said.

"And now," Anan continued softly, "I must insist upon a far less pleasant conversation."

Hiro stepped between the abbot and Father Mateo. "We did not kill your priest."

"Did I accuse you of it?" Anan raised his eyebrows.

"We will gladly talk with you," the Jesuit interjected. "In fact, if you'll accept our aid, we want to help you learn what happened here."

CHAPTER 5

Hiro stared at the Jesuit in disbelief.

"We have investigated other murders," Father Mateo said, "we know—"

"When to keep our noses out of other people's business," Hiro hissed in Portuguese. "At least, I know it—and you should."

Even as he spoke the words, he realized he had no choice. No matter how much he loathed involving himself—and Father Mateo—the timing and circumstances of Ringa's death concerned him deeply.

Anan raised a wrinkled hand. "I believe we should have this conversation elsewhere."

Hiro weighed the threat of ambush against the abbot's age and frailty.

Not a difficult decision. "Lead the way."

They followed the abbot down the creaking hallway, around the bend in the corridor, and past their guest room. When they reached the latticed exit at the end of the hallway, Anan gestured to a row of sandals on a narrow shelf beside the door. "Temple sandals. If you please."

He slipped a pair on his feet as Hiro and Father Mateo followed suit.

Sandals on, they followed the abbot through the door and onto the narrow, covered veranda that circled the building. The hondō loomed directly ahead, on the opposite side of the temple yard. A squat stone lantern guttered feebly beside the steps of the worship hall, barely managing to stay alight against the wind. Hiro found it strange that the lantern was lit at all. Fuel was expensive, and the hour was late.

"Please follow me." Anan closed the door behind them, stepped off the veranda, and turned to his right.

Two buildings lay ahead, to the north, across another narrow yard. The one on the right was little more than a deeper shadow against the darkness, but lanterns burned at the base of the steps near the entrance to the building on the left.

"The structure on the right is Myo-in's meditation hall." Anan raised his lantern as he gestured to the shadowed building. "This other one"—he shifted the lantern left—"is my home, the abbot's hall."

A flash of lightning gave them a momentary glimpse of the building, a humble but well-built structure with a raised foundation and peaked thatch roof, encircled by a covered wooden veranda.

Thunder rumbled.

As they crossed the yard, a hailstone struck Hiro's head. Another stung his cheek. Around him, tiny balls of ice began to bounce and clatter on the ground.

"Hurry!" Anan increased his pace, the lantern bobbing in his hand.

The clattering became a roar as the clouds released a thunderous fall of hail. Father Mateo raised his arms above his head and ran for the abbot's porch.

Once they reached the safety of the eaves, the three men faced the yard.

Hailstones fell with startling force, as if the gods were flinging icy gravel from the sky. They bounced off the roof of the abbot's home and across the ground like swarms of frightened crickets.

The flame in the lantern outside the hondō guttered one last time and disappeared.

"Inside, quickly!" Anan opened the door and gestured for Hiro and Father Mateo to lead the way. Behind him, lightning flashed and thunder cracked. The sound of hail increased.

Leaving their sandals on the porch, Hiro and Father Mateo hurried through the door.

The one-room house had a sunken hearth at the center. Tatami covered the rest of the floor. A kettle hung above the hearth, suspended from a ceiling beam by a length of rope and chain. On the floor beside the hearth, a low wooden table held an ink well, writing brushes, and a stack of sutra books.

Across from the entrance, a recess in the wall held an altar, upon which sat a cross-legged Buddha carved so skillfully that, except for its visible grain, it might have been flesh instead of wood. An enigmatic smile played across the Buddha's lips. Its eyes were closed, and its wooden hands lay in its lap, palms up and fingers open, with its right hand resting partially atop the left one.

A lantern shaped like a lotus blossom hung beside the Buddha, bathing the statue in golden light. Tendrils of smoke rose from an incense burner at the Buddha's feet, perfuming the room with the cloying, peppery odor Hiro associated with temples—and with death.

Anan shut the door, reducing the sound of the hail a fraction, and transferred the fire from his lantern into a brazier on the left side of the door. After setting the empty lantern down, he walked to the hearth and knelt with his back to the Buddha.

"Please." He gestured to the space around the hearth. "Would you like tea? It is no trouble. I was awake, and studying, when Shokai came to bear the news."

Thunder cracked, more loudly than before. Hail hammered the roof with a sound like a thousand sticks in the hands of overexcited children.

"Not at this hour, but thank you for the offer." Father Mateo knelt to Anan's left as the abbot stirred the coals to life in the hearth and added a stick of wood from the nearby pile.

Hiro took the place across from Anan. The position left his back to the entrance, vulnerable to an attack from the door, but he did not consider the risk unreasonable. Ringa's killer had likely left the temple. Unless . . .

He realized, with concern, that Ringa could have revealed his true identity—and Hiro's—to the murderer before he died.

"How well did you know Ringa?" Anan asked.

Hiro raised an eyebrow at the abbot's directness.

"Given the hour," Anan said, "I trust you will forgive my skipping the usual formalities."

"Ringa-*san*?" Father Mateo echoed, though adding the honorific. "I met him just last night, when we arrived."

"While I appreciate your answer, you are not the one I asked." The abbot gazed at Hiro.

A well-timed rumble of thunder shook the house.

"I did not know him," Hiro said.

"Ringa told me otherwise, just hours ago, when he informed me of his plans to leave the temple."

Though surprised by this revelation, Hiro gave no outward sign. "Why ask me, then?"

Anan indicated Father Mateo. "I trust your companion knows the truth?"

"As much as you do, if not more."

The abbot nodded. "I know you carried a message from Hattori Hanzō, of the Iga ryu."

"Do you know Hattori Hanzō?" Father Mateo leaned back slightly.

"Many years ago, I asked him to provide a guardian for Myo-in, a man who could pass as a warrior-priest, but with additional . . . skills . . . to protect the temple and to train its priests in self-defense."

"May I ask," Father Mateo said, "why a Buddhist temple needs to hire an assassin?"

"You find my concern for our safety unexpected?" A flickering smile played over the abbot's lips, but disappeared as he continued, "Shingon is a peaceful way, but not all temples implement Kōbō Daishi's teachings as they should. Many have adopted a more martial approach to life in recent years. As abbot, I am responsible for the safety of the temple and its priests. We needed help. I sought the best.

"When Ringa arrived, he presented himself to the other priests as a warrior-monk from Shikoku who had come to Kōya for further study in Shingon doctrine. After his arrival, I asked him to train our priests in the ways of self-defense. Only I knew his true origin and purpose.

He guarded Myo-in with the dedication of Fudō—as I believe I mentioned, 'Fudō' became his nickname."

"You allowed the nickname, even though he only impersonated a priest?" the Jesuit asked.

"Impersonated? On the contrary, Ringa completed the formal training to become *ajari*—a priest who is qualified to take disciples and perform the role of teacher. He may have come from Iga, but he was as true and dedicated a priest as any man I have ever known."

And yet, he also remained a loyal spy, Hiro thought. "Did people call him Fudō in public?"

"You wonder if the name was known to men outside of Myo-in." Anan considered the question. "Ringa did not use or claim the name in public, and we did not use it there. He was a humble man."

"Then he was killed by a priest of Myo-in," Father Mateo said.

Anan's face grew solemn. "No priest in this temple had the strength or skill to overwhelm him physically."

"Even a talented fighter can be caught off guard," Hiro said.

"More importantly," Anan continued, "Ringa had no enemies and no quarrels."

"With respect," Hiro replied, "his death says otherwise."

CHAPTER 6

"Would you tell me more about Fudō Myō-ō?" Father Mateo asked. "With apologies, I do not know about him."

"Why would you?" Anan shrugged and added another stick to the fire. "You serve a different god. Fudō is one of the jusanbutsu—thirteen deities who have great importance in Shingon practice. Some, like Fudō, are manifestations of the Buddha, while others are *bodhisattvas*, enlightened souls who chose to forego nirvana in order to help others reach enlightenment."

"Manifestations of the Buddha?" Father Mateo echoed. "I thought Buddha was a man who lived in India two thousand years ago."

The abbot gave an affirming nod. "You refer to Shaka-*sama*, known in life as Prince Gautama. Although he died many centuries ago, he continues to reveal the path to enlightenment through various manifestations and incarnations—including that of Fudō Myō-ō. Fudō, 'the immoveable one,' manifests the Buddha's *dharma* body and helps remove obstacles to enlightenment."

"Dharma body?" Father Mateo wrinkled his forehead in confusion.

"The essence of Buddhahood and the law." Anan smiled. "This is a difficult and confusing concept, especially for a person without training in our doctrine. Normally, Shingon teachings are passed from teacher to student over many years."

"The solution to Ringa's murder does not require an in-depth knowledge of Buddhism," Hiro said. "We simply need to identify who wanted him dead, and why."

"I would like to think no priest in this temple would have killed him," Anan repeated. "Which leaves only the pilgrim, his young son, and you."

"Why bring us here, alone, if you think we killed him?" Hiro asked.

Thunder cracked and rumbled. The sound of hail on the roof increased. Father Mateo glanced uneasily at the rafters, as if concerned the weather might break through.

"Because I know that you did not kill Ringa," Anan said. "In fact, despite my earnest desire to believe that no one at Myo-in would commit such an evil deed, the two of you are the only men in the temple I do not suspect."

"Why not?" Father Mateo asked before Hiro could.

"I find it unlikely that the men who delivered Ringa an assignment from the Iga ryu would also kill him."

"What makes you think we brought him an assignment?" Hiro asked.

"Ringa told me he had received an urgent message and had to leave the temple immediately. He could not tell me when, or if, he would return to Myo-in. Although he did not divulge the content of the message, or identify its bearer, only orders from Hattori Hanzō could have made him leave. Moreover, the message arrived when you did. Thus, it stands to reason you delivered it."

"When did the pilgrim arrive?" Hiro asked.

"Soro? Also yesterday," Anan acknowledged, "but several hours before the two of you. Had Ringa received the message then, he would have told me before my evening meditation."

"Possibly." Hiro kept his expression neutral.

"I knew Ringa as well as I know the grain on Shaka-*sama*'s face." The abbot gestured to the statue in the alcove. "The message did not arrive with Soro, which means it came with you. Now, will you help me identify Ringa's killer?"

Hiro's thoughts returned to Oda Nobunaga's recent attacks on Iga. Hanzō believed that Oda was hunting Iga shinobi, in hopes of exterminating every obstacle between himself and the shogunate. Based on the evidence, Hiro agreed.

Although he would never admit it to the elderly abbot, Hiro had already decided to investigate Ringa's murder, if only to determine whether Oda Nobunaga was involved. Hatred for the power-hungry *daimyō* smoldered in Hiro's chest. Part of him almost hoped to discover—and capture—one of Oda's spies, and make the man suffer for his allegiance. . . .

"Of course we will help you." Father Mateo gave Hiro a look of concern that made the shinobi realize his face must have revealed his thoughts. "But, if I may ask, doesn't it seem suspicious that the pilgrim has a son? Especially since you don't allow women on your sacred mountains."

"Not all Shingon priests adhere to Kōya's precepts. Some are married. Others had children before becoming priests. As for the rest"—an impish smile spread across the abbot's face—"priests can father children as effectively as any other man, if opportunity arises."

Hiro stifled a smile at the double meaning, which he took as very much intentional.

The abbot's face grew serious. "You may have access to the entire temple, though I hope you will respect our sacred buildings and traditions."

"We will try." Hiro paused. "If you truly believe no priest of Myo-in would have murdered Ringa, why not accuse the pilgrim?"

"Without evidence?" Anan tipped his head to the side. "Shingon exists to promote the search for truth and understanding. I cannot accuse a man of murder without any proof."

"He wants to find the real killer." Father Mateo sounded triumphant. "Not just someone to take the blame."

"Indeed." Anan studied the fire, which flickered brightly in the hearth. "Ringa's death confuses and concerns me, and not only because my friend is dead. I do not believe he would let a stranger close enough to kill him."

Hiro agreed.

"Which means," the abbot continued, staring at Hiro across the fire, "as much as I hate to say it, I believe he was murdered by someone he knew."

A rumble of thunder underscored the comment and made Hiro realize the rattle of hail on the roof had ceased.

"You called him the temple guardian," Father Mateo said. "I'm still confused. This mountain is so isolated. Do you truly require warrior-priests?"

"How long have you lived in Japan?" the abbot inquired.

The Jesuit looked at the rafters as he calculated. "Four years, and a little more."

"And yet, you still inquire about the need for protection?" Amusement quirked the abbot's lips.

"In Kyoto, I would understand, but here? On a sacred mountain?"

"Not all men respect the sacred places. Sometimes, samurai attempt to infringe upon our independence. Sometimes, the temples' disagreements flare into violence, despite our dedication to a life of peace. And, sometimes, sacred treasures lure thieves."

"A thief did not kill Ringa," Hiro said.

"Nor an outsider," the abbot replied. "We secure the temple gates at sunset. Shokai said the bar remained in place across the gates when he found the body."

Hiro found it curious that Shokai even noticed the gate, given the condition of the corpse.

"The killer could have climbed the wall, both to enter and to leave," Father Mateo pointed out.

Thunder rumbled, softer than before, as Anan replied, "Not without damaging the shingles on the wall. We'll know in the morning if that's the case, but I do not think so." He gestured upward. "Kōya's winter storms are fierce and deadly. Unless this one lets up within an hour or two, the path down the mountain will remain impassable for days."

"The killer could have fled to another temple," the Jesuit offered.

"At this hour?" Anan shook his head. "No one answers a stranger's knock so late at night. Not even in a storm."

Unless the one who knocks is not a stranger, Hiro thought.

Iga had spies on the sacred mountain. Others doubtless had them, too. If Ringa's killer was a spy who lived in another temple, and had already escaped across the wall, they would never find him.

However, Hiro had no intention of relying on that assumption.

"What will you do with the killer, once we find him?" Father Mateo asked. "Is there a magistrate on Kōya?"

"We have no need of magistrates."

Hiro raised an eyebrow. "Ringa's ghost might disagree."

"The abbot of the head temple mediates disputes among the temples. More private matters, we handle on our own." The abbot's tone suggested he considered Ringa's death the latter.

"We should examine the body as soon as possible," Hiro said. "If you do not mind."

Anan rose. "I will take you to the room where we lay the dead."

"You have a room for it?" Father Mateo stood. "Do many people die here?"

"Everyone who lives must die," the abbot said. "And when they do, we need a place to lay them."

CHAPTER 7

A nan lit his lantern from the brazier and opened the door. An icy wind swept in, along with a sound like the pattering of a thousand kittens running across tatami.

The hail had changed to a combination of rain and snow.

"Is it safe to go out there?" Father Mateo peered cautiously into the darkness, as if expecting a bolt of lightning to strike him through the doorway.

"The storm appears to be lessening, and the hondō is not far." Anan stepped into his sandals without touching his *tabi*-clad feet to the porch.

Hiro and Father Mateo slipped on sandals and followed the abbot off the veranda. They crossed the yard toward the hondō, sandals crunching and sliding on the slippery ground. Hiro remembered the abbot's warning about the weather rendering the mountain paths impassable. Even had they wished to leave and forego an investigation, the hailstorm had now foreclosed that option.

More immediately, it also dampened his tabi through the temple sandals. He regretted traveling with only a single change of socks.

Rather than leading them down the side of the building to the hondō's large front entrance, Anan took a right and approached a second, smaller wing that jutted off the north end of the worship hall. Three wooden steps led up to a paneled door in the side of the hondō annex.

As he followed the abbot and Father Mateo up the stairs, Hiro noticed pale light emerging through the crack at the base of the sliding door.

A gust of incense-laden air escaped from the worship hall as Anan opened the door. Hiro stifled a cough and paused to draw a final breath of cold, fresh air before following Father Mateo and the abbot into the hondō annex.

Braziers burned in every corner of the rectangular, twelve-mat room. Glowing bronze lanterns hung from the ceiling, illuminating the open, tatami-covered floor and three alcoves in the western wall, directly opposite the entrance. Each of the alcoves held a wooden Buddha. The statues on the right and left, though different, had a uniformity of style that suggested the same artist carved them both.

The unusual Buddha in the center drew Hiro's eye. In addition to being carved by a different hand, the figure was standing instead of seated in meditation like the others. One foot rested slightly in front of the other, as if the Buddha tried to leave the alcove. The statue's right hand was raised to shoulder level, palm facing forward and fingers extended. Its left hand cupped a small, round jar.

Incense burners sat before the Buddhas, sending coils of pale, fragrant smoke into the air. The flickering, hazy light transformed the statues' benevolent expressions to something sinister, as they gazed with sightless eyes upon the corpse.

Ringa's body lay on a narrow mat, face up, with his head oriented toward the west, in the direction of the Buddha statues. His hands lay at his sides. His eyes were closed. He wore a plain, dark robe with sharp creases across the front and sleeves.

Kenshin and Shokai knelt on either side of the body, heads bowed, as they chanted in haunting monotone. Although they could not have missed the rattle of the door or the swirl of wind that made the lanterns flicker and dropped the temperature in the room, they did not hesitate or miss a single syllable.

Anan closed the door, and the annex suddenly felt hot and stifling.

As they waited for the chanting to conclude, Hiro surveyed the room more closely. Rows of inscribed funerary tablets lined the southern wall, to the left of the entrance. At the end of that wall, a pair of wooden steps led up to a paneled door. Presumably, it led to the main worship hall beyond.

Elaborate tapestries covered the wall to the right of the door. Each contained dozens of different Buddhas arranged in intricate patterns. Smoke and time had faded the brilliant silks to brooding hues, making the images harder to comprehend.

The prayer concluded with a final, wavering syllable.

Kenshin and Shokai stood and bowed to Anan.

The abbot returned the gesture, but less deeply. "Have you learned how Ringa died?"

Kenshin gestured to the body. "Someone stabbed him from behind."

"Repeatedly," Shokai added. "The back of his robe was soaked in blood. But it makes no sense. Ringa taught us to listen for footsteps, to remain alert in the yard at night. How could someone have caught him unaware?"

"Perhaps he knew the killer, and did not consider him a threat," Father Mateo suggested.

Hiro hoped the facts would prove this true. Ringa's death at the hands of another priest, though tragic, created less concern than a hired assassin sent to eliminate agents of the Iga ryu. Unfortunately, the latter seemed more likely.

"None of us would kill him." Shokai drew back as if offended.

"We are a family," Kenshin agreed.

"Even families have secrets," Hiro said.

"May we examine the body?" Father Mateo gestured to the corpse.

"We told you how he died." The young priest crossed his arms. "What more could you learn by disturbing his rest?"

"Shokai." Kenshin's voice held a reproach, though the younger man showed no remorse.

"I give you my word, we will not harm him," Father Mateo said. "My faith, like yours, respects the dead, whose souls have gone to judgment."

"By our tradition, he has not been judged." Anan regarded Ringa's body. "Each seven days, for the next forty-nine, Ringa's soul will be judged by the jusanbutsu. On the forty-ninth day, they will render a final judgment, and Ringa's soul will experience rebirth, release, or torment in hell."

"So they judge him every seven days, and finish on the forty-ninth?" the Jesuit asked. "Do you believe, during that time, his spirit can change its fate somehow?"

"This is a complicated question," Anan said. "The jusanbutsu render judgment as a group, on the forty-ninth day. However, each of the thirteen also has a specific funerary observance that corresponds to, and is conducted on, a specific day after a person's death. The final judgment takes place on the forty-ninth day after death, although only seven of the Buddhas' observances take place before that judgment happens."

"And the others?" Father Mateo asked.

"We perform them on specific annual anniversaries of a person's death." Anan paused. "This greatly oversimplifies our teachings, but I fear the details would only confuse you more."

Father Mateo frowned. "With respect, how can prayers conducted after judgment help a spirit escape condemnation?"

"In Ringa's case, it does not matter." Kenshin spoke with confidence. "The kings of hell will not condemn him. He has earned release."

"Or a good rebirth, at least," Anan agreed. "However, we can help his fate by performing the funeral rites and prayers properly, and by learning his killer's identity."

"How does learning the murderer's identity help Ringa's soul?" Father Mateo asked. "God already knows what happened."

"Your god will not be judging Ringa-*san*." Shokai spoke with unexpected vehemence.

"The investigation helps because it shows we cared for Ringa-*san*," Anan explained. "Moreover, it reveals he made a good impression on the rest of us, and that we care about him still."

Turning to Kenshin, the abbot continued, "I have asked the visitors to help with our investigation."

"Regrettably, there is not much to investigate," Kenshin replied. "We found no weapon, and the wounds could have been made with many different blades."

"Perhaps we could examine him anyway," Father Mateo said.

Hiro expected the physician to object, but Kenshin nodded. "Shokai, add more fuel to the braziers. Our guests will need sufficient light to see."

Thunder rumbled faintly in the distance as Hiro knelt beside the body. An unwanted lump of emotion rose in his throat as the memory of Neko's corpse made painful pressure build behind his eyes and in his throat. He pushed the thought away, although his throat and chest remained uncomfortably tight.

In this position, Ringa's body gave no hint of his traumatic death. Had Hiro not known otherwise, he would have thought the priest was merely sleeping.

Kenshin knelt on the other side of Ringa. After untying the obi that bound the dead man's robe, the physician slipped the sleeve from the corpse's right arm and carefully rolled the body over, drawing the robe away to reveal Ringa's naked back.

Slender vertical cuts sliced through the dead man's back on either side of his spine. The bleeding had stopped, but the open wounds still oozed dark blood that smeared around the edges.

"Why is he bleeding?" Shokai pointed. "He is dead, and we washed him clean!"

"Even after death, blood seeps toward the ground until it clots," Hiro said.

"Which wound killed him?" Father Mateo asked.

"We cannot tell for certain," Kenshin said. "Any one of them could have proven fatal."

The physician indicated each of the injuries as he spoke. "This one likely pierced his heart, these two his lungs, and this one"—he extended a slender finger toward the lowest wound—"probably cut his stomach. Not immediately fatal, but eventually it would have killed him also."

"You know anatomy," Hiro observed.

"I would be a poor physician if I did not."

"Did you train in medicine before you became a priest?" Father Mateo asked.

"I received my training here," Kenshin replied. "My father brought me to Mount Kōya when I was eleven years old. I have not left the mountain since."

Before the Jesuit could distract the physician any further, Hiro asked, "Which wound was inflicted first?"

He had a theory of his own, but wondered whether Kenshin had one too.

CHAPTER 8

Kenshin regarded the body as if thinking hard. "The lungs. If the killer had not pierced them first, Ringa-*san* would have shouted."

Hiro agreed but feigned surprise. "The temple guardian would have called for help?"

"No," Kenshin replied, "he would have raised an alarm to warn us of the danger."

"A fact the killer must have known," the Jesuit observed.

"How many people live at Myo-in?" Hiro asked.

"Ten"—Anan hesitated—"now nine."

"And how many visitors on the grounds tonight?"

"Four," the abbot said. "The two of you, the pilgrim, and his son."

"How much do you know about the pilgrim?" A flicker of movement drew Hiro's eye to the Buddhas at the front of the room. He knew it was only a trick of the light—wooden statues did not move—but he could not shake the feeling that the Buddhas were watching them, and judging.

"Only his name," Anan replied, "and that he came to Kōya to inter his abbot at Okunoin."

"He carried a body up the mountain?" Father Mateo sounded shocked.

"Only his ashes, in a wooden box. The cremation was performed at his home temple."

"The pilgrim must have murdered Ringa-*san*." Shokai's fury drew a warning glance from Kenshin, but the younger man continued, undeterred. "None of us would ever hurt him."

"What makes you certain no one here would kill him?" Hiro asked.

Shokai gave Kenshin a look that fell halfway between a request for approval and a dare to keep him silent.

The physician sighed but nodded.

"Doyu-*san* was abbot here before Anan-*sama*," Shokai began. "Now his mind is like a child's, his eyes so dim he barely sees. Bussho leads him everywhere, and watches to ensure the former abbot does not hurt himself—so clearly he is not the killer."

Blindness and feeblemindedness could be faked, though Hiro said nothing.

"Nichiyo-*san* is the custodian of our sacred objects," the young priest continued. "He cares only for his own study and meditation, as does Jorin-*san*, who does not notice anything unless it's written in a book of sutras or a scroll. As for Gensho, he may handle many knives, but the only things he cuts with them are vegetables."

A fleeting look of disapproval passed over Anan's face, but it disappeared so quickly Hiro wasn't certain which of Shokai's observations caused it.

"Do all of the priests have equal status?" Father Mateo asked. "Aside from the abbot, of course."

"In one sense, yes," Anan replied, "although we recognize that some have reached a higher plane of study. For example, only those who qualify as ajari may teach others, or take students."

"I believe your faith refers to them as *disciples*," Kenshin added.

Anan seemed uncertain about the parallel but continued, "In most cases, students learn primarily from a single teacher, though there are exceptions."

"Like me. Until Myokan arrived." Shokai's bitterness carried clearly, despite the muttered words.

"Myokan was samurai, and already trained as a warrior." Anan spoke with compassion, though his tone suggested he had said the words before. "Teachers and students must be matched with care. . . ." He trailed off, as if aware the young man was not listening.

Shokai clenched his jaw. His cheeks flushed red.

"Do samurai often become priests?" Father Mateo asked.

"It is not uncommon," Anan said, "especially for younger sons. Myokan is an only child, but his family lost their lands when Od—a daimyō—seized their province."

Hiro noticed the abbot's stammer, and that the stifled name was likely *Oda*.

"Had he not come here, he would have become *ronin*." Shokai sounded smug. "And, like all masterless samurai, devoid of honor."

"You have a problem with ronin?" Hiro leaned forward slightly and let a threat infuse his voice.

"N-no." Shokai's left eye twitched. His scar stood out against his pale skin.

Father Mateo pressed his lips together in disapproval. "What about Bussho-*san*? Might he have sneaked out after Doyu-*sama* fell asleep?"

Kenshin smiled. "Bussho is only eight years old."

"An eight-year-old priest?" The Jesuit blinked.

"Bussho has not been ordained. He is not yet a priest." Shokai's voice held an edge of disdain that grated on Hiro's temper.

"Even so," Anan put in, "his comprehension of our teachings far surpasses that of many priests."

"Is that why his father sent him here so young?" Confusion, and a hint of disapproval, colored Father Mateo's question.

"Buddha, not his father, sent him here," Kenshin replied.

Father Mateo looked even more confused.

"After an earthquake collapsed his parents' home," Anan explained, "the neighbors heard an infant crying in the rubble. They found the child deep in the wreckage, yet unharmed. The family shrine had fallen across his cradle, and an image of the Buddha lay across the baby's body, shielding him as the house collapsed around him. Rescuers found the infant clutching an amulet bearing the image of Kōbō Daishi. Since *Ō-daishi-sama* saved the child, and he had no living relatives, the rescuers delivered him to Koya. He has lived among us ever since."

"He has no family?" Father Mateo asked.

"We are his family," Kenshin said. "Even his name, Bussho, is one we gave him."

The abbot nodded. "I believe the child is a reincarnation of a *bodhisattva*, reborn in human form for some great purpose. Which *bodhisattva*, and why he returned to earth, we do not know, because the boy does not yet remember his true nature."

Shokai clenched his jaw. Father Mateo did also. Hiro noted the similar expressions with mild amusement.

Kenshin indicated the corpse. "With respect, if you have finished your examination, we should leave Ringa-*san* in peace."

Instead of answering, Hiro knelt to help him dress the body.

After Ringa was dressed and resting on his back once more, Father Mateo asked, "Can you tell us anything about the position of his body?"

Kenshin regarded the corpse as if puzzled. "In what position do Kirishitans lay the dead?"

The Jesuit flushed. "No . . . I meant the position . . . when we found him, in the yard."

Anan gestured to one of the statues on the far side of the room. "That is Fudō Myō-ō."

The Buddha glared across the room, fanged mouth turned down in an angry scowl. Its right hand held a golden sword, the left a coil of rope. An elaborate aura of wooden flames arched up behind the figure's head, eerily similar in shape and proportion to the ones that had burned above Ringa's corpse.

Father Mateo's mouth dropped open, though no sound emerged.

"We will need to speak privately with everyone in the temple," Hiro said.

"No one who knew Ringa would have killed him," Shokai insisted.

"And yet," Hiro commented, "he is dead."

Suddenly, Shokai turned to the abbot. "Who will conduct the fire ritual, now that Ringa-*san* is gone?"

It wasn't a question Hiro expected, though Anan seemed unsurprised.

"Nichiyo conducted the *goma* before Ringa came to Myo-in. He will resume the duty."

"I know the ritual also," Shokai said. "I studied—"

"While I appreciate your offer, the duty falls to Nichiyo."

"And Myokan will play the drum, as always." Shokai lowered his face, but Hiro saw the disappointment in the young man's eyes.

A sudden crack of thunder shook the building. Father Mateo cried out in alarm, and for an instant, it felt as if an earthquake had struck the mountain. The drumming of rain increased as if someone had poured an ocean on the roof.

Anan looked upward. "Even heaven mourns our loss."

Hiro did not believe in gods, but if he had, he would have thought them angry—not in tears.

CHAPTER 9

Thunder boomed again, and the chatter of hail on the roof resumed.

"Please excuse me," Anan said. "I need to purify myself, and meditate, before the morning rituals."

"Shokai and I can escort the guests back to their room," Kenshin offered. "We have finished here for now."

The drum of hail increased as Anan opened the outer door. The five men hurried across the yard. Anan took the longer path to his home, while the others raced across the narrow strip of ground between the hondō annex and the residence hall.

Kenshin paused in the doorway to Hiro and Father Mateo's guest room. "Given the hour, and the storm, perhaps your conversations with the priests could wait until after the morning rituals and meal?"

"I see no need to wake them up again tonight," the Jesuit agreed. "Do you allow outsiders to observe your worship services?"

"Would you like to?" Kenshin's face lit up. "All pilgrims may participate. Perhaps you could offer prayers for the shogun. And for Ringa-san, of course."

"He is not a pilgrim," Shokai protested. "He prays to a foreign god."

"Any man who seeks the truth is a pilgrim," Kenshin corrected, more gently than the younger man deserved. "Kōbō Daishi would not have refused him access. We won't either."

51

After an hour, the thunder faded. Some time later, the drum of hail on the roof gave way to a silence even louder than the storm.

Hiro lay on his futon in the darkened room. His mind replayed the scene of Ringa's corpse propped up on stakes and surrounded by fire, stabbed and bleeding from behind but facing the world in the image of a god. He remembered that same body in the annex of the worship hall, laid out beneath the wooden glare of statue gods who judged, but did not save.

Gato twitched in her sleep. Her body shifted on Hiro's legs as she curled more tightly but did not awake. Across the room, Father Mateo's peaceful breathing hitched and then resumed.

Hiro envied their ability to rest. Every time he fell asleep, he relived Neko's death, except that in his dreams, he held the blade. He felt it sink into her flesh, watched crimson blood flow from the wound, and saw the spirit leave her eyes. He awoke in fury and despair, aware for the first time in his life that nothing—not even vengeance—would heal the chasm in his soul.

Even so, the desire for vengeance burned within him like molten steel waiting to be forged.

The bronze bell in the temple yard began to toll, its peals deep and resonant as it called the priests of Myo-in to prayer.

Father Mateo stirred and rose. Hiro pulled his feet from beneath the cat, stood up, and slipped his swords into his obi. Buddhists did not normally carry weapons in the worship hall, but he doubted anyone would object to a samurai wearing the symbols of his rank—especially on the morning after the murder of the temple guardian.

Shoji rattled in the hall. The floorboards creaked as feet walked past the guest room door.

Hiro double-checked his swords and ensured his *shuriken* were hidden in the pocket up his sleeve. Religious men might trust in gods, but he preferred to put his faith in steel.

He laid a hand on the door. "If you want to attend the ritual, we should go."

A couple of minutes later, Hiro knelt on a woven rug at the back of Myo-in's worship hall, breath pluming out before his face in clouds that quickly dissipated in the chilly air. The hail had changed to snow in the night, and during his short walk to the hondō thick snowflakes had covered his hair and robe. As they melted, trickles of icy water ran down the back of his neck and behind his ears.

Cold air seeped in through the crack beneath the wooden doors behind him. Unlike the annex where Ringa's body lay, which had only a single door, Myo-in's main hondō had a pair of swinging wooden doors that opened onto an inner set of sliding shoji, thus offering two layers of defense against the elements. However, the shoji were left open during rituals, and the outer doors alone did not provide a thorough seal against the cold.

Ordinarily, Hiro would have found the draft unpleasant, but this morning the frigid air provided his nose a welcome respite from the cloying incense smoke that filled the room.

Father Mateo knelt to Hiro's right, wide-eyed and mouth agape with wonder.

The enormous worship hall measured at least forty mats in size and had no interior walls to divide the space. The formal entrance opened onto the back of the hall, where visitors knelt on cold tatami mats that covered the wooden floor. About ten feet from the entry doors, a knee-high wooden railing separated the worshippers' area from the sacred space beyond. Directly in front of the railing, on the worshippers' side, a small bronze burner and a bowl of powdered incense sat on a table the height of the barrier rail.

On the far side of the railing, at the center of the room, an elaborate golden pagoda stood at the center of a wide, square table. The three-tiered structure rose almost four feet into the air, its curving eaves tapering to a pointed peak. Candles, bowls, and other golden objects sat around the base of the pagoda in deliberate, but esoteric, patterns.

Bulbous, waist-high lanterns shaped like lotus buds stood at the corners of the table. Directly above them, four more lotus lanterns hung suspended from the ceiling. They filled the room with glowing, golden light but no noticeable heat.

Several feet behind the pagoda, an enormous gold-leafed altar rose along the back wall of the hondō. A life-sized golden Buddha sat cross-legged in its central alcove, staring down across the room with one hand raised and the other resting gently in his lap. The Buddha's half-closed eyes and benevolent smile reminded Hiro of the childhood hours he spent beneath the stare of similar statues, waiting as his mother offered prayers.

Resentment welled within him. Neko too had offered prayers, but the Buddha had not saved her life.

"What are those paintings?" Father Mateo's whisper drew Hiro's attention to a pair of scrolls on either side of the statue, in the altar's other alcoves. "I saw some like them in the other room." The Jesuit nodded to the northern wall, beyond which lay the annex.

As he opened his mouth to answer, Hiro realized Father Mateo had spoken to Kenshin and Shokai, who knelt on the Jesuit's other side.

"Mandalas," the physician whispered back. "The one on the left is the Womb Mandala, the other the Diamond Mandala. Together, they express the entire dharma, as a map for meditation and enlightenment."

"Dharma?" Father Mateo asked.

Kenshin raised his hands, lowered them to his lap again, and sighed. "It is difficult to explain. Perhaps—"

The doors behind them opened, letting in a blast of freezing wind and a swirl of snow.

Priests filed into the hondō and knelt around them on the floor. Hiro recognized the muscular Gensho, as well as Myokan, and guessed the elderly priest who held the hand of a child was probably Doyu, which would make the boy Bussho. The pilgrim, Soro, and his son followed the others through the doors. They knelt on the far end of the hall, where dim light and smoky air obscured their faces.

The wooden doors swung closed with a thump. A skeletal priest with slender hands and the squint of degrading sight slid a metal latch across the doors to hold them closed before joining his fellows on the tatami. *Jorin*, Hiro thought, remembering the man from the night before.

A moment later, Anan and a portly, red-faced priest entered the worship hall through a door at the back of the room, to the right of the altar. For a moment, Hiro thought they had come from the annex, but realized there was in fact a second door, even farther back, that led to a different room, which the priests must use to prepare for various rituals.

Anan walked across the back of the room, between the pagoda and the Buddha. After he reached the far side of the table, he and the other priest walked toward the worshippers, their footsteps falling precisely in unison as they approached the railing on opposite sides of the pagoda table. Just before they reached the wooden barrier, they stopped and knelt on the wooden floor, facing the pagoda.

The abbot lit a candle as the other priest reached under the table and withdrew a pair of cymbals, each one larger than his head. Without a visible signal, but again in perfect unison, Anan and the red-faced priest began to chant.

CHAPTER 10

The other priests took up the chant, their voices blending into one. Hiro observed the service with detachment, letting the words flow over him. He watched the priests for signs of unease that might suggest guilt over Ringa's murder. Only the pilgrim's tiny son was stumbling in the chant, and the child's trouble clearly stemmed from lack of knowledge rather than a guilty mind.

The chanting continued for several minutes. Hiro heard the names of various Buddhas repeated, mantra-style, though since the chant was conducted in Sanskrit he understood little else. At intervals, the red-faced priest raised the cymbals and rubbed them together or, more rarely, clanged them like a gong.

Just as Hiro hoped the service might be coming to an end, Kenshin stood and approached the table beside the wooden barrier. Placing his palms together, he bowed to the Buddha, knelt, and took a pinch of incense from the bowl beside the burner with the thumb and first two fingers of his hand. He raised those fingers to his forehead, closed his eyes, and mouthed a silent prayer as he lowered his hand and dropped the incense into the smoldering burner. He repeated the gesture two more times before clasping his hands, bowing his head, and rising to return to his former position on the floor.

When Kenshin finished, Gensho stood and approached the table. Hiro's stomach growled, as impatient for breakfast as his mind was for the ritual to end.

One by one the priests advanced to the table, prayed, and offered incense. Even Doyu performed the ritual, with Bussho at his side.

Watching him bow before the altar, Hiro wondered whether the former abbot prayed or merely copied the familiar motions, muscles remembering what his brain did not.

As Soro took his turn to pray, Kenshin touched Father Mateo's sleeve and tipped his head toward the table with a gesture of invitation. Father Mateo clasped his hands before him, closed his eyes, and lowered his face as if in prayer, which appeared to satisfy the physician. Kenshin tried to catch Hiro's eye, but the shinobi looked away. His reasons for refusing differed from the Jesuit's, but Hiro, like Father Mateo, had no intention of making offerings to a god in whom he did not believe.

The cymbals clashed.

Anan snuffed out the candle with a sudden snap of his hand.

He and the red-faced priest stood up, bowed deeply toward the Buddha, and departed from the hondō through the door at the back of the worship hall.

The other priests stood up, bowed to the Buddha, and departed in order of seniority, with Kenshin leading and the pilgrim, Soro, bringing up the rear with his young son.

"How much of that did you understand?" Father Mateo asked when he and Hiro returned to the guest room.

"Nothing except for the incense ritual," Hiro replied, "a prayer for the dead. As for the rest . . . I don't speak Sanskrit, and I'm not a Buddhist."

"Then it was Sanskrit." Father Mateo nodded to himself, then asked, "You truly have no faith at all?"

"I have faith in those I trust. I have yet to find a god who's worthy of that honor."

And I doubt I ever will.

Father Mateo gazed at him with sorrowful eyes. "Do you blame God for Neko's death?"

Hiro made a sharp, derisive noise. "Of course not. I blame no one but myself."

The Jesuit's face grew stern. "You did not kill her." He raised a hand, abruptly. "No man is responsible for the choices another man—or woman—makes."

Hiro disagreed, but argument would not change the past.

"Have you a plan for interviewing the priests?" The Jesuit's rapid subject change was worthy of a samurai.

"We start with the person who gained the most from Ringa's death." When Father Mateo looked confused, Hiro added, "His student, Myokan."

Someone knocked on the frame of the guest room door.

"Forgive my interruption," Shokai called, "but Kenshin-*san* sent me to escort you to the goma, if you wish to see it."

Hiro and Father Mateo followed Shokai through the residence hall, across the yard, and to the smaller worship hall whose steps had concealed Hiro's conversation with Ringa the night before. Heavy snow fell all around them, muffling sound and already covering the ground to a depth that allowed for footprints.

"How does this ritual differ from the one we attended earlier?" the Jesuit asked as they climbed the steps to the goma hall and left their sandals in a wooden rack beside the door.

Unexpectedly, the young priest's answer held no trace of his usual rudeness.

"The goma is a ritual of consecrated fire, sacred to Fudō Myō-ō. The wood we burn is a symbol of desire, which causes suffering. Each day, we write special prayers on slender sticks, which we use to fuel the goma."

"What kind of prayers?" Father Mateo asked.

"Mostly for the dead, but others also. As the fire consumes the wood, it carries the prayers to heaven as sacred smoke. Of course, this oversimplifies the goma, and its meaning, but you would need to advance much further on the path to enlightenment in order to understand a deeper teaching."

"As you should advance to the rank of ajari before assuming the role of teacher." The red-faced priest who played the cymbals at the early service appeared in the entrance to the goma hall. "You forget your place, Shokai."

"I . . ." The young priest's cheeks flushed red, making his scars stand out. He bowed.

"You may go." The portly priest bowed to Father Mateo. "I am Nichiyo. Have you come to attend the goma?"

The Jesuit returned the bow. "We would like to, if our presence will not offend."

Shokai disappeared into the falling snow.

"Please." Nichiyo gestured for Hiro and Father Mateo to follow him inside.

The goma hall consisted of a single darkened room with a raised foundation and a platform at the center that served as an altar. Even with the doors flung wide open, the air smelled dense and smoky.

A trio of Buddhas sat in alcoves on the far wall of the room, behind the platform. Scowling, fanged Fudō Myō-ō stood beside a peaceful, cross-legged Shaka and another Buddha Hiro did not recognize, who held a scroll.

The knee-high ceremonial altar, three feet wide and six feet long, extended from the central Buddha's platform toward the door. It held a cluster of ritual implements, including two bronze candlesticks with flickering tapers. At its center, a tower of narrow wooden sticks rose from the center of a wide bronze bowl.

To the left of the altar, Myokan knelt in front of a *taikō* that sat upright on a wooden stand. The drum's smooth surface almost seemed to glow in the candlelight.

Myokan bowed as the others entered, touching his forehead to the tatami that covered the wooden floor of the goma hall.

Nichiyo gestured to the right side of the platform. "Please, be seated."

As Hiro and Father Mateo knelt on the floor, the red-faced priest continued, "I will kneel here"—he gestured to an open space at the near end of the altar platform—"and ignite the sacred fire, which transforms the prayers written on these sticks to sacred smoke."

With that brief explanation, Nichiyo knelt on the platform, arranged his robes, and began to chant in Sanskrit as he ladled various liquids from a set of small bronze bowls onto the pile of sacred sticks. Myokan's voice joined the chant, as he beat a complex accompaniment on the drum.

Setting the ladle down, Nichiyo held a strip of pale wood in a candle's flame. When it caught fire, he slipped it underneath the pile of sticks.

Instantly, a three-foot flame flared up from the bowl like a striking snake. It danced like a living creature, feasting on the sacred wood and oils. More tongues of flame appeared and grew, their snapping, weaving dance so mesmerizing Hiro could not look away. Fragrant smoke rose from the fire and gathered in the rafters, filling the room with the scent of burning pine.

The tower of sticks collapsed in a massive shower of glittering sparks. Nichiyo fanned the flames with a book of sutras, bringing them back one final time before they died to flickering tongues. In minutes these, too, died away, leaving a layer of fine black ash in the bottom of the bowl.

Nichiyo continued chanting, but more softly, as the final embers faded out among the ashes. When the last glow disappeared, the chanting and the taikō's beat abruptly and simultaneously ended.

The silence that followed was so complete that Hiro could hear the featherlight patter of snow on the ground outside the hall.

And then, as happens at such moments, his stomach gave a loud, insistent gurgle.

CHAPTER 11

Hiro's cheeks grew warm as his stomach continued its loud complaints.

Father Mateo turned to look, but Nichiyo merely said, "Myokan, escort our visitors to the morning meal."

Myokan stood up. "Please follow me."

Outside, the snow fell harder, obscuring the hondō and the towering cedars beyond the temple walls. Hiro and Father Mateo stayed close to Myokan, who led them through the blizzard to the kitchen building, east of the residence hall.

As they stepped inside and removed their sandals, Myokan wiped his hand across his head, removing the layer of snow that topped his stubbly scalp. Hiro didn't envy the younger man's clean-shaven head, but the trickle of icy liquid that ran down beneath his samurai knot reminded him that baldness had at least a few advantages.

The front half of the kitchen building had a raised, tatami-covered floor and several knee-high wooden tables. Beyond the seating area, two wooden steps led down to the packed-earth floor of the cooking space, which featured a long brick stove and two large fermentation barrels. Shelves along the far wall held supplies and cooking tools. The delicious scents of miso and steamed rice perfumed the air, a pleasant change from the smoke and incense of the temple's worship halls.

Once more, Hiro's stomach rumbled.

Gensho stood beside the stove. He held a giant bamboo paddle, which he used to stir a steaming pot.

Myokan led Hiro and Father Mateo to a table near the door, across the room from one where Bussho sat beside a nodding Doyu. The former abbot's eyes were closed. His nose hovered precariously close to his bowl of rice.

Myokan waited for Hiro and Father Mateo to kneel on one side of the table before taking a place across from the foreign priest.

A moment later, Gensho approached, carrying a stack of lacquered trays. The top one held an enormous bowl of rice, a teapot, and three lacquered wooden cups. The ones beneath held dishes, though their contents were obscured.

Gensho knelt beside Myokan and set the stack of trays on the floor. After lifting the tea tray off the top, he set it gently in the center of the table. "Rice and tea for everyone."

After setting one of the next three trays in front of each man, he bowed, stood up, and returned to the stove.

Myokan and Father Mateo bowed their heads in silent prayer as Hiro surveyed his breakfast tray.

In addition to chopsticks, a small wooden spoon, and an empty bowl for rice, the tray held a steaming cup of miso soup, a dish of vegetable slaw, and a shallow bowl containing a square of silky tofu topped with a dab of *matcha* paste. To the left of the tofu, one last tiny dish held *tsukemono*: a pickled plum and a paper-thin slice of fermented radish.

Myokan murmured, "*Itadakimasu*," clapped his hands, and reached for his chopsticks.

Hiro repeated the word, an expression of gratitude for the meal, and used the wooden spoon at the edge of his tray to take a bite of the creamy tofu. The unexpected flavor of sesame filled his mouth, and when he swallowed, unusual sweetness lingered on his tongue.

Father Mateo tasted the tofu, too, and inhaled sharply with delight.

Myokan smiled with joy and pride. He gestured to his own small bowl. "*Gomadofu*, made from sesame seeds instead of soy. A specialty of Kōya."

"It's delicious." Father Mateo stared lovingly at the tofu.

"A humble food, for humble people . . . but quite delicious also." Myokan raised his bowl and began to eat, as if suddenly aware that theirs were the only voices in the room.

Father Mateo began to speak, but Hiro caught the Jesuit's eye and shook his head. Clearly, meals were not the place for extensive conversation.

When they finished eating, Myokan stood up. "Gensho will remove the trays. May I escort you to your room?"

"Please come inside," Hiro said when they reached the guest room.

Someone had removed the futons and returned the little table to the center of the room. Gato sat upon it, licking her stomach, with her left hind leg stuck straight out toward the ceiling.

"Do you need assistance with something more?" Myokan followed the Jesuit through the door as Hiro removed the cat from the table. After he set her on the floor, Gato stalked to the corner, tail lashing, and resumed her bath.

"We would like to speak with you about Ringa's murder." Hiro removed his swords from his obi, knelt, and placed the weapons beside him on the floor.

Myokan looked confused but knelt. "I don't know what happened. Only that my teacher is dead, and I am unprepared to take his place."

"Yet you do expect to take his place," Hiro said.

"The temple needs a guardian. With Ringa gone, the task will fall to me."

"Do you know who might have killed him?" Father Mateo sounded apologetic.

Myokan shook his head. "Most of us hoped that Ringa-*san* would succeed Anan-*sama* as abbot."

Hiro found that interesting. "Is Anan ill?"

"Not that I know of. Abbots customarily choose and train their successors before the need arises. However, Anan-*sama* had not yet done so. . . ." Myokan trailed off as if deciding to omit the rest of the thought.

"Anan-*sama* did not mention this." Father Mateo looked at Hiro as if for confirmation.

"Please forgive me." Myokan bowed his head. "I may have given you the wrong impression. Anan-*sama* has not named a successor. He has not even taken a student for several years. Not since Ringa-*san* advanced to ajari. Also, several other priests have been here longer than Ringa-*san*, which makes them more likely candidates for the abbot's role."

He glanced uneasily at the door and lowered his voice. "It's just that . . . some of us believed . . . Ringa-*san* would make a better abbot than the men who outrank him."

"Who outranks him?" Hiro stifled the urge to add, *And why do you find them wanting?*

"Nichiyo-*san*, Kenshin-*san*, and Gensho-*san*. Gensho is disqualified, despite his seniority, but Kenshin and Nichiyo both outrank—that is, outranked—Ringa in age and training."

"Gensho-*san* cannot become the abbot?" Father Mateo clarified.

"He has failed, three times, to achieve the rank of ajari." Myokan shrugged. "After the last attempt, he elected to forego any further study. Since he cannot train students, he cannot rise any higher within the temple."

"And the others?" Hiro asked. "What's wrong with them?"

"Nothing is wrong with Kenshin-*san*," Myokan replied at once, "except that he doesn't want to become the abbot. Anan-*sama* asked him to train for the position, but Kenshin-*san* refused to accept any higher role than that of physician-priest."

"When did this happen?" Hiro asked.

"Last spring," Myokan replied, "shortly before I came to Myo-in."

"How do you know it happened, then?" Hiro suspected he knew the answer. Rumors sprang up in closed communities like weeds in a summer garden.

Myokan bit his lip, as if considering an answer.

Hiro waited patiently. Most men would speak to fill a silence, even if they opted for a lie.

To his relief, Father Mateo also held his tongue.

"I was angry when I came here," Myokan said at last. "I resented that I, a man of samurai blood, must spend my life in poverty because Oda Nobunaga killed my father and stole my birthright."

"You escaped alive?" Hiro struggled to keep his question neutral, though he found it difficult to understand how a warrior could flee. He knew it happened, but considered cowardice unforgivable in a samurai.

"I was visiting friends in Kyoto when it happened," Myokan replied. "By the time I learned of the attack, Oda's men had seized our land and my family was dead."

Despite the youth's defensive tone, the tale had the ring of truth.

"I did not want to live as ronin." Myokan bowed his head to Hiro. "With apologies for any offense that statement causes you."

Hiro nodded, stifling a smile at the young man's awkward turn of phrase. He had not introduced himself as ronin, but only a masterless samurai would work for a foreigner.

"At first, I could not adjust to temple life. I struggled with the discipline, and argued with Shokai." Myokan blushed and hurried on. "Although Ringa-*san* was my official teacher, Kenshin-*san* taught me that anger would not solve my problems."

"How did he do that?" Father Mateo asked.

"By explaining that ambition is a poison in the soul, and that only by placing the needs of others before himself can any man find peace."

CHAPTER 12

"Can you tell us where you were last night, at the time of the murder?" Father Mateo asked.

Hiro was glad the Jesuit took the lead. The question would sound less threatening if asked by a fellow priest instead of a samurai.

Myokan's cheeks flushed scarlet. "In the meditation hall, studying the image of Fudō in search of enlightenment."

"All night long?" Hiro asked.

"Until midnight." Myokan forced an embarrassed smile. "Ringa-*san* ordered it . . . after I lost my temper with Shokai."

An understandable error, Hiro thought.

"What made you lose your temper?" Father Mateo asked.

Myokan's flush deepened at the question. He looked away and mumbled, "Shokai cheated." Steeling himself, he spoke again, more clearly. "Yesterday afternoon, we sparred in the courtyard. Shokai cannot beat me fairly, so he cheated. He wants—wanted—to replace me as Ringa-*san*'s primary student."

"I thought Ringa taught all the priests," Father Mateo said.

"In self-defense, yes, but he was also training me to succeed him as temple guardian. Shokai trains primarily with the temple physician, Kenshin-*san*."

"But Shokai would rather be a warrior than a physician?" the Jesuit asked.

"Who wouldn't?" Myokan's cheeks returned to their normal color. "But Shokai was not born samurai. His father is a merchant." Myokan gave Hiro a knowing look.

Hiro did not return it. "Do you think he murdered Ringa?"

Myokan made a dismissive sound. "Impossible. He did not have the skill."

It didn't take much skill to stab a man in the back when he believed you harmless. "Who then?" Hiro asked.

Myokan lowered his voice to a whisper and looked at the wall that separated their guest room from the next one over. "Soro is no normal pilgrim. When he arrived, he insisted on speaking privately with Ringa-*san*. Afterward Ringa told us all not to disturb the pilgrim, or his son, for any reason."

"Perhaps his pilgrimage requires isolation," Father Mateo suggested.

"No man would bring a child on such a pilgrimage," Myokan replied.

"But he would bring a child to an assassination?" Hiro paused to let the words sink in.

Myokan looked offended. "Perhaps, as a distraction."

Gato rose from her place in the corner and padded across the room. She raised her head and sniffed at the table's surface. When she tensed to jump onto it, Hiro grabbed her.

The cat's protest came out as a squeak, but it quickly dissolved into a purr as Hiro pulled her onto his lap and began to stroke her back.

A bell clanged in the distance and continued ringing.

"That's the gate." Myokan jumped to his feet. "But who . . . ? Excuse me."

He left the room and hurried away.

Before his footsteps, and the squeaking floorboards, faded, Hiro set the cat aside, picked up his swords, and followed.

Father Mateo hurried after him. "Why are we . . . ? Hiro, wait."

"Anything unusual is relevant," Hiro answered over his shoulder, "until the facts prove otherwise."

In the doorway of the residence hall, Hiro stopped and watched as Myokan hurried toward the temple gate—or, at least, the place where the gate had been, before it disappeared into the blizzard. After a moment, the young priest also vanished into the snow.

"Shouldn't we go with him?" Father Mateo shivered as a swirl of snowy air blew through the entry.

Hiro weighed the risk of exposure to whoever waited at the gate against the need to defend himself and the priest against a threat that had already breached the walls. Between the two, he opted to defend the gate. He slipped on a pair of sandals and headed out into the yard. Although he could not hear the Jesuit following, he had no doubt that Father Mateo shuffled through the snow in his wake.

They reached the gate as Myokan pulled it open and peered through the crack.

The young priest raised his hands in alarm. "Go away! You must not be here!"

Hiro drew his sword.

"Please . . ." A single word swirled in on the wind from the far side of the gate. The speaker sounded elderly—and female.

"That's a woman, and she needs help!" Father Mateo approached the gate.

Hiro sheathed his sword, shaking his head at the Jesuit's need to involve himself in other people's problems.

Myokan stood in the narrow opening. His right hand gripped the gate so hard his knuckles paled.

On the other side of the gate, three women huddled in the cold. Their robes were torn and filthy, streaked with soot from hem to sleeve. Patchy spots of red and white on their hands and faces suggested frostbite from exposure to the cold.

The woman closest to the gate was bald, and wore a nun's dark robe. The two behind her both had hair. One held a pilgrim's wooden staff. All three shared the rumpled, wide-eyed look of tragedy.

"Ana!" Father Mateo pushed Myokan aside—succeeding only

because the younger man did not expect it. "What are you doing here? Why aren't you at the nyonindo?"

Hiro recognized the Jesuit's housekeeper standing behind the nun and next to a woman whose long dark hair and silk kimono suggested samurai birth—or would have, had they not been ripped and tangled, frosted with snow and clumps of ice.

"A tree fell on the hall and collapsed the roof." Ana spoke unusually loudly. "The hall caught fire—"

"In the snow?" Myokan sounded suspicious.

"It happened late last night, during the worst of the thunderstorm," the nun replied. "Lightning struck the tree. Our braziers set the nyonindo ablaze when the roof fell in, despite the storm."

"The hall is burning?" Father Mateo craned his neck as if to see, though the gesture was futile. The nyonindo lay a ten-minute walk back up the hill, on the crest of the mountain valley.

"Not any longer." The old nun sighed. "We could not save the nyonindo, or the women who were trapped when the roof fell in."

"How many died?" Horror spread across Father Mateo's face.

"Five." The nun pressed her palms together as if in prayer. "If Buddha was merciful, they were crushed before the flames took hold."

"We tried to save them." The woman beside Ana raised her chin defiantly. An angry, bloody scratch ran down her forehead and across her cheek. "We stayed until daylight, f-fighting the fire and searching." Her lips chattered in the cold.

"You should not be here," Myokan declared. "It is forbidden."

"Hm." Ana's disapproval carried clearly through the snow.

"Where would you have us go?" The samurai woman raised her staff and pointed it back up the hill. "The nyonindo now lies in ruins."

The nun frowned as the samurai woman approached the gate. "W-we cannot leave the mountain in this storm, and without shelter we will freeze to death."

"I cannot let you in . . . it is forbidden." Myokan's voice quavered.

"Please allow us to speak with the abbot," the elderly nun said softly.

Myokan shook his head. "Anan-*sama* has not spoken with a woman since—"

Father Mateo rounded on the younger priest. "I thought the Buddha advocated mercy and compassion. Would you really leave these women in the snow?"

"They can't come in. . . ."

"That decision belongs to the abbot," Father Mateo said forcefully. "Not to you."

Myokan opened his mouth, shut it again, and scurried away across the yard.

"Please come inside." Father Mateo forced the gate open against a growing pile of snow.

The samurai woman started forward, but the nun laid a hand on the taller woman's sleeve. "We will wait for the abbot here. We must not violate the sacred laws any more than necessary."

With a sigh, the samurai woman stepped behind the nun.

Minutes passed. Snow gathered on the women's heads and fell to the ground around them.

Father Mateo switched to Portuguese. "They can't just stand there."

Before Hiro could answer, Myokan flew toward them through the snow. "Come quickly! Please! Anan is dead!"

CHAPTER 13

"Dead?" Father Mateo repeated. "Are you certain?"

Myokan's sandal slid out from beneath him. He tumbled to the ground in a spray of snow. Rolling over, he struggled to his feet, his breathing hard and shallow. "Please, I need your help."

The young priest reached for Hiro's sleeve, but Hiro backed away.

"The abbot is dead." Myokan's voice broke on the final word.

"What of the women?" Father Mateo cast a frightened look at the gate. "We cannot leave them here."

"Anan is *dead*!" Myokan raised his hands in a pleading gesture.

"Perhaps the women could wait in the entry to the residence hall while we see about the abbot," Hiro suggested. Ordinarily, he would not have advocated for their cause, but Father Mateo would not leave the women in the snow, and Hiro would not leave the priest alone with a killer on the loose.

Myokan gripped his hands together. The ends of his fingers were turning red.

"We can close the gates," Hiro added, "and the women can ensure that no one enters or leaves the yard while we are gone."

He decided not to mention that the blizzard made it impossible to see the gates from the residence hall.

"Whatever you wish. Just hurry, please." Myokan sounded desperate.

The women followed Hiro and Father Mateo across the yard as Myokan closed and barred the gates behind them. Hiro did not disagree with securing the temple, but the gesture also struck him as less than helpful.

Death was already inside the gates.

After leaving the women in the entry, Myokan led Hiro and Father Mateo through the residence hall and across the snowy yard to the abbot's home. The three men slipped off their sandals on the veranda.

Myokan slid the door open and stepped aside. "He is in there. . . ."

Hiro surveyed the room from the threshold, hand on his sword, and prepared for an ambush.

Anan sat on the far side of the hearth, legs crossed in the lotus position and head slumped forward against his chest. His hands rested in his lap, palms upward and fingers extended, with the right hand resting slightly atop the left one.

An inverted wooden bowl sat on the abbot's head. Two delicate trails of bright red blood emerged from under the rim of the bowl and ran down the abbot's face from his forehead to his chin. A pair of bloody droplets formed on either side of the abbot's mouth, elongated slowly, and then dripped into his lap. They struck his palm, spattering the puddle of blood that had already gathered in his open hand.

Seeing no one else in the room, Hiro stepped through the door. The others followed.

"Did you touch him?" Hiro asked.

"No." Myokan gestured to the abbot. "This is exactly how I found him."

Hiro walked around the hearth and laid two fingers on the abbot's neck. "Then how did you know for certain he was dead?"

"You doubt it?" Myokan's voice rose in disbelief. "All that blood . . . he didn't move. . . ."

Hiro felt no pulse, and the abbot's skin had begun to lose its warmth. He recognized the clammy texture of the abbot's skin and fading body heat as evidence of recent death.

Gently, he raised the edge of the bowl that covered Anan's forehead. When he saw what lay beneath, he lifted the bowl away.

Someone had carved a bloody circle in the center of the abbot's forehead.

"What is that?" Father Mateo gasped.

"The *urna*." Myokan covered his mouth with his hands.

"What does it mean?" Father Mateo asked. "Could that have killed him?"

Myokan lowered his hands and clasped them together. "The third eye symbolizes the ability to see beyond this world, into the realm of the divine. But why would someone do this?"

"I don't know why the killer did it," Hiro replied, "but the injury was not fatal. In fact, it probably wasn't even cut until after he was dead."

"How can you tell?" Myokan looked at the floor, as if avoiding the sight of the corpse.

"Head wounds normally bleed profusely." Hiro studied the abbot's face. "This one bled, but not enough, unless his heart had stopped already. Also, living victims move. The trails down his face would not have been this clean if he was cut before he died."

Using his thumb, he raised the abbot's eyelid. Tiny scarlet spots and streaks discolored the whites of the abbot's eye. He checked, and the other eye looked the same.

Before he could mention this, Father Mateo spoke in Portuguese. "Is it just me, or does his position remind you of . . . ?"

The Jesuit fell silent, but Hiro already knew the final words: *a Buddha*. Just like Ringa's corpse.

"What did he say?" Myokan pointed an accusing finger at Father Mateo. "Did he do this? I've heard about foreigners stealing treasures and defiling temples, claiming Buddha is a demon in disguise. Did he come here to murder us, and ruin Myo-in?"

Hiro gently lowered the abbot's eyelid and stepped away, still holding the bowl. Unfortunately, it was made of wood and too lightweight to make an effective weapon. "He merely mentioned that the position of your abbot's body resembles that of a Buddha."

Myokan had not stopped speaking. "Foreigners call Shingon 'false religion.' They say their god is the only god, their faith the only real faith. They want us all to say the same. I heard them say so, in Kyoto—" He cut himself off abruptly and glared at the Jesuit. "Do you deny it?"

"I believe—"

Hiro spoke over him. "He denies it."

Myokan looked back and forth between them, unconvinced.

"My faith decrees that murder is a mortal sin," the Jesuit continued, "for which God will send a man to hell for all eternity. God does not permit his priests—or anyone—to take a human life."

"You lie!" Myokan stabbed a finger at Father Mateo. "Your faith condemns all Buddhists. You came to Japan to destroy our way of life."

Hiro stepped between them. "With respect, this is not the time for theological arguments. This man did not kill Ringa or Anan. I swear it on my honor."

"Ronin have no honor," Myokan said bitterly.

Hiro laid a hand on the hilt of his katana. "Unless you wish to join your abbot in the afterlife, I recommend you not say that again."

"Who would do this?" Panic edged the young man's voice. "No Buddhist would defile a temple, or its priests, this way."

"I agree with you," Father Mateo said. "Someone here is not who he claims to be."

Myokan's eyes flew wide. "The pilgrim—Soro. He will pay."

Hiro stepped sideways, barring the exit. "Do not make assumptions before we know the facts."

"If the foreigner is not guilty, there is no other reasonable conclusion."

"Give us time to prove it," Father Mateo said. "Do you want the death of an innocent man on your conscience?"

Myokan wheeled on the Jesuit. "He could escape before you learn the truth."

"No one can leave the mountain while the storm persists." Father Mateo spoke softly, though his eyes were sharp. "We have at least until the blizzard breaks."

Myokan stared at the Jesuit in a way that made Hiro tighten his grip on the katana.

Finally, the young priest nodded. "Very well, but only if Kenshin-*san* and Nichiyo-*san* agree. I will get them now and bring them here. Do not leave this room, and do not touch Anan-*sama*, until the three of us return."

CHAPTER 14

As the door slid shut behind Myokan, Father Mateo said, "I think he's right. The pilgrim must be an assassin, traveling with a child as a disguise."

"Unlikely," Hiro answered. "A shinobi would have waited out the storm before attacking, to ensure he could escape without detection." He looked around the room but noticed nothing out of place. If theft had also been a motive, Anan's killer left no sign.

"Unless his orders required haste," the Jesuit suggested.

"Speed achieves nothing in this situation except increasing the odds of discovery." Hiro stared at the abbot's corpse. "However, this does suggest a motive for Ringa's murder."

"You think Anan was the target all along?"

Hiro nodded, impressed that the Jesuit had followed his deduction. "Ringa's death left the abbot vulnerable. Unfortunately, that does not rule out an assassin."

"Or Lord Oda's interference, though I don't see what he would gain from striking in such a remote location."

"Any strike against an enemy—" Hiro cut himself off and faced the door as footsteps thumped on the porch outside.

Myokan entered the house a moment later, followed by Kenshin, Nichiyo, and Shokai. The last three paused in the doorway as they saw the abbot's corpse.

"He's truly dead." Nichiyo was out of breath, his face more red than usual.

"What killed him?" Kenshin asked.

"I have a theory," Hiro said, "but I need to examine the body to know for certain."

"Examine the abbot of Myo-in?" Nichiyo shook his head. His jowls wobbled. "Out of the question."

"I knew you would not allow a foreigner to defile his corpse." Myokan sounded smug.

"Examination will not defile him," Kenshin said. "They examined Ringa, and did no harm."

"Who let them see Ringa?" Nichiyo demanded. "Only the abbot can grant permission—"

"The abbot did." Kenshin nodded to Anan. "Shortly after we found the body."

"He also asked us to help him find the killer," Father Mateo added.

"Anan-*sama* trusted you to investigate Ringa's death?" Nichiyo raised a hand and rubbed his double chin thoughtfully. "If he did, perhaps I should trust you also."

Myokan and Shokai frowned, but neither man objected.

Finally, Nichiyo lowered his hand and gave a decisive nod. "As the highest-ranking priest at Myo-in, I grant you permission to investigate the abbot's death, as well as Ringa's."

"Only the abbot—" Myokan cut himself off.

Nichiyo rounded on the younger man. "Do you disagree that I am the obvious choice to succeed Anan as abbot?"

Kenshin opened his mouth, but Nichiyo spoke over him. "You had your chance, Kenshin-*san*, and you refused."

"I merely wished to say—"

"If the killer is still on the temple grounds," Nichiyo added, "we are in danger. More of us could die. These men—"

Myokan pointed at Father Mateo. "He wants us dead. Him and all his kind."

Hiro stepped in front of the Jesuit as Father Mateo raised his hands and protested, "That's not true."

Myokan ignored him. "When I lived in Kyoto, I heard the foreign priests tell samurai to cease supporting Buddhist temples and worship the foreign god instead. They want to destroy our way of life."

Nichiyo leaned sideways to see Father Mateo. "Is this true?"

"Of course not. I respect your beliefs."

"Liar!" Myokan hissed.

Father Mateo raised his eyebrows as Hiro took a threatening step toward the younger man, hand once more on the hilt of his sword.

"Please wait." Kenshin raised his hands as if to plead for peace as he stepped between Hiro and Myokan. "I spoke with the Kirishitan at length, last night, about his faith and about his foreign god. His prayers involve wine and bread, like Buddhist offerings. His Jesus argues for forgiveness of the dead, like our Jizō. You see, the deities are even similar!"

Myokan's scowl had not abated, but Nichiyo appeared to be listening.

"He answered my questions thoroughly," Kenshin continued, "and showed no hostility to our Shingon ways. In fact, he asked many curious questions. He even agreed to help us pray for Shogun Ashikaga's soul. A man like that . . . I cannot believe he is a murderer."

Nichiyo raised a hand to his chin again and rubbed it thoughtfully. "Kenshin-*san*, please supervise these men while they examine the body. When you finish, come to the meditation hall. With a killer on the loose, I think we should all gather there for safety."

"Forgive me," Myokan said, "but if everyone goes to the meditation hall, that means the killer will be there too."

Hiro agreed with the observation, despite his irritation with the man who made it.

"Possibly," Nichiyo admitted, "but each of the men he killed was alone. I doubt he will attack a group, if we remain together."

Hiro suspected the killer had fulfilled his objective and would not strike again. However, gathering the priests together would make the investigation simpler, so he did not argue.

"There is another matter." Father Mateo spoke tentatively. "The storm destroyed the nyonindo. The nun—the women—came here seeking shelter."

"Women cannot enter Myo-in," Nichiyo said. "It is forbidden."

"We could not leave them in the storm," the Jesuit replied. "They asked to see the abbot. Myokan—"

Nichiyo's nostrils flared. His cheeks flushed purple. "You let women inside the gate?"

"He insisted!" Myokan pointed at Father Mateo. "He said they would die. . . ."

"I let them in." The Jesuit's voice held a challenge. "They cannot descend the mountain in this storm, and they will die outside."

"Where are they now?" Nichiyo seemed more frightened by the prospect of women in the temple than he had been at the sight of the abbot's corpse.

Myokan gave Father Mateo a guilty glance.

"In the entrance to the residence hall," the Jesuit answered. "Until you find a more suitable place to shelter them."

"There is no suitable place for women in a Shingon temple!" Nichiyo's chin wobbled.

"Forgive me." Kenshin dipped his head in apology. "Perhaps I can offer a solution. This building will require a thorough purification before the new abbot can take up residence. Since that must happen anyway, the women could stay here— only until the storm has passed, of course. If we lead them here through the yard, they would not need to pass through any other temple buildings. We could even leave a bucket. . . ."

He trailed off as if unwilling to broach the topic of women's latrines in any more detail.

Shokai scowled. Myokan looked horrified. Father Mateo's face looked hopeful, though once again he did not intervene.

Nichiyo's forehead furrowed.

"Gensho-*san* could leave their food on the veranda," Kenshin added. "If they do not leave the building, the defilement will spread no further. Did not Kōbō Daishi say, 'With the heart of Fudō I would preach to people. Wear the clothes of the Buddha's great compassion'?"

Nichiyo sighed. "The women may shelter here, but only until the storm has passed. And they must take their—bucket—with them when they go."

Shokai gestured toward the abbot's corpse. "They may object to sleeping underneath a roof defiled by death."

"They may perform a cleansing ritual, if they wish." Nichiyo made a dismissive gesture. "Myokan, tell them of my decision. Shokai will inform you when the body has been moved, so you can lead them through the yard, as Kenshin-*san* suggested."

Neither of the younger priests looked pleased, but neither one objected. Hiro wondered whether any of them realized that Nichiyo had just assumed the role, and authority, of the abbot.

Myokan opened the door, slipped on his sandals, and hurried off into the snow.

"Examine him quickly," Nichiyo told Hiro, "and with respect. When you finish, help them move the body, and then join us in the meditation hall."

CHAPTER 15

After Nichiyo departed, Hiro approached the corpse and bent to examine the murdered abbot's face.

"What happened to him?" Shokai frowned. "Why does he have a third eye like Shaka Nyorai?"

"The historical Buddha?" Father Mateo asked.

Kenshin looked surprised. "You know the Buddha's incarnations?"

"I have heard of Prince Gautama Siddhartha, as we call him in the West. What makes you think he looks like that particular Buddha?"

"The urna, and his hands." Shokai opened his hands, palms up, and laid the right hand partially atop the left one. "This is the *mudra* of meditation—most often associated with Shaka Nyorai."

"By chance, did people call the abbot *Nyorai*?" Father Mateo gestured to Anan.

Kenshin and Shokai exchanged a look of confusion.

"Do you mean Shaka-*sama*?" Kenshin asked. "*Nyorai* just means 'Buddha.'"

"I meant, did you call the abbot after that Buddha," Father Mateo said, "in the way you called Ringa *Fudō Myō-ō*?"

"In all the years I've lived here," Kenshin said, "no one has ever called Anan-*sama* anything but his proper name or 'abbot.'"

Shokai frowned at the corpse. "You think the killer posed them as the incarnations they most resembled."

"Buddha leads your faith, just like an abbot leads a temple," Father Mateo said.

Kenshin pressed his lips together. "I believe you misinterpret

Shaka's role. He does not lead directly, like an abbot leads a temple or a merchant runs his store. Rather, Shaka shows the way for those who wish to learn and follow him toward enlightenment."

Shokai gave the Jesuit a suspicious look. "But a killer who did not know our ways could easily make a mistake like that, and pose the abbot as Shaka-*sama* because he thought their roles were similar."

Ignoring the accusation, Kenshin said, "The abbot more closely resembles Kōbō Daishi: a spiritual father, who leads the way and teaches by example."

"When we spoke last night, you mentioned that Kōbō Daishi reached enlightenment, and became a Buddha during his lifetime," Father Mateo pointed out. "Doesn't that mean the abbot is like a Buddha?"

"Philosophical debates won't help us find the killer," Hiro said. "We need to know who benefits from Anan-*sama*'s death."

"Myokan," Shokai said at once. More slowly, he added, "And Nichiyo-*san*, I suppose. At least, he does if he becomes the abbot."

"If?" Hiro asked.

"Anan-*sama* had not named a successor," Kenshin explained, "so the choice will fall to the priests of Myo-in. If we cannot decide, the abbot of the head temple—the senior temple on Mount Kōya—will mediate until a choice is made. However, Nichiyo-*san* seems the most likely choice, at least for now."

And assuming he is not the killer, Hiro thought. "How does Myokan benefit?"

"By becoming the temple's new guardian." Bitterness edged Shokai's words.

"That remains uncertain also." Kenshin's voice held disapproval. "Shokai, go fetch cloths and water. I will prepare the abbot's body here, before we move him."

After the young priest left, the physician removed a folded purple robe from the cabinet beside the door. "Please begin your examination. I will wash and dress him when you finish."

Hiro gently lowered Anan's upper body backward to the floor.

Kenshin moved closer for a better look. "Do you know what killed him?"

"No, but I have a theory." Hiro untied the abbot's robe and lifted the cloth away from the dead man's chest. No injuries or bruises marred Anan's smooth skin.

Hiro rolled the body over, slipping the robe off the abbot's arm as he did so, to expose the dead man's back. As expected, Anan's back was as unblemished as his chest.

"He was not stabbed." Kenshin sounded surprised.

"Is it possible that a different person murdered him?" Father Mateo asked.

"Killers need not limit themselves to a single method." Hiro rolled Anan's body over so it faced the ceiling once again.

Kenshin bowed his head. "May the kings of hell have mercy."

"You mentioned them earlier," Father Mateo said. "Who are these kings of hell?"

"Most people refer to them as the jusanbutsu—the thirteen Buddhas. Among other roles, they act as judges of the dead." The physician smiled at Father Mateo. "When we were young, a friend and I referred to them as the kings of hell. At least, we did when no one else could hear us. The jusanbutsu judge the soul of the deceased each seven days—"

"Anan already explained it to him." Hiro studied the corpse as if the killer's name might appear on its skin if he continued staring long enough.

"He did not explain how the judging works, however," Father Mateo said.

"In many ways, it differs little from the way your Kirishitan god judges the dead. Except, of course, that you have only one deity, and we have many."

"Also, Jesus intervened to save believers from condemnation," the Jesuit said.

Kenshin smiled. "Jizō performs that function, too. He argues on behalf of the dead before the other kings of hell."

The door slid open. Shokai stomped the snow from his feet, slipped off his sandals, and stepped inside, carrying a steaming bucket and a stack of folded cloths. He set the bucket down and closed the door.

Kenshin gestured. "Bring it here."

"Do you know what killed him?" Shokai set the bucket down beside the corpse and bent down for a better look.

Hiro reached out and raised Anan's left eyelid.

"His eyes are full of blood!" A cloth fell off the stack in Shokai's arms and landed on the floor.

Kenshin examined the abbot's eye more closely. "How did that happen?" He opened the abbot's other eye. "This one is bloody too."

Hiro nodded. "The killer likely smothered him to death."

Father Mateo looked confused. "I thought strangulation caused the victim's eyes to bleed."

"Both modes of death can cause this kind of bleeding, but a strangled man will normally have marks on his neck"—Hiro gestured— "and Anan has none. For that reason, I suspect suffocation. It can also cause this kind of bleeding."

"How do you know this?" Kenshin asked.

"How do you not know it?" Hiro countered.

The physician shrugged. "My training focused on brewing medicinal teas and healing minor wounds—the illnesses and injuries that happen commonly in Shingon temples." He extended a hand toward Anan's body. "I have never seen a death like this."

"Regrettably, we have seen several." Father Mateo sighed. "It gets no easier with repetition."

Waves of pain crashed over Hiro. His chest constricted. His throat closed off, and the room felt suddenly devoid of air. Panic rose inside him at his inability to breathe. He closed his eyes and inhaled slowly, letting the pain wash over him like a wave.

He opened his eyes as the moment passed. His throat still hurt, but his airway opened, allowing him to breathe.

"Is something wrong?" Kenshin stared at Hiro's face.

"No." He stood. "We have seen what we need to see."

"Are you certain?"

Hiro started toward the door. "Let us know if you find anything unusual when you wash and dress him, though I doubt you will."

"Thank you for allowing us to examine the body." Father Mateo bowed to the other priests but kept his eyes on Hiro.

Kenshin returned the bow. "Shokai, show them to the meditation hall while I bathe Anan."

"That won't be necessary," Hiro said. "We know the way."

CHAPTER 16

Thunder rumbled overhead as they left the abbot's hall.

Father Mateo looked upward. "Thunder and snow? Is that even possible?"

"Considering it just happened, I'd say yes."

Hiro slipped on a pair of sandals, stepped off the veranda, and turned left toward the meditation hall. He could not see it through the snow, but knew it lay in that direction. As he walked, he remembered a similar storm, many years before, when he and Neko had played hide-and-seek among the trees of Iga village until his mother forced them inside, with a warning that lightning could kill despite the snow.

His sandal slipped, and he almost fell.

"Hiro." Father Mateo hurried to his side. "What's going on?"

"Someone is killing priests—or hadn't you noticed?"

"That's not what I mean, and you know it." The Jesuit paused. "You're thinking of Neko. Did she like the snow?"

"Do not say her name." The words came out harshly, but Hiro didn't care.

He did not want the Jesuit's compassion.

"You should talk about her. It will help."

"Do not presume to understand my grief!" Hiro whirled on the priest as another crack of thunder split the sky.

"I would not dare, but I can share your burden, if you let me."

"Neither of us can afford the distraction." Hiro jabbed a finger at the abbot's home. "Two men are dead, and not at random."

"Of course they weren't random." Father Mateo wrapped his arms around himself. "Can we discuss this where it isn't snowing?"

Hiro lowered his voice to a whisper and spoke in Portuguese. "Ringa was the real target."

"Ringa? Not the abbot? But you said—"

Hiro looked around before answering. They seemed to be alone, but falling snow obscured everything farther than a katana strike away. "Hanzō has reason to believe that Oda Nobunaga's spies have learned the identities of several vital Iga agents."

"And you think Ringa's name was on that list?" The Jesuit's face grew grim.

"That, or Oda somehow learned that Hanzō sent us here with orders for Ringa to leave and warn them. . . ." Hiro looked over his shoulder, unable to shake the feeling that someone was watching them through the storm.

"If Lord Oda knew that Hanzō sent us, we would be in danger too."

"Precisely."

"How could he know?" The Jesuit stomped his feet against the ground. "We took an indirect path from Iga. No one but the two of us and Hanzō even knew our destination, let alone the message we carried. Besides, if Ringa was the target, why did the assassin kill the abbot?"

"To hide the crime and throw us off the trail." Hiro gestured to the meditation hall. "Aside from us, only Anan knew Ringa came from Iga."

"Surely the assassin would have waited until we left, to lower the risk and avoid the need to kill us also. Besides, last night you said assassins didn't strike in storms." Father Mateo tucked his hands into his sleeves. "Please don't take offense, but I'm afraid your hatred for Lord Oda may have compromised your judgment."

Heat rushed into Hiro's cheeks. "That has nothing to do with this!"

"If you say so, but when it comes to these killings, I think a madman makes more sense than an attack by Lord Oda's spies."

Hiro would not waste his time and breath in fruitless argument. He stomped away across the yard. Unfortunately, the slippery ground

required too much attention for a satisfying stomp, and the extra care
he paid to his footing let his anger bleed away. By the time he reached
the meditation hall, his rage had lost its satisfying edge.

Father Mateo caught up with him as he stepped onto the covered
veranda encircling the hall. "Wait," he said, continuing in Portuguese.
"The pilgrim is the only stranger here, aside from us. Does that make
him the killer, if your theory is correct?"

"Not necessarily," Hiro replied. "The assassin could have been
living here, and masquerading as a priest."

"Two spies in one temple? That seems doubtful. Wouldn't Rin—
someone—have suspected?"

"How many years did we live in the capital? And no one ever suspected me."

The outer door to the meditation hall opened onto a foyer with a
wooden floor and a sandal rack built into the left-hand wall. On the
far side of the entry, a single wooden step led up to sliding shoji that
separated the foyer from the main meditation room.

Hiro and Father Mateo left their shoes on the rack and stepped up
into the larger room. The open, tatami-covered floor would easily hold
four dozen priests, despite the fact that Myo-in had barely a quarter of
that number.

Mandala tapestries hung from the walls on the right and left of the
entrance. Just beyond them, braziers burned, setting the room ablaze
with light. At the far end of the hall, two more braziers cast their glow
over an enormous built-in altar that housed a trio of wooden Buddhas.
Hiro recognized the grouping: Shaka, flanked by Monju and Fugen,
the Buddhas who represented wisdom and virtue, respectively. He
found it strange that he remembered his mother referring to the group
as a Shaka Triad. He also had a faint memory of her explaining something else about these Buddhas, but that part was lost to him.

Nichiyo stood in front of the altar, addressing a quartet of priests who knelt before him, backs to the door. In the front row, muscular Gensho sat beside spindly Jorin. Behind them, Bussho knelt beside Doyu, whose ancient head was dotted with silvery stubble and purple liver spots. The old man's head tipped forward. He nodded gently as if in sleep.

Nichiyo noticed Hiro and Father Mateo. "You have arrived."

The others—except for Doyu—turned to look.

"These men have agreed to help us find the person who murdered our guardian and abbot," Nichiyo said.

Gensho stood up. "Was the abbot also posed as Fudō Myō-ō?"

Father Mateo indicated Bussho. "Perhaps we should wait to discuss . . ." He trailed off as if hoping the muscular priest would take the hint.

Hiro did not share the Jesuit's concern about discussing death in front of children, but preferred to keep the details secret anyway. "Too much talk could harm our investigation."

Gensho frowned. "With respect, who authorized investigation of the abbot's murder?" He gestured to the assembled priests. "With Anan-*sama* dead, we should have had a voice in that decision."

"No one here has greater seniority than I." Nichiyo paused. "Except for Doyu-*sama*, and—"

"I am Doyu." The ancient priest's head jerked up. He raised a liver-spotted hand and swiveled his head from side to side, revealing a pair of clouded eyes. "I am Doyu."

"Yes, Doyu-*sama*." Bussho patted the old man's arm.

"I am Doyu," he said once more, with a nod.

"Clearly, he cannot resume the abbot's role," Nichiyo concluded.

"Seniority alone does not assure you the position." Gensho's voice held a challenge. "There is a process—"

"Which will be followed, when time permits." Nichiyo looked around, including the others in his words. "However, someone needs to protect the temple, and its priests, from the murderous threat that stalks the halls right now."

"The fact that someone killed the abbot—"

"And the guardian," Nichiyo put in.

"—does not necessarily put the rest of us in danger." Gensho narrowed his eyes at the red-faced priest. "Especially if the killer's objective was to take the abbot's place."

The seated priests exchanged startled looks. Only Doyu did not react. His eyelids drooped, and his head bent forward.

Nichiyo stepped backward. "Are you accusing me of murder?"

"Merely pointing out that, in the absence of the abbot, important decisions—and the investigation of the abbot's death most certainly qualifies—are made by consensus." Gensho gave the red-faced priest a defiant look.

Nichiyo looked at the others as if for support. "Do any of you object to me assuming the role of abbot until we find the person who murdered Ringa and Anan?"

Hiro noted that, as phrased, Nichiyo's tenure as abbot would continue indefinitely if the killer escaped or remained unknown. Thus far, the jowly priest had not struck Hiro as particularly smart or calculating, but Nichiyo's current actions made the shinobi reconsider that assessment.

Without warning, Bussho stood up. "May I speak honestly?"

CHAPTER 17

Nichiyo stared at the boy, mouth open, though no words came out.

Except for Doyu, who appeared to have fallen back asleep, the priests leaned toward Bussho as if intensely curious what the child would say.

Bussho stood with his hands at his sides. His sock-clad feet were slightly pigeon-toed. He spoke with a silent confidence that belied his age. "Kōbō Daishi said, 'Do not seek to follow in the footsteps of the men of old; instead, seek what they sought.' Anan-*sama* sought to keep us safe, and to foster unity at Myo-in. He would not want his death to create enmity among us."

Gensho's face flushed as red as Nichiyo's. The other priests exchanged embarrassed glances. Slowly, each one nodded in agreement.

"If we seek to do as Anan-*sama* would have done," Bussho continued, "we must either agree upon a leader or send word to the head temple, requesting assistance from the abbot there."

"That is in accordance with the law, and our traditions." Jorin raised his hand, revealing a scroll. "Perhaps we should send word to the head temple."

"In this storm?" Nichiyo asked. "Jorin, you know as well as I do that the slopes are far too treacherous. Even if the messenger survived the trip, the head temple's abbot would not dare to risk the storm. While we wait for it to pass, the killer walks among us."

"We do not know the killer is still here." Jorin cast a worried look at his scroll.

The door in the entry shut with a bang, as if blown closed by the storm. Hiro tensed, but relaxed again as a snowy Myokan entered the hall and bowed.

Nichiyo looked unusually pleased to see him. "Have you seen any sign of someone climbing over the temple walls since the storm began?"

Myokan drew back as if confused. "N-no. The snow on the walls is undisturbed."

"Perhaps we should leave the temple together," Jorin suggested. "We cannot reach the head temple, but one of the closer temples would give us shelter."

"If we do," Nichiyo said, "the killer will go with us."

"Unless he has escaped already," Gensho countered, "or is hiding on the temple grounds and planning to escape when the storm dies down, or when we sleep."

"I just searched the grounds, and I found no one." Myokan glanced at Nichiyo and continued hesitantly, "Our other guests are in the abbot's house."

"Nichiyo-*san* told us about the women." Gensho nodded approval. "We all agreed that we should give them shelter."

"What are we going to do about the leadership of Myo-in?" A deeper flush of scarlet rose in Nichiyo's neck and cheeks.

"I think we should wait on that decision until the abbot's killer is brought to justice, to ensure our new abbot does not have blood on his hands." Gensho gave the red-faced priest a meaningful look and crossed his arms. He looked around quickly. "Where is the pilgrim? I just realized he's not here."

"Soro?" Nichiyo shrugged. "When I asked him to join us, he said he preferred to remain in his guest room, with his son."

"That, or he planned to escape while the rest of us were gathered here." Gensho started toward the door.

"Wait!"

The muscular priest turned back at Nichiyo's objection. "Perhaps I should ask why you trusted him to remain alone, and why you object to me checking on him now? Have you some reason . . . ?"

"It is you I am concerned about, not him," Nichiyo snapped. "Yes, I let him stay in his room. He's a stranger here, and I realized—as you did—that he arrived just hours before someone murdered Ringa. If he wants to escape, let him do it! It means no one else will die."

"And you, conveniently, survive to take the abbot's role," Gensho retorted.

"Are you implying I had a part in this?"

Gensho took a threatening step toward the red-faced man. "Merely noting your willingness to take the abbot's place before his body is even cold."

Nichiyo raised a hand to his chest. "I merely wish to ensure this temple, and its priests, survive."

"May I suggest a compromise?" Father Mateo asked.

Hiro wished the Jesuit had let the argument run its course.

"Perhaps Nichiyo-*san* could become abbot temporarily," the Jesuit suggested. "Just until the storm has passed and we find the killer. Once you know what happened to the former abbot, and to Ringa-*san*, you can send for the abbot of the head temple and make a permanent decision."

Gensho narrowed his eyes at Nichiyo and waited for the other man's response.

The red-faced priest gave a nod of approval. "This sounds like a wise proposal."

"Of course, because it keeps you in control," Gensho retorted.

"I merely wish to protect the temple, and its priests," Nichiyo repeated. "Jorin, you know the laws. What do you say?"

"I cannot think of any procedural objections." The skeletal priest spoke slowly, as if thinking. "We could appoint a temporary abbot, if we chose."

"But not until Kenshin-*san* and Shokai-*san* arrive," Gensho said.

Jorin considered this. "A temporary appointment requires only majority consent. As long as no one here objects, their presence is not strictly required, so long as we make no permanent decisions."

Gensho nodded. "A temporary appointment only, until we know who the killer is, or that he has escaped."

Hiro's impression of the muscled priest went up a notch. Apparently, he noticed the loophole in Nichiyo's first suggestion.

"Does anyone else object?" Nichiyo asked.

Bussho knelt at Doyu's side. "Doyu-*sama*," he whispered.

The elderly man's head jerked up. He blinked like an owl caught in sunlight.

"Do you want Nichiyo-*san* to become the temporary abbot?" Bussho asked.

"Anan-*san* is the abbot." Doyu blinked.

"Anan-*sama* is . . . dead." The child's voice wobbled on the word. "Do you think Nichiyo-*san* should replace him?"

"Nichiyo-*san* is well-behaved since coming to the temple." Doyu nodded sagely.

"Indeed." Nichiyo spoke quickly. "I accept the role of abbot. Temporarily, of course."

Hiro doubted the red-faced priest had any intention of stepping down, but by the time that issue required resolution, he planned to be halfway down the mountain—if not farther.

"How can we help your investigation?" Gensho sounded determined to find an answer as soon as possible.

"Speak with us honestly," Father Mateo said. "Do not conceal information."

"You think the killer will confess?" Gensho sounded incredulous. "That's your strategy?"

"Our strategy is to interview everyone and learn the facts," Hiro said. "Will you consent to an interview?"

"Of course." Gensho crossed his arms. "I have nothing to hide. But don't you think it might be wise to check on the pilgrim first? To ensure he's safe." He cut his eyes to Nichiyo.

"Are we in danger?" Bussho's forehead wrinkled with concern. Surprisingly, his eyes were not afraid.

The entry door opened and closed again.

"We have returned," Kenshin called from the entry. A moment later, he appeared in the doorway with Shokai on his heels.

"I hope you are not in danger," Father Mateo told Bussho. "However, I think it wise for you to remain in the meditation hall with the other priests, at least for now."

"Because the killer is less likely to attack a group." Bussho nodded. "Yes, I understand."

The Jesuit's eyes grew wide at the child's perceptive answer.

"But you will leave, to conduct the investigation?" Bussho tipped his head to the side. "Why should you bear the risk on our behalf?"

"He volunteered." Nichiyo's answer lowered Hiro's opinion of the acting abbot yet again.

Kenshin laid a hand on Bussho's shoulder. "The foreign god requires his priests to sacrifice themselves for others. It is an important tenet of his dharma."

Bussho nodded thoughtfully. "I see." He bowed to Father Mateo. "Thank you."

"We wanted to let you know that we had moved the abbot's body safely," Kenshin said, "but Shokai and I must return to the hondō and commence the prayers for the dead."

Nichiyo nodded. "Stay together for safety." After a pause, he added, "Before you arrived, the other priests asked me to assume the role of abbot—temporarily, of course—until we find the killer." His voice held a hint of challenge.

"A wise decision." Kenshin bowed.

Shokai frowned but did not object.

"And I have decided to elevate Myokan to the role of temple guardian—again, until we find the killer."

Shokai's scowl deepened.

"Killer or no, I need to finish cleaning the kitchen and start preparing the evening meal." Gensho stared at the abbot as if expecting an argument, but Nichiyo merely nodded.

Hiro gestured to Father Mateo. "We will check on Soro."

CHAPTER 18

"Who is there?" Soro called through the door in response to Hiro's knock. "What do you want?"

"We wish to speak with you about the recent murders," Hiro said.

"With respect, please go away. I will not risk myself or my son for the sake of conversation."

"A priest does not refuse samurai," Hiro growled. "Open this door or face the consequences."

The door slid open. "Welcome, *samurai*. Please come inside." Though polite, Soro's voice held a hostile edge.

"We appreciate the invitation." Hiro strode across the threshold with a frowning Father Mateo in his wake.

"Please do not worry," the Jesuit said. "We mean no harm. We merely wish to talk."

Soro's room was identical in size and layout to the one that Hiro and Father Mateo shared, except that the scroll in the tokonoma featured an image of the Buddha rather than calligraphy. Noting the similarity, Hiro wondered whether the priests told all guests their room was the "finest" in the temple, and whether the lie increased donations to the temple coffers.

The pilgrim's son knelt on the far side of the wooden table, studying a book of sutras.

"Ippen." Soro slid the shoji closed.

When the child looked up, the pilgrim nodded to the corner farthest from the door.

Ippen rose, picked up his book, and retreated to the corner. There, he knelt and opened the book once more.

Soro placed himself between the boy and the visitors. He did not invite them to sit or kneel.

Hiro knelt beside the table anyway, a deliberate insult—both because he was uninvited and because the action suggested the pilgrim was no threat. "Why did you refuse to join the priests in the meditation hall?"

"Ippen and I are safer here." Soro shifted his weight. Although his robe made it impossible to judge his strength, his build and stance suggested martial training.

Hiro pretended not to notice. "Why did you come to Myo-in?"

"To inter our abbot's bones at Okunoin, the cemetery here on Kōya," Soro said.

"What killed him?"

"Age." Soro met Hiro's gaze without blinking.

"Show me his ashes."

Father Mateo gave Hiro a horrified look, but Soro approached the built-in cabinet, opened it, and withdrew a simple wooden box.

He extended it to Hiro. "Do you wish to look inside?"

A faint gasp sounded from the corner, followed by a thump as the book of sutras hit the floor. Ippen covered his mouth with his hands. His eyes filled up with tears.

Hiro did not doubt the box held charred bone fragments similar in size and shape to a cremated body. If Soro was shinobi, the ashes might be those of an animal. If not, they were likely human. Either way, examination would prove nothing but Hiro's distrust of Soro and disrespect for the dead.

Hiro felt no need to prove either.

Father Mateo flushed. "We do not question your honesty."

Hiro did but didn't say so. "Did you leave this room at all last night, or early this morning?"

Soro returned the box to the cabinet and closed the door. "You saw me in the hall last night. I heard yelling, and went to see the cause. This morning, Ippen and I attended the morning service and used the latrine. The young priest brought our meals to the room, as I requested when we arrived. I do not know who killed the abbot or the other priest."

"How did you know Anan was dead?" Hiro asked.

"The priest who asked me to go to the meditation hall explained what happened," Soro said, "but I heard running and yelling again this morning, and guessed that something was amiss."

Hiro found the flippant answer irritating. "Why did you refuse to join the others?"

"Two priests are dead in less than a day. Only a fool would trust a stranger now." He paused. "And I am a stranger here, myself. For all I know, these men will turn against me."

"A reasonable concern," Hiro said, "especially if you are not the killer."

"Which, fortunately, I am not. But I do appreciate your concern." Soro gestured to the door as if inviting them to leave.

Although tempted to stay and press the issue, Hiro could not think of questions likely to reveal a useful truth. He stood up.

"Thank you for talking with us." Father Mateo looked at the cabinet. "We apologize for . . ."

Soro nodded.

"Have the priests at Okunoin selected a day for your abbot's interment?" Hiro asked.

"Originally, we planned it for tomorrow," Soro said. "With the storm, the ceremony will have to wait."

"An unfortunate inconvenience." Hiro nodded and left the room.

Father Mateo followed him out of the room and closed the door.

Instead of turning right, toward their guest room, Hiro started down the hall in the opposite direction.

The Jesuit followed. "Where are we going?" He lowered his voice to a whisper. "And that was rude. I can't believe you almost made him show the ashes!"

"It's time to find out more about our temporary abbot. As for the ashes . . ." Hiro shrugged. He didn't really care.

"The meditation hall is that way." Father Mateo pointed backward down the hall.

"But the kitchen is this way," Hiro said, "and while I don't trust Nichiyo to tell us much about himself, I do think Gensho will be glad to fill the gaps."

Hiro paused to remove his sandals in the kitchen entrance.

"So?" Gensho called from the other side of the room, near the oven. "Did the pilgrim escape?" He stood in front of a steaming kettle. A pile of dirty bowls sat stacked beside him on the oven's edge.

"Soro and his son are safe." Father Mateo placed his sandals next to Hiro's on the rack. The two men crossed the room, but paused at the edge of the raised, tatami-covered platform.

"We hoped to speak with you about the killings," Hiro said.

Gensho dunked a bowl in the kettle, swished it around, and pulled it out. The steaming water turned his hands a brilliant, angry red. Satisfied that the bowl was clean, he wiped it off with a cloth, set it upside down on a nearby shelf, and started toward them, drying his hands.

When he reached them, he asked, "Would you like tea?"

"No, thank you," Father Mateo said, though Hiro would have liked a cup.

The three men knelt near the edge of the floor. Gensho took care to leave his feet hanging over the edge, to ensure their dirty soles did not touch the tatami.

"Where were you last night when Ringa died, and this morning after the prayer service?" Hiro asked.

"You think I killed them?" Gensho shook his head. "If the pilgrim is innocent, you should talk to Nichiyo, not me."

"Why did you agree to him becoming the abbot, if you think he's guilty?" Father Mateo asked.

"You were there." Gensho looked at the cloth in his hands. "It would have happened no matter what I said. I'm not smart when it comes to books or doctrine. I can cook, and clean, and fix the temple, but when it comes to important decisions, no one but Anan-*sama* considers my opinions of any worth."

"Is there anything about Nichiyo you think we should know?" Hiro asked.

Gensho looked up with concern in his eyes. "You won't say that I'm the one who told you?"

Given the physical contrast between muscular Gensho and jowly Nichiyo, Hiro found the reaction intriguing enough to answer directly. "We will say nothing."

CHAPTER 19

"I do not know the circumstances of Nichiyo-*san*'s arrival at Myo-in," Gensho said, "because I was away at the time, on a pilgrimage in Shikoku. Doyu-*sama* was abbot then, though he will not remember. Kenshin-*san* knows more than me, but he disapproves of gossip, so he may not tell you anything."

"We will speak with him," Hiro said, "but tell us what you know as well."

"It isn't much," Gensho admitted. "Just that Nichiyo-*san* won't talk about his life before Myo-in."

"Many men prefer to break with former lives completely when they join the priesthood," Father Mateo said. "At least, it is that way in my religion."

"This is also true of Shingon priests," Gensho agreed, "but even so, Nichiyo-*san*'s behavior is not normal. When the topic comes up, he starts sweating and always finds an excuse to leave the room. I think he's hiding something."

"And this makes you think he murdered Ringa and Anan?" Hiro asked.

"Anan-*sama* was barely dead before that . . . *pretender* was putting on the abbot's robes."

"Yes, but have you any evidence linking him to the killings?" Hiro had noticed Nichiyo's eagerness to grasp control, but selfishness and a thirst for power, though motives for murder, did not necessarily prove guilt. "Did he behave strangely last night or this morning?"

"I wouldn't know. I spent yesterday meditating and preparing meals. Before you ask, I wasn't alone, at least not in the evening hours. Shokai helped me cook the meals and wash the bowls. After that I took a bath and went to bed. I sleep early, because I have to cook before the morning service."

"Can anyone confirm the hours you spent in the meditation hall?"

As Hiro hoped, Gensho replied, "Myokan was there when I arrived, and when I left." He snorted a laugh. "Probably had to stay all night, like last time."

"Last time?" Hiro prompted.

"Every time he fought with Shokai, Ringa-*san* required him to meditate on anger." Gensho sighed. "Not that it helped."

"Did they fight often?" Hiro asked.

"No more than many young men do. Young priests are still young men, you know, despite their hope to overcome attachment to the world." Gensho's face grew serious. "It took me many years to surrender dreams of advancing beyond my skills. However, once I accepted my role and purpose, I found great peace in its fulfillment. This is a deceptively simple teaching, and a difficult one for young men to accept."

"Are you referring to Myokan or Shokai?" Hiro asked.

"Both."

"We heard that Shokai wanted to become a temple guardian, and that he argued with Myokan," Father Mateo said. "Can you tell us, why did Ringa train them both to fight, if Shokai was not Ringa's student?"

"Anan-*sama* asked the guardian to train every priest in self-defense and rudimentary combat to ensure that, if needed, all of us can help defend the temple. Shokai came to Myo-in two years ago. He hoped to become a warrior-priest, and showed real promise in martial studies, despite his common birth—his father is a merchant in Osaka."

"But when Myokan arrived, the abbot made him Ringa's student and forced Shokai to learn medicine instead." Father Mateo nodded sagely.

Hiro wished the Jesuit would just let Gensho tell the story.

"Yes." The muscular priest folded the cloth into a tidy square and laid it in his lap. "Anan-*sama* is the one who decided to alter Shokai's training, but Shokai resents Myokan anyway."

"You said Ringa ordered Myokan to spend the night in medita-tion," Father Mateo said. "Did Shokai escape punishment for the fight?"

"Not at all," Gensho replied. "His punishment will last a week, not just an evening. Kenshin-*san* declared that Shokai must help me in the kitchen, morning and night, for seven days, to learn humility and med-itation through physical labor."

Hiro found the divergent punishments interesting, and wondered whether Shokai's penance might have triggered an even more violent outburst—not only against Ringa, but against the abbot also. The young priest seemed a less likely suspect than an assassin hired by Oda Nobunaga, but the theory was still worth a closer look.

"Where were you this morning during the fire ceremony?" Hiro asked.

"Preparing the morning meal, with Shokai's help." Gensho stood up. "As I mentioned earlier, I do not know who murdered Ringa and Anan, and don't believe the killer will admit his guilt when you ask him to."

"One final question," Hiro said as he and the Jesuit stood up also. "Who benefits the most from the deaths of Ringa and Anan?"

"No one." Gensho's nose flushed red. He blinked as if fighting tears. "Every one of us is poorer for the loss of our guardian and our abbot."

"Despite your harsh opinion of Nichiyo?" Father Mateo asked.

"No man so eager to lead can do it properly," Gensho replied. "I do not like him much, but upon reflection, I do not believe Nichiyo-*san* killed Anan-*sama*. More importantly, I know he could not overpower Ringa-*san*. That is the question you were really asking, isn't it?"

Hiro nodded. "Thank you for your time."

He started toward the door, but stopped when Gensho asked, "What killed Anan-*sama*?"

"He was smothered," Father Mateo said.

"And posed as an incarnation of the Buddha?" Gensho asked.

"What makes you think so?" Hiro kept the question conversational.

"Why else would you think the same man killed them both?"

"Does anyone else in the temple have a violent streak?" Hiro asked. "Doyu-*sama*, perhaps?"

"Between his fading sight and fading mind, Doyu-*sama* is like a little child."

"And Jorin?"

"Spends every waking hour studying sutras. His room is filled with spiderwebs because he will not sweep them down. He would not harm an ant, much less a man."

Gensho indicated the boiling pot, still steaming on the stove. "Now, please excuse me, I have work to do."

The kitchen lay only a short walk from the residence hall, but the blizzard had grown so intense that neither building was visible from the other. The ground and air had turned a uniform shade of white, obscuring distance, muffling sound, and draining all color from the world.

Hiro ducked his head against the driving snow, relying on his memory of the temple grounds and the reassuring knowledge that the walls around the temple yard, though now invisible in the snow, would prevent him from becoming permanently lost.

By the time the wooden doors to the residence hall appeared in front of him, his ears had begun to numb. He stepped into the hall, alongside Father Mateo, and closed the entry door. Gray light seeped in through the slatted window next to the entrance, casting the room in ghostly hues. The air felt stale and ancient, trapped within the incense-scented walls like the bones of priests in wooden boxes under the ground at Okunoin.

Hiro shook off the mental image along with the snow that had gathered on his robes. Leaving his sandals on the rack, he started down the passage. Floorboards creaked beneath his feet. The shutters moaned.

When he opened the guest room door, he stopped on the threshold. The remnants of a fire burned in the brazier, offering feeble light.

The room was empty.

Far too empty.

"Is something wrong?" Father Mateo asked behind him.

"Gato." Hiro looked around the room a second time. "She's gone."

"Gone?" The Jesuit peered over his shoulder. "You're certain?"

"Her basket is missing." Hiro pointed to the corner. "There's no place for her to hide."

Father Mateo looked down the darkened hall. "Perhaps she escaped."

"And took the basket with her?"

"It might be in the cupboard." Father Mateo entered the room and flung the cabinet wide. He searched the folded bedding, but found neither cat nor basket. "Who would take her? Probably, we let her out and didn't see her go."

Hiro imagined Gato, limp and cold, neck broken by the killer's hands. His stomach dropped, and his knees felt weak. The priests of Myo-in would not have harmed her. Buddhists did not kill. . . .

He felt an overwhelming need to feel Gato's silky coat and hear her purr.

His hands clenched into fists.

"We need to find her," Father Mateo said, "before she eats a sacred scroll or uses a holy urn as a latrine."

Hiro smiled despite his churning stomach.

"Remember the day she used the hearth instead of going outside in the rain?" the Jesuit continued. "Ana was furious. I can only imagine what the priests will think—"

"Ana!" Relief flowed through Hiro's limbs like a river at spring thaw. "Ana must have taken her."

"But the rules prohibit women in the temple."

"Who else would take our cat away?" Hiro hoped the Jesuit wouldn't answer.

Father Mateo shrugged. "It's worth a try."

CHAPTER 20

"Hm." Ana pressed her lips together in disapproval. "One night here, and you've already lost the cat?"

"She isn't lost . . . exactly. . . ." Father Mateo trailed off.

"Someone took her," Hiro said. "Her basket is also missing."

"You thought I did it?" Ana looked down her nose at Hiro—a significant feat, given her diminutive size. "Hm. *You* might defile a sacred space, but some of us were raised with more respect."

A vision of the abbot's forehead, carved and bloody, entered Hiro's mind. He thought of Gato—and then pushed both thoughts away. The cat was fine. She had to be.

"Are you comfortable here?" Father Mateo looked past Ana to the nun and the samurai woman sitting beside the abbot's hearth.

Hiro was torn between the desire to flee the room in search of his cat and the knowledge that he could not do so without offending the women and the priest.

The elderly nun bowed. "We are grateful to have shelter from the storm."

"Then you find the accommodations . . . satisfactory?" Father Mateo asked.

A smile crept through the nun's deep wrinkles. "Did you think we would object to sheltering in a room that held the dead? As between this storm and superstition, only one will kill."

"Speaking of killing, did someone actually murder the abbot of Myo-in?" The question came from the samurai woman, who knelt by the hearth on the nun's right side. Her hair, now dry and neatly combed, cascaded down her back like an ebony waterfall. Despite the stains that marred her robe, her regal bearing and polished accent would have been at home in the shogun's palace.

"And, if so," she added, "are the rest of us in danger?"

The question held no hint of fear.

Hiro wondered whether she was foolish, brave, or involved in the killings. "We believe the abbot was murdered. As to your second question, I don't know."

"In that case, I'll need a sword." She nodded to the scabbards at his waist.

"You can use one?" As he spoke, he realized the question might offend.

She stood and gave a formal bow. "I am Endō Hatsuko, sister to Endō Naotsune. My brother is a retainer of Daimyō Azai of Ōmi Province. And yes, I do know how to use a sword."

"Are your brother and the daimyō on the mountain?" Hiro kept his tone conversational, though alarm ran through his thoughts at the mention of Ōmi—a province currently allied with Oda Nobunaga.

She narrowed her eyes and raised her chin. "You think a woman cannot take a pilgrimage alone?"

"Most female pilgrims opt for destinations where they are not banned."

"I do not care that women cannot enter the temple precincts. I wished to see Kōbō Daishi's sacred mountain." Hatsuko nodded to Hiro's swords. "I need a weapon to protect myself—and these other women, too. I ask again: will you lend me a sword?"

She extended her hand.

Hiro stepped away. Furious with himself for reacting visibly, he forced a smile. "Regrettably, I cannot lend you one of mine. However, I will ask the priests if Myo-in has one that you can borrow."

Hatsuko smiled. "I suspect they will object to a woman touching their sacred blades."

Before Hiro could decide if she intended the double meaning, the samurai woman laughed, bent down, and grasped the pilgrim's staff that lay beside her feet. "No samurai worth his blood would lend his sword, let alone to a stranger. Do not worry. This is all I need."

Although she looked nothing like Neko, Hatsuko's voice held a similar taunting confidence. They also shared an inappropriate sense of humor—and inconvenient timing.

"A staff?" Father Mateo sounded incredulous. "What if the killer has a sword?"

"Then I will kill him and take it." She bowed to Hiro. "We appreciate your concern for our safety, but do not wish to detain you any longer."

After a pause just long enough to make the dismissal clear, she added, "And I hope you find your cat."

"Shouldn't we have gone to the meditation hall, to ask for a sword for Hatsuko?" Father Mateo asked as they stepped back inside the residence hall.

Hiro shut the door and left his sandals on the rack. Only a dim gray, cloudy light penetrated the latticed door, leaving most of the corridor steeped in darkness.

"I have no intention of arming that woman." He started down the creaking hall. "We're going to look for Gato."

Father Mateo refused to follow. "You care more for the cat than Ana's safety?"

Hiro returned to the priest and lowered his voice to a whisper. "Daimyō Azai of Ōmi is the brother-in-law of Oda Nobunaga."

"You suspect Hatsuko?" the Jesuit whispered back. "But she was at the nyonindo with the other women when Ringa and Anan were killed."

Hiro looked down the hall toward Soro's guest room. Pale light seeped out beneath the door. Where light could travel, sound could too. He lowered his voice still more and switched to Portuguese. "She could have slipped away in the night to murder Ringa, and returned for Anan in the confusion after the tree fell down—though I admit that seems unlikely."

Father Mateo switched languages also. "'Impossible' seems more accurate to me. Did you see her cuts, and the state of her robe? That wasn't faked."

"She could have brought an assassin to the mountain in her retinue, or carried instructions to one already here."

"You didn't ask if anyone came with her to the mountain," Father Mateo said.

"She claimed she came on a pilgrimage. Had I questioned her further, she might have grown suspicious."

The Jesuit glanced at the latticed door. "The other women could be in danger, then."

"Only if Hatsuko is guilty," Hiro said. "And even then, she is unlikely to attack unless provoked. Right now, I'd like to find my cat."

Just then, the outer door swung open, letting in a blast of frigid air. The wide veranda roof prevented most of the snow from blowing in, but several handfuls' worth spilled off the shoulders of Gensho's robe as he stepped inside.

He held a stack of logs split into narrow lengths, and stopped so quickly at the sight of Hiro and Father Mateo that a few fell off and clattered to the floor.

The Jesuit bent to retrieve them. "I am sorry we surprised you."

"Thank you," Gensho said as the priest set the sticks atop the pile. "I thought you'd have returned to the meditation hall by now."

"Our cat has disappeared." Hiro squinted, hoping to catch a change in the other man's expression.

"You brought a cat on a pilgrimage?" Gensho sounded confused, but recovered quickly. "It must be hiding in the building. Animals know better than to go outside in such a storm. After I deliver this to the pilgrim's room"—he shifted the wood in his arms—"I'll help you look."

"Thank you," Father Mateo said.

Gensho nodded. "By the way, I thought of something, but . . . I don't want to give you the wrong impression."

"Tell us anyway," Hiro said. "If it's not relevant, we will ignore it."

"I was thinking about your question: who would benefit from the abbot's death. I don't know if it's important, but . . . last summer, Nichiyo-*san* pressed Anan-*sama* to name a successor. He kept mentioning that Doyu-*sama* was smart enough to do it before his mind began to fade. At first it sounded reasonable, but as time went on it started getting . . . pushy."

"Did Nichiyo say who Anan should choose?" Hiro asked.

"Not that I ever heard," the muscular priest admitted, "but he didn't really need to. Since Kenshin-*san* refused the role, Nichiyo-*san* was the only remaining candidate."

Hiro remembered Myokan saying something similar. "Why didn't Kenshin want to become the abbot?"

"He thinks his past disqualifies him." Gensho frowned. "I disagree. I've known Kenshin-*san* for many years, and though I understand his reasons I assure you he is wrong."

"Then why does he think so?" Hiro asked.

"He cannot forgive himself for the sins of his past, even though he has grown beyond them," Gensho said. "In that way alone, he remains samurai."

"Samurai?" Given Kenshin's slender fingers and vestigial Kyoto accent, Hiro had taken the physician for the son of an artisan.

"What clan did he come from?" Father Mateo asked.

"He doesn't like to mention it." Gensho glanced over his shoulder as if expecting the physician to appear. Lowering his voice, he whispered, "But Kenshin-*san* was born an Ashikaga."

CHAPTER 21

"Kenshin-*san* belongs to the shogun's clan?" Father Mateo sounded as shocked as Hiro felt.

"The former shogun, anyway," Gensho replied. "I heard the emperor hasn't confirmed a successor yet."

"Kenshin-*san* thought being from the Ashikaga clan disqualified him from becoming abbot?" Father Mateo asked. "I would have thought the opposite."

"Not his birth. . . ." Gensho shuffled his feet. "You should ask him yourself. And it isn't him I was concerned about, just so it's clear. I've known Kenshin-*san* for many years, and though he had a rough beginning here, his dedication to Shingon practice is both faithful and sincere. Nichiyo-*san* is the one to investigate."

"We understand, and thank you," Hiro said.

"Don't worry," Father Mateo added, "we will not reveal your concerns."

As Gensho started down the hall, Hiro stepped into a pair of temple sandals. "I still want to find Gato, but I think it's time we had a talk with Kenshin."

They found the physician in the annex of the worship hall. He knelt beside Anan's body, chanting softly in a monotone. Shokai knelt beside him, also chanting, though where Kenshin knew the words by heart, the younger priest was holding a book and reading the sutra off the page. Outside, the storm winds wailed in counterpoint.

Across the room, the Buddhas smiled knowingly. The lanterns' golden light had a feeble, sickly cast compared with the vibrant snow outside. The room felt small and close.

Spicy incense flooded Hiro's nose as he closed the door. He exhaled sharply, but it didn't help.

Kenshin opened his eyes as the door rattled shut. His features darkened in alarm. "Has something happened?" He jumped to his feet.

Shokai stammered, paused, and shut the sutra book.

Father Mateo raised his hands. "There is no emergency."

"However, we hoped to speak with you alone." Hiro cast a meaningful glance at Shokai.

The young priest clutched the book of sutras to his chest.

Kenshin studied Hiro's face. "Of course. Shokai, we will stand in the doorway as you return to the meditation hall. That way, if you encounter trouble, we will hear you call."

Shokai stood abruptly, bowed to Kenshin and the Buddhas, and left the annex. Kenshin followed the younger man to the door.

"We apologize for disrupting your prayers," Father Mateo said.

The physician watched Shokai disappear into the snow, then slowly closed the wooden door and turned to face them once again.

Kenshin considered the corpses. "I sincerely hope they do not need the rituals, although we will perform them anyway."

"Do not need them?" the Jesuit echoed.

"I was . . . being polite." Kenshin shifted awkwardly. "I respect that your beliefs are different."

"Not so different, truly." Father Mateo smiled. "God judges souls at the moment of death, not over time, but, in your doctrine, how does a soul earn entry into heaven?"

Hiro stifled a sigh. The Jesuit took any chance to talk about religion—regardless of the gods in question. More importantly, Gato was still missing and a killer moving freely through the halls of Myo-in.

The wind wailed louder. Shutters rattled. A chill ran up Hiro's spine.

"Every soul is weighed according to actions taken, and merit earned, in life," Kenshin explained. "Souls who achieve enlightenment receive release from the cycle of life, death, and rebirth. They become one with the Buddha nature in the heavenly realm, where no suffering exists." He paused. "You understand, this is a simplification of the dharma. With apologies, your mind is not prepared to comprehend its fullness."

"Of course," Father Mateo said. "Good teachers offer explanations listeners understand."

With a nod, Kenshin continued, "After death, a person's soul remains in the earthly realm for forty-nine days, during which time the jusanbutsu conduct a trial of the deceased. Each seven days, they render another judgment; on the forty-ninth day, the kings of hell deliver their final verdict and judge the soul."

"Where does the spirit go for the forty-nine days?" the Jesuit asked.

"It wanders the earth," Kenshin replied, "normally near the location where it died."

"Are your prayers said for the dead or for the Buddhas?"

Neither, Hiro thought. *It is the living they appease.* Smoke burned his eyes and throat. His chest grew tight. He thought of Neko's body, burned to ash.

His heart beat faster. He would never see her face again.

"We say the prayers to demonstrate our love for the deceased," Kenshin replied, "and in the hope the jusanbutsu will show mercy."

The opening snapped Hiro from his thoughts. "Speaking of mercy, we hear you use your past to help the younger priests learn self-control."

"I struggled with anger for many years. Helping others gives my struggle meaning."

"Tell me," Hiro said, "what made a son of the Ashikaga clan so angry?"

Kenshin's eyes went stony. "Someone told you who I am."

"Only that you are an Ashikaga," Father Mateo said.

"*Was* Ashikaga." Kenshin crossed the room and stopped in front of the standing Buddha in the central alcove. "But that was a very long time ago."

He raised his face to the statue.

Languid curls of smoke rose from the incense burners. Hiro longed to fling them out the door into the yard. Their stench reminded him of chrysanthemums—dusty, sweet, and loathsome.

The wind blew through the rafters with a wail like a dying breath.

Hiro clenched his fist, annoyed by his inability to focus. None of the suspects had obvious ties to Oda Nobunaga except for the woman, Hatsuko, and she could not have committed the crimes. One of the priests was guilty. He wondered whether Kenshin's ties to the Ashikaga clan could lure the murderer from hiding.

"Of all the incarnations of the Buddha"—Kenshin gestured to the standing statue—"this one is my favorite. Do you know him?"

Father Mateo joined him in front of the Buddha. "With apologies, I have trouble telling them apart."

"Yakushi-*sama* is the Buddha of medicine and healing." Kenshin raised his hand to his chest. "My patron."

"Is he normally carved in a standing position?" Father Mateo asked.

"The style is relatively new, and mostly seen in temples of the Tendai School. They carve him standing to demonstrate his active involvement in the world."

Hiro stifled a frown. The physician had shifted the topic back to theology.

"Does this temple belong to the Tendai School?" Father Mateo asked.

"All the temples on Mount Kōya, including Myo-in, belong to the Shingon School, which follows the teachings of Kōbō Daishi," Kenshin explained. "Tendai temples follow the teachings of a different priest, named Saichō."

"Please forgive the question," Father Mateo asked, "but why do you display a statue that belongs to a different sect? In my faith, this would not happen."

"The statue was a gift from my father." Kenshin's face grew pensive as he studied the Buddha. "He was not a religious man, and did not understand its symbolism. He knew only that it was expensive."

He shifted his gaze to Father Mateo, eyes suddenly sharp and focused. "Whoever told you I was born samurai clearly thinks my past is relevant to your investigation."

CHAPTER 22

"I have nothing to hide." Kenshin made a gesture of invitation as he knelt on the floor. "In fact, I think you would benefit from hearing the entire story."

Hiro knelt with his back to the Buddhas, and Father Mateo knelt beside him.

The physician smoothed his robe across his knees. "My father is a distant cousin of the shogun. He bears the surname 'Ashikaga,' but is not in the line of succession. However, he was a loyal retainer of Shogun Ashikaga Yoshiharu."

"Yoshiharu?" Father Mateo asked. "I thought the shogun's name was Yoshiteru."

"Yoshiteru died last June," Kenshin confirmed. "Ashikaga Yoshiharu was his father, who served as shogun before his son. My father served in Yoshiharu's personal guard, and they became close friends after my father saved the shogun's life.

"Yoshiteru and I were born a month apart and grew up together in the shogun's palace. He was my closest friend."

"I am so sorry," Father Mateo said. "His death must have been difficult for you."

"I pray for his spirit every day, even though the forty-ninth day, and even the hundredth day, after his death has come and gone. I will pray for him as long as I draw breath." After a thoughtful pause, Kenshin continued, "We were inseparable as children, learning the ways of sword and bow, horsemanship and etiquette. We were closer than friends. We were brothers, as truly as if we shared a womb."

Kenshin's voice grew soft. "The year we turned eleven, Yoshiharu abdicated the shogunate—a negotiated resignation, designed to resolve a political conflict. As a result, Yoshiteru became the shogun."

"At eleven years old?" Father Mateo's voice rose in disbelief.

"It was one of the terms of his father's abdication. On the day Yoshiharu resigned the shogunate, he fled to Ōmi. My father and the other bodyguards willingly followed him into exile. A few young samurai remained in Kyoto as Yoshiteru's personal guard, but I was too young to swear the oath." Kenshin clenched his jaw. His eyes reddened with unshed tears.

"A touching story," Hiro said, "but it doesn't explain how you ended up in a temple."

The comment drew a scolding look from Father Mateo, but Hiro didn't care. His eyes itched. His lungs were filled with smoke. The wind was howling with a sound like Gato made when Ana accidentally locked her out at night, and the story was wasting time he could use to find his cat and stop the killer.

Kenshin blinked. "Of course. I will get to the point. Since I could not swear the oath, my father and Yoshiharu decided that I should become a Shingon priest, and spend my life in prayer for the shogun's health, success, and wisdom."

"But your father was not religious," Hiro objected.

"Shogun Yoshiharu was, although most people did not know. He hid the depth of his beliefs because he feared people would think him weak.

"Apparently, the idea for his abdication came from a dream in which the Buddha told him that resigning the shogunate in favor of Yoshiteru would ensure not only their survival, but continuation of the Ashikaga shogunate. When his political enemies agreed to the suggested terms, Yoshiharu wished to send a generous gift to the temples on Mount Kōya—including a priest whose primary role would be to pray for the health and success of the Ashikaga clan, and Yoshiteru in particular."

"And you became the sacrificial lamb." Father Mateo spoke the final words in Portuguese.

Kenshin scratched his head. "I do not know this term. However, I was Yoshiteru's closest friend, and so my father offered me to Kōya." He looked up at the standing statue. "This image of Yakushi-*sama* and a bag of silver bought me a position here."

The words sounded genuine, but Hiro found them difficult to believe. "A man who was not religious allowed his son to become a priest?"

"More than just allowed it, he required it, against my will." All emotion disappeared from Kenshin's voice. "My father was samurai, loyal to his lord. Had the shogun asked him to kill me, he would have done it without hesitation. As it was, I merely had to walk beside his horse from Kyoto to the summit of Mount Kōya."

"You walked all that way? At eleven years old?" Father Mateo sounded shocked. "He didn't have another horse for you to ride?"

Kenshin smiled. "Traditionally, a man who wants to become a priest can prove his worthiness to join the temple, and earn substantial merit toward enlightenment, by undertaking the arduous journey on foot. The shogun requested that I follow the traditional way."

"And you agreed?" The Jesuit sounded doubtful.

"I did not." Kenshin seemed on the verge of either tears or laughter. "I did not understand why my father stripped me of not only my birthright—my future as a warrior of the ruling Ashikaga clan—but also of my closest friend. That was the part that angered me most—that I would never again lay eyes on Yoshiteru, who I loved as deeply as a brother. I could have completed *genpuku* and earned my swords in another year, or two at most. Instead, he condemned me to a life of prayer, bells, and solitude. The unfairness struck me to the core."

The physician spoke with an eerie lack of emotion, almost as if the events had happened to someone else. "By the time we reached Mount Kōya, I was filled with bitterness and rage."

"You didn't tell your father how you felt? Or ask to stay in Kyoto with the shogun?" Father Mateo rubbed the back of his scarred left hand with his right thumb.

"A samurai does not question his father, or the shogun," Kenshin said. "My words would not have changed his mind. They merely would have shamed us both.

"When we arrived on Kōya, my father gave the abbot—Doyu-*sama*—a bag of silver and departed. The statue of Yakushi-*sama* arrived six months later, along with a letter from my father—the only one I have received."

"What did it say?" Father Mateo asked.

"I do not know. I burned it." Kenshin smiled. "As I said, I was an angry child. Doyu-*sama* appointed Anan-*sama* as my teacher, but at first I would not listen. I ignored his words, tore sutra books, and dripped hot candle wax on anything I thought that it would ruin. I refused to study, and yelled in the yard when other priests were meditating."

Father Mateo nodded shrewdly. "You thought they would kick you out, and you could return to Kyoto."

"That is so." The physician ran a hand across his cleanly shaven scalp. "Fortunately, it did not work. Anan-*sama* remained as calm as Buddha. The worse I behaved, the more serene and patient he became. In time, I grew to see him as a father, and loved him more than the man who gave me life."

"And as your love grew, your anger faded," Father Mateo said.

"No. If anything, it grew worse. As I grew older, I realized I could never return to Kyoto. I had taken vows dedicating my life to prayer on behalf of Yoshiteru and the Ashikaga clan. As a child, I had not understood their significance, but as I grew older . . .

"When I turned eighteen, the oldest priest in the temple died. As I watched his body burn on its funeral pyre, I realized that I, like him, would never leave this mountain. For a short time after that, I thought of suicide, but feared the judgment I would face before the kings of hell.

"The following year, I learned of my father's death. As I said the funeral prayers for him, I knew I could no longer blame him for my misery. I did not choose this life, but I could choose the way I lived it. Anan-*sama* had told me many times that study and meditation could free me from anger, but only if I wanted to embrace a different way.

"I began to study the sutras in earnest. I approached Doyu-*sama* and asked to study with the temple physician. He granted my request, and when the physician eventually died, I took his place. Anger, like fire, cannot survive in the absence of fuel. When I stopped feeding mine, it died. I still miss Yoshiteru. I will miss him until the day I die. But, at least, I am no longer angry."

"Why did you refuse to become the abbot?" Father Mateo asked.

Kenshin seemed to expect the question. "As a child, I equated worldly power with greatness. Now, I recognize it as an unwelcome and oppressive burden. Also, it would interfere with my duty to the shogun."

"But the shogun died." Father Mateo sounded uncertain.

"A fact that does not diminish my obligation to offer prayers. If anything, I must be even more diligent, to ensure the emperor names an Ashikaga to succeed him."

"Do you approve of Nichiyo becoming the abbot of Myo-in?" Hiro asked.

"A man who does not wish to do a job himself must not impede the man who undertakes it."

"Kenshin-*san*!" Shokai's panicked cry rang out from the worship hall next door. Footsteps pounded toward the shoji separating the annex from the larger space.

Hiro sprang to his feet and stepped in front of Father Mateo as the door slid open. Wind rattled the building. A high, thin wail echoed through the hall.

Shokai's eyes were wild. He held a fighting staff. "Come quickly! Jorin-*san* is here—and dead!"

CHAPTER 23

"Jorin?" Kenshin repeated.

As he spoke, the wail intensified—and Hiro realized the sound was not the wind. He glanced at Father Mateo.

"That's Gato!" both men said.

Hiro ran for the narrow stairs. Father Mateo followed a step behind.

Shokai jumped to clear the door as Hiro barreled through.

He paused to let his eyes adjust to the dim interior of the worship hall. Two bronze lanterns burned on either side of the pagoda table in the center of the room. Aside from this, the hall was dark and gloomy. Shadows gathered in the corners, obscuring most of the room.

"Gato!" he called.

She wailed, her crying heavily muffled but clearly somewhere in the room. His stomach dropped. The wind was not the only howling he'd been hearing in the annex.

"It really is—" Father Mateo gasped and made the sign of the cross.

Hiro followed the Jesuit's stare to the alcove behind the altar table. During the morning worship service, a gilded wooden Buddha had filled the space.

Now it held the body of a priest.

The dead man wore a plain, dark robe and a cap embroidered with golden swirls. His chin rested on his chest, and shadows hid his face and neck. His right hand held a sword. The left one clutched a well-worn scroll. He sat cross-legged atop a lacquered box.

"It's Jorin." Shokai sounded strangled.

The box emitted an angry yowl.

Hiro's muscles loosened with relief. The cat sounded furious, but unhurt. He started toward the alcove, but stopped abruptly. "Shokai—did you check this room?"

"For what?" the young priest asked. "I just came in this way to check the lanterns—sometimes they go out—and saw—" He glanced at the alcove and looked away quickly.

"The killer might still be here." Hiro laid a hand on his katana and surveyed the shadowed room. The gloomy light of the lanterns barely reached the alcove, and sides and back of the room were steeped in darkness. Hiro squinted, but his vision could not penetrate the shadows.

He looked back over his shoulder at Father Mateo. "Stay here, by the door." He widened the look to include the other priests. "Everyone, stay here."

He gripped his katana but changed his mind and drew the shorter *wakizashi*. Given the elaborate clutter of lamps, pagodas, Buddhist statues, candlesticks, and other holy detritus that filled the room, the longer sword would prove a liability.

Slowly, Hiro circled the altar table. He stayed within the light. It made him a target, but if the killer was hiding here, he already knew where Hiro was—and, also, that his presence was suspected. By remaining within the lanterns' glow, Hiro reduced the chance of successful ambush.

After every step, he stopped. He slowed his breathing, listening for any motion in the room. It wasn't easy. Gato's wails intensified. She clawed at the inside of the box with determined fury, and her scratching covered any other silent sounds.

Hiro doubted the killer had remained in the hall, but only a fool would make assumptions.

And Hiro was no fool.

Three steps past the end of the altar table, he stopped at the edge of the light. Directly ahead, the southern wall of the worship hall was lined with shelves. Each one held rows of tiny wooden Buddhas and memorial tablets, marching along in perfect lines, a cemetery in miniature.

"A squirrel couldn't hide in there," Shokai said from across the room.

Hiro did not answer. He heard something to his right, near the alcove. Quickly, he took three steps forward and spun around, pressing his back against the shelves.

Across the room, Father Mateo gave him a nervous nod.

Hiro raised his sword and sidestepped down the wall until he reached the knee-high wooden barrier between the altars and the open, tatami-covered area for worshippers. Shadows filled the space, but Hiro's eyes had now adjusted just enough to reveal that it was empty.

"He's not here." Shokai's voice held a hint of derision. "We need to see to Jorin."

"In a minute," Hiro snapped.

Keeping his back to the shelves, he moved in the other direction, toward the alcove where the body sat. As he passed the table, he bent and looked beneath it.

He saw not even a dust ball on the floor.

To his left, a bulky shadow loomed. Hiro froze. The shadow didn't move. He took a step forward, wakizashi ready.

It was only the gilded Buddha, sitting upright on the floor.

Hiro took a breath and exhaled slowly.

Walking normally, he made his way to the end of the shelves. They stopped three feet before the rear wall of the worship hall, leaving a narrow alcove that wasn't visible from the front of the hall.

It was also deep enough to conceal a man.

Gripping his wakizashi firmly, Hiro leaped around the corner, expecting the area to be empty.

A tall, robed figure huddled in the space between the cabinet and the wall.

Hiro slashed, but felt the blade slice only air.

An instant later, he realized his mistake.

A ceremonial robe hung on a hook against the wall. In the darkness, he mistook it for a man.

"Hiro!" Father Mateo's frightened cry rang out.

"I'm fine." A rush of heat filled Hiro's cheeks. He raised his empty hand. "There's no one here."

He faced the others. "The room is clear."

"Of course it is." Shokai followed Kenshin and Father Mateo to the alcove. "Had the killer been here, he'd have murdered me when I found Jorin."

Gato's howling grew louder and her clawing more insistent.

"The cat is in the box beneath the body." Father Mateo gestured. "Why?"

"*Who* is the more important question," Hiro said. "Who put her there?"

"Her basket's here." Father Mateo picked it up from where it lay discarded in the shadows on the floor.

"Can there be any doubt who did this?" Shokai asked. "Everyone who stood between Nichiyo-*san* and the office of abbot is dead. Ringa, Anan, now Jorin—"

"Jorin-*san* did not object to Nichiyo-*san* becoming abbot," Kenshin said.

"Not openly, but no one knew the laws as well as he did. If he did object, his words would carry weight."

"Three men are dead, and you make baseless accusations?" Kenshin frowned. "Yours are not the words of a physician or a priest."

Shokai narrowed his eyes at the rebuke.

An awkward silence fell, but only for a moment.

Gato yowled and scrabbled at the inside of the box.

Kenshin gestured. "We should tend to Jorin-*san*—and free the cat."

CHAPTER 24

"Wait." Hiro sheathed his wakizashi. "Before we move him, we should figure out which Buddha he's supposed to represent."

"You think—" Kenshin fell silent as he gazed at the body. "You may be right."

"Another Buddha?" Father Mateo asked. "Are you certain?"

"This time, it's obvious." Hiro gestured to the wooden statue sitting on the floor. "The killer moved this one to make it clear."

"He has a sword," the Jesuit observed. "Perhaps Fudō again?"

"Fudō has a rope, not a scroll," Kenshin replied.

"I recognize him!" Shokai's voice rose with excitement. "Sword and scroll, and seated on a tiger—well, a cat—he's Monju Bosatsu, the Voice of the Law."

Kenshin nodded. "That makes sense, considering who Jorin was in life."

Hiro raised the dead man's head. The darkening bruises on the corpse's throat were visible despite the gloom. "Most interesting, considering he was choked to death." He looked over his shoulder at Shokai.

"That looks like the Perfection of Wisdom sutra." Shokai gestured to the scroll in the corpse's hand. "Jorin had it with him in the meditation hall."

Kenshin took the scroll from the dead man's hand and unrolled it carefully. "Correct."

Hiro lowered the corpse's head and stepped away. He felt as if he was missing something critical. It hovered just beyond his conscious thoughts, frustratingly out of reach.

Gato's angry howling split the air.

Hiro disliked the killer's use of his cat—and not only because he cared so deeply for her. The decision raised the dangerous possibility that the killer knew, or at least suspected, Hiro's true identity. The choice might be coincidental, but the murders had begun the night they arrived at Myo-in. . . .

The connection that had danced around the edges of Hiro's conscious mind snapped sharply into focus.

It didn't get him closer to the killer's name, but the reason for the Buddhas now made horrifying sense.

He longed to discuss it with Father Mateo, but would not risk a word around the priests. Shokai's willingness to gossip made him untrustworthy, even if Hiro hadn't also suspected him of the killings. As for Kenshin, his true loyalties remained in question also.

Keeping his expression neutral, Hiro said, "Now that we know which Buddha he represents, let's get him down and free the cat."

Gato yowled as if in agreement.

Hiro removed the sword from the dead man's hand and passed the weapon to Kenshin. As between the physician and Shokai, the former seemed less likely to use it against the others in the room. Kenshin accepted the weapon and promptly handed it off to Shokai.

So much for safety.

Kenshin moved to Hiro's side. "Let's carry him to the annex."

The two men gently lifted Jorin down from the alcove and around the altar table, taking care not to knock over the pagoda, lamps, or other ritual objects.

"Don't open the box," Hiro said to the Jesuit.

Father Mateo paused, his hands already on the lid. "Why not?"

"If she gets out in here, we'll never catch her." *And she'll break or ruin something irreplaceable.*

"Good thinking." The Jesuit picked up the box and followed.

As Hiro helped the physician carry the body through the doorway and down the steps to the annex floor, he wondered where the killing occurred. Strangulation victims struggled, but the worship hall appeared intact. With ritual objects covering every surface, something would have broken, or at least fallen over, if the killing had taken place beside the altar.

Ordinarily, Hiro would have wondered how the killer managed to move a body across the temple yard without being seen. However, the blizzard answered that question too. With the snow so thick, the killer could pass within a few feet of another person—or a building—without ever being noticed.

As they rested Jorin's body on the floor about six feet from Anan's corpse, the cap fell off his head, revealing his shiny scalp but no additional injuries. Hiro hadn't expected any, given the extensive bruises on the dead man's throat. Reaching down, he opened Jorin's eyes. The whites were now a shocking red.

Father Mateo looked down, still holding the howling box. "Strangled, as you said."

Shokai looked and jumped away. "His eyes look like the abbot's—only worse."

"Strangulation causes the eyes to bleed, especially if the victim struggles." Hiro lowered Jorin's eyelids. "This confirms the cause of death."

Father Mateo gave the corpse a puzzled look. "I don't understand why he didn't yell when the killer attacked. More importantly, didn't we just leave him in the meditation hall?" The Jesuit's eyes went wide. "The other priests might all be dead!"

"Unlikely." Hiro straightened. "Why would the killer bother moving a single body to the hondō? More likely, Jorin left the hall and ran into the murderer while alone."

"Why would he leave?" the Jesuit asked.

"The latrine?" Shokai shrugged. "Eventually, everyone needs it."

Gato howled, joining her voice to the storm that whistled through the rafters and rattled the outer door to the annex room.

"The killer could have followed him, too," Shokai pointed out. "It might not have been an accident."

"The death was not accidental," Hiro said.

"Perhaps you should talk with Gensho-*san*," Shokai said. "He claimed he had chores to do. He's been alone all morning."

"Five minutes ago, you accused Nichiyo-*san*. Now Gensho?" Kenshin paused. "Such accusations are dangerous—"

"So is the killer!" Shokai's voice grew shrill. "Besides, I simply pointed out that Gensho was alone, and that he's strong enough to strangle a man barehanded, if he wants to."

Hiro found it interesting that Shokai recognized the marks on Jorin's neck were made by fingers rather than a rope.

"What does Gensho-*san* gain from Jorin-*san*'s death?" Kenshin demanded. "Or the deaths of Ringa and the abbot?"

"I don't know," Shokai admitted.

Inside the box, Gato grew strangely silent. A moment later, she gave a plaintive mew.

"We should take her back to the room." Hiro appreciated the excuse to speak with the Jesuit privately.

"May we remove this box from the hondō?" Father Mateo asked as Hiro relieved him of the burden.

"It isn't holy," Shokai said. "It's just a box we use for storing sutras."

"We will return it, when we can." Hiro started toward the door.

"Shokai," Kenshin said. "Come with me to notify Nichiyo-*san* and the others of Jorin's death. After that, we can prepare his body for the funeral rites."

CHAPTER 25

Outside, the blizzard filled the air with snow that caught on Hiro's lashes. Wind and snowfall muted sound, including his own footsteps, and despite the fresh, cold air around him, Hiro felt almost as smothered as he did inside the smoky halls.

The smooth-soled temple sandals slipped and skidded on the ground. More snow fell into them with every step, soaking his tabi and his toes.

Gato jumped inside the box. Between the sandals and the cat, Hiro struggled not to fall.

The air inside the residence hall felt strangely still after the howling storm. Hiro's ears and face felt hot, despite the chilly temperature. The new snow on his tabi melted, soaking in and making them even wetter, if that was possible.

He hurried to the guest room as, inside the box, Gato renewed her wailing.

As soon as Father Mateo shut the guest room door behind them, Hiro raised the lid.

For a moment, nothing happened.

Slowly, Gato's head appeared, ears laid back and whiskers tight against her face. She glared at Hiro, leaped from the box, and raced around the room. When she finished, she leaped onto the table and licked her side with angry vigor.

"She seems unhurt," Father Mateo said, with audible relief.

"Regrettably, the rest of us are not. The killer will strike again, and more than once."

"Did I miss a clue?"

Hiro revealed the insight that had struck him with such force. "The killer is posing the victims' corpses as the jusanbutsu."

"The judges of the dead?" The Jesuit drew back. "You're certain?"

Hiro raised a finger for each victim, counting them off as he explained, "Ringa, posed as Fudō Myō-ō—first to die, and representing the incarnation that oversees the judgment on the seventh day, the first that takes place after death. Anan—the historical Buddha, Shaka, who judges the soul on the fourteenth day. Second to die, and second to judge. Now we have Jorin, posed as Monju, the one who presides on the twenty-first day after death."

"So the killer not only chooses his victims based on their resemblance to the judges of the afterlife—he's killing them in order?"

"In the order the incarnations judge the dead."

Gato stretched, jumped off the table, and arched her back against Hiro's legs. He bent and stroked her fur, considering how to explain the greater significance of the killer's choice.

"Hiro." Father Mateo sounded grave. "There are thirteen kings of hell. When the killings began, there were fourteen people in this temple."

Hiro straightened. "Precisely."

"Unless we stop him, he will kill everyone in the temple, including the children."

"Giving further weight to my belief that Oda is behind the deaths, and wants Myo-in destroyed."

"Why would he destroy an entire temple to eliminate an Iga spy?" the Jesuit asked. "It makes no sense. And even if he did, why pose the dead as Buddhas? Why not set a fire and kill them all at once?"

"Oda Nobunaga destroys what he cannot control, and not just samurai. He would not hesitate to destroy a temple to eliminate a threat. He does not care if innocents suffer. Burning the temple outright carries too high a risk of the targets escaping, though I do suspect the killer plans to burn the buildings after all the priests are dead, to hide the evidence or at least obscure its cause.

"As for the poses"—Hiro shrugged—"people who kill for a living are often strange."

"But how would a stranger know the victims' personalities well enough to match them to the deities?"

"That is not what I meant by strange."

Father Mateo crossed his arms.

"Oda's assassin would have received detailed information about the priests of Myo-in," Hiro said, "unless he was living here already. And, of course, we cannot make assumptions."

"So we can't eliminate anyone." Father Mateo raised his hands. "How will we identify the killer?"

"You must not reveal what we've deduced to anyone."

"But they're at risk," the Jesuit objected. "We must warn them. Bussho and Ippen are only children!"

"The risk will increase if the killer knows we've figured out his plan." Gato coiled around Hiro's legs, purring more insistently. He picked her up. "For the moment, he's using a recognizable pattern, killing solitary victims several hours apart from one another. If he thinks we're close to catching him, he could easily change or escalate his efforts, making him more difficult to stop."

"Why kill children?" Father Mateo demanded. "Position corpses as Buddhas? It makes no sense. He must be insane, or possessed by a demon, and no one in this temple acts that way."

Hiro raised an eyebrow. "Possessed by a demon?"

The Jesuit crossed his arms again. "It happens."

"If you say so."

"A madman, then. Do you disagree?"

"Men are more than capable of evil without the excuse of madness or superstition." Hiro sighed and stroked the cat. "I almost wish the murderer was suffering from madness. We would catch him much more easily."

"Which Buddha comes next in the funeral rites?" The Jesuit paused. "And how did you see the pattern so quickly? You're not a Buddhist."

"But my mother is." Hiro bent over and put Gato back inside the box. Holding her down with his hand, he set the lid back into place. "She made me go to the temple with her when I was a child. The belief didn't stick, but the information did."

Inside the box, the cat began to cry.

"What are you doing?" Father Mateo asked.

Hiro lifted the box and straightened. "The next victim will represent Fugen, the bodhisattva of goodness and virtue." He started toward the door. "Gato will be safer with Ana than in our room alone. Also, if we leave her there we'll have an excuse to check on the women frequently."

"Because no one would believe we cared about the women's welfare."

Hiro ignored the Jesuit's sarcasm. "We have no reason to worry about their welfare. They are safe from the storm, and none of the jusanbutsu are female." He reconsidered the statement as he adjusted his grip on the wooden box. "Kannon, whose observance occurs on the hundredth day, is sometimes shown in female form, but the killer could not have known the nyonindo would burn."

"Unless the fallen tree was not an accident."

Hiro's mind swam with the additional complications that created.

"No assumptions," the Jesuit said. "Remember?"

"Given Hatsuko's connection to Ōmi, we cannot rule out her involvement. I don't think she's the killer, but she could easily be working with someone else."

"Like Kenshin?" Father Mateo suggested. "His father lived in Ōmi too, remember?"

"That was before the daimyō aligned with Oda Nobunaga. The province was loyal to the Ashikaga clan at that time, and Kenshin seems loyal to them now, though, as you say, we cannot make assumptions. We'll talk with Hatsuko when we leave the cat, and after that, we'll speak to Nichiyo and Shokai."

"How can we keep the children safe?" Father Mateo opened the door.

"The same way we protect the others," Hiro said. "We find the killer quickly."

CHAPTER 26

"Of course we will keep Gato." Ana accepted the box from Hiro and set it on the floor beside the abbot's hearth. When she raised the lid, the cat sprang out immediately.

"Shouldn't she consult the other women?" Father Mateo murmured in Portuguese.

A smile elongated the nun's wrinkles. "What a lovely cat. Of course we will watch her for you." She extended a hand to Gato, who sniffed and then butted the elderly woman's knuckles. "I hope my cat survived the fire. She often hunted in the woods, and sometimes stayed out overnight, so I suspect she has a place to hide. If not, at least she caught enough mice in the nyonindo to earn a good rebirth."

Hatsuko knelt and made a clicking noise. Gato's ears twitched. She trotted over and rubbed her body along the samurai woman's robe as Hatsuko stroked the black-and-orange fur. "I had a cat this color when I was a child. She was my favorite."

Gato pawed at Hatsuko's kimono and jumped onto the samurai woman's lap. After circling once, the cat lay down and purred.

Hiro hid his surprise beneath a banal question. "You grew up in Ōmi?"

Hatsuko met his gaze and held it. "My family has served alongside the Azai for generations." She ran her fingers over Gato's fur.

Hiro felt a flicker of frustration at her nonresponsive answer.

"Another priest has died," Father Mateo said. "You should be wary of anyone who tries to enter this room, aside from Hiro and me."

Hatsuko fixed her gaze on Hiro. "We should simply trust that you are safe?" The hint of flirtation in her question irritated him even more.

"Hiro-*san*?" Ana snorted. "Unless you're a sake flask, he's harmless."
Hiro frowned.

"I see." The glimmer left Hatsuko's eyes. "He is a common samurai."

I am anything but common. Hiro blinked, dismayed by his own reaction, and not only for its vehemence. He should not—did not—care what this woman, or any other, thought of him. He affected commonality as a disguise, to avoid attention. That was all.

"We believe—" Father Mateo started over. "We suspect the killer remains in the temple, hiding among the priests. For safety, please do not trust anyone."

"Except for you," Hatsuko said drily. She continued to stroke the cat and indicated the wooden staff that lay on the floor beside her. "I assure you, I will not."

Hiro and Father Mateo fought through the blizzard to the meditation hall. Driving snow obscured the yard. Winds gusted hard enough to knock an unsuspecting person off his feet. The sense of isolation, always present in the mountains, seemed more amplified than normal in the storm. Hiro tucked his chin into his robe and bent his head against the wind. Icy crystals stung his face like sand. By the time he and the Jesuit reached the meditation hall, his eyes felt gritty and his ears began to burn.

As he paused to remove his sandals in the wood-floored entry, Hiro noticed a spider spinning its delicate web in a corner between the rafters and the wall. He felt a flash of unexpected pity. So late in the year, the web would trap no moths or flies. Delicate insects died in winter's cold.

Unfortunately, the killer suffered no similar lack of victims.

Rhythmic chanting flowed into the entry from the hall beyond. Several voices blended into one with a hypnotic quality that intrigued and repulsed Hiro in equal measure.

He followed Father Mateo into the meditation hall.

The surviving priests of Myo-in, except for Gensho, knelt on the far side of the room before the Buddhas. Everyone but Nichiyo and Myokan faced the statues. The guardian knelt at the back of the group, angled sideways to watch the door.

Nichiyo sat cross-legged in front of the group, with his back to the statutes. He held a book of sutras, and his eyes were closed. Although his position suggested leadership, the voices rose and fell as one, with no apparent cues or instructions.

Father Mateo caught Hiro's eye and nodded to Kenshin and Shokai, who knelt among the priests. Hiro recognized them, even from behind, and agreed with the Jesuit's silent observation: those two should not be here. Preparing a body for funeral rites took longer than he and Father Mateo had spent in the abbot's home with the women, even allowing for their earlier conversation in the guest room.

Hiro debated interrupting, but before he could the priests fell silent. Nichiyo opened his eyes and saw them standing near the entrance.

"Bussho, please take over." He stood up, handed the book to the boy, and walked toward Hiro and Father Mateo.

Myokan began to rise, but sank back down at a look from the abbot.

After Nichiyo passed by, Kenshin stood up and followed him, drawing frowns from Myokan and Shokai. A moment later, Shokai rose and followed his teacher.

Myokan's frown deepened, but he stayed in place.

Nichiyo bowed to Hiro and Father Mateo, who returned the greeting.

Behind the abbot, Bussho's reedy voice began to chant. The other priests joined in a moment later, voices blending with and then disguising the child's softer tones.

"Is it true?" Nichiyo asked softly. "Jorin-*san* is dead?"

Hiro found the question odd. "Kenshin-*san* did not explain?"

"Of course he did." Nichiyo's tone, though silent, revealed irritation. "Why do you think I ordered him to stay with us instead of going back to the hondō?"

"With respect," Kenshin put in, "we need to return and prepare the body—"

"I told you, it is not safe," Nichiyo hissed. He pointed to the Jesuit. "You told me you could find the killer. Now another priest is dead. I begin to wonder if Myokan was correct about you wanting to destroy our temple."

Hiro placed himself between the Jesuit and the abbot. "He had nothing to do with—"

"Truly, you cannot believe such nonsense." Father Mateo stepped around Hiro and advanced on Nichiyo. He towered over the abbot. "God abhors murder, and so do I. More importantly, why would a Christian priest position the dead as Buddhist saints?"

"What are 'saints'?" Shokai whispered.

Nichiyo ignored the question. "Assuming you are a priest at all. We have only your word, and that of your ronin translator."

Behind them, chanting rose and fell, the priests unaware of the argument. Hiro considered the irony. Most Buddhist prayers were offered in hope of peace.

Father Mateo gestured toward the front of the room. "Even if I wanted you to accept my religion, murder is hardly an effective way to achieve that goal. Especially for a man alone."

"You are not one man alone." Nichiyo looked meaningfully at Hiro.

"While I appreciate the compliment," the Jesuit said, "if I planned to kill you, I would have brought more samurai."

"Why did you come to Kōya?" Nichiyo asked. "Foreigners have no business on this mountain."

"With respect," Kenshin said, "I disagree. He came to learn, as many people do."

"To learn our weaknesses." Nichiyo glanced at Myokan, who began to rise, but sank back to his knees again at a shake of the abbot's head.

"This foreigner could not have known that we called Ringa Fudō Myō-ō," Kenshin continued, "or that Jorin's expertise was law."

"Jorin was posed as Monju?" Nichiyo looked alarmed.

So much for keeping that part a secret, Hiro thought—and, just as quickly, realized Kenshin had also initially held that information back.

"Fudō, Shaka, Monju . . . the first three of the jusanbutsu." Nichiyo surveyed the chanting priests, nodding slightly as if counting. Slowly, his cheeks grew pale. "Only eleven men remain alive in this temple, including the two of you, the pilgrim, and his son. Unless you stop the killer, all of us are going to die!"

CHAPTER 27

"I suspect not all of us will die," Hiro said. "Most likely, the murderer plans to live."

"Only the killer would find that amusing," Nichiyo snapped.

Hiro narrowed his eyes at the abbot. "Facts or steel?"

"Pardon me?"

"Such a deadly accusation must be backed by facts or steel. Which one do you plan to use?"

Nichiyo shrank back in fear, as Hiro knew he would. Petty men and cowards growled like tigers, but they ran like rats when real threats appeared.

Father Mateo deftly changed the subject. "Where is Gensho-*san*?"

Nichiyo nodded toward one of the braziers at the back of the room. "We cannot survive the storm without food and heat. Gensho-*san* volunteered to continue preparing meals as usual, and to replenish the fuel so no one else would need to leave the hall."

Hiro noted the lack of concern in the acting abbot's voice.

"What of the pilgrim?" Shokai frowned. "Where is he?"

"Soro chose to remain in his guest room, with his son," the Jesuit explained.

"Still? But he might be the killer," Shokai protested. "If so, he could leave his room at any time to kill again."

"A valid point," the abbot said. "Perhaps we should require him to join us after all."

Hiro tried to imagine jowly, red-faced Nichiyo requiring anything of Soro, and failed miserably. An amusing line of thought, but it wouldn't catch a killer. "Aside from Gensho-*san* and Jorin-*san*, did anyone leave the meditation hall after we did?"

"When you went to speak with Soro?" Nichiyo rubbed his chin in thought. "Myokan went out to check the gates and inspect the walls. I used the latrine, as did Doyu-*sama* and Bussho. But surely you don't think one of us would murder our fellow priests?"

"I merely asked who left the building," Hiro said.

"Implying you believe that we are guilty." Nichiyo stared at Hiro as if daring him to contradict.

"As a factual matter, someone here *is* guilty." Hiro spoke without emotion. "Neither Bussho nor the pilgrim's son has the physical strength to commit the crimes, but everyone else in the temple remains a suspect."

Including Hatsuko.

"Even Doyu-*sama*?" Nichiyo scoffed. "He barely remembers his own name."

"Last I checked, that is not a prerequisite to murder."

"Three days ago, he wandered into the yard while Bussho was sleeping and almost fell to his death while attempting to rescue a cat from the temple roof." Nichiyo looked at the elderly former abbot, who once again appeared to be dozing. "It was a *tanuki*, not a cat"— he shifted his gaze to Father Mateo—"an animal of similar size, but masked, with a bushy tail."

The Jesuit nodded. "I have seen them."

"Doyu-*sama*'s fading eyes could not tell the difference, and his addled brain no longer seems to understand when danger threatens. When he climbed onto the roof, the creature ran away. He tried to follow, fell, and struck his head on the stones at the edge of the pond."

"You are certain that's what happened?" Hiro stared at the back of Doyu's nodding head. Between the discoloration of age and liver spots, he couldn't tell if the priest had suffered injuries.

"That is what he told us, when he regained consciousness," Nichiyo said. "Except, of course, that he insists the creature was a cat."

"How do you know it wasn't?" Hiro asked.

"Tanuki are common on Kōya. Cats are not." Nichiyo turned to Kenshin. "You and Shokai may tend to Jorin's body, but stay together and in sight of one another at all times. It is no longer safe for us to leave the hall alone."

Relief relaxed the physician's face. "Would you like us to check on Gensho-*san* as well?"

"I would appreciate that, thank you."

Hiro marked how deftly the abbot had shifted the topic away from the people who had left the meditation hall, but did not press the issue. A man who diverted a conversation would also lie, if pressed. Besides, the abbot's comments had given Hiro another idea he wanted to discuss with Father Mateo privately and soon.

Fortunately, Nichiyo had also provided a way to make that happen.

Hiro gestured to Father Mateo. "We will find Soro, and bring him here."

Nichiyo raised his chin and nodded once to grant permission. "Thank you. Bring his son as well."

In the residence hall, Hiro paused in front of the guest room he shared with the Jesuit.

"What about Soro?" Father Mateo asked.

"In a minute." Hiro drew the door open.

As expected, Father Mateo followed him inside. Hiro closed the door, switched to Portuguese, and lowered his voice to a whisper. "I've been trying to figure out the order in which the remaining priests will die—"

The Jesuit's face lit up. "So we can save them. Good idea."

"Let me finish. Fugen represents goodness and virtue—"

"The children." Father Mateo raised a hand and gripped the wooden cross that hung from a leather thong around his neck.

"Possibly, but that's not my point. Several candidates could fill the role of Fugen, but the Buddha who comes after that—Jizō—when the killer gets there, he's going to come for you."

"Me? I'm not a Buddhist—"

"Jizō is unlike the other jusanbutsu. He argues on behalf of the dead, just like the Jesus god you serve. Jizō is the Buddha who forgives."

"I assure you, they are not the same. Jesus Christ is God incarnate, in human form. He died to save humanity from judgment."

"As Jizō intercedes with the jusanbutsu, requesting mercy for the deceased."

"Yes, but . . . never mind. I see your point." The Jesuit paused. "In fact, Kenshin-*san* has made that same mistake. Do you think— What if he merely pretended not to want the abbot's role? Perhaps to cover that he's working for Lord Oda?"

"No man loyal to the Ashikaga shoguns would have anything but enmity for Oda," Hiro said. "An intelligent spy might feign such loyalty, but Gensho and the others trust him, and Ringa was willing to leave you alone together, the night we arrived. Also, Oda's spy would want the abbot's role. He would not decline it, even as a ploy."

"Ringa had no reason to worry about me," Father Mateo said.

"He knew we came from Iga. Because you traveled with me, he would not have left you alone with anyone he did not trust. Especially someone he suspected of having ties to Oda Nobunaga." Hiro looked for Gato, but remembered almost instantly that they had taken her to the abbot's home. He also remembered, with chagrin, the way the cat purred in Hatsuko's lap.

"We do not know the killer works for Oda," Father Mateo said. "In fact, I find it most unlikely. Lord Oda doesn't control this province, and doesn't need to murder a dozen innocent men to eliminate a spy."

"Oda could not care less about priests, innocent or not, and killing everyone disguises his true target. People who hear about the killings will attribute them to a madman, or a fire, if the killer destroys the temple as well as the men within its walls."

Father Mateo hesitated. "Hiro . . . I understand your desire for vengeance, but I fear it may be impacting your judgment."

The Jesuit's accusation made anger rise like magma in Hiro's chest. However, unlike a volcano, he could and did prevent its release. "You do not understand."

"I understand far better than you know. You see Lord Oda's men in every shadow—"

"That is not true!" Hiro snapped. In the silence that followed, he heard his mother's voice inside his head: *Your lack of control proves otherwise.*

CHAPTER 28

Father Mateo ignored the outburst. "What makes more sense: a madman killing priests, or an assassin planning thirteen murders to distract attention from his target?"

"Perhaps the entire temple is the target," Hiro said. "At first I thought he came for Ringa or the abbot. Now I wonder. Maybe Oda Nobunaga has a grudge against Myo-in."

"Then why not send his samurai to burn the temple openly, or multiple assassins who could murder all the priests at once? Killing them in sequence seems so . . . inefficient. Also, but for the storm, the priests would have left the temple. Surely a man like Oda would prefer a plan with fewer risks of failure."

"Kōya is known for winter storms. The killer could have waited for a blizzard, knowing it would isolate the temple and give him time to carry out his plan."

"That sounds unnecessarily complicated," Father Mateo said. "A madman's game."

"Assassin or madman, he will die when he comes for you, if not before." Hiro laid a hand on the door. "For now, we need to talk with Soro."

Hiro knocked on the wooden frame of the shoji that led to the pilgrim's guest room. "Soro, we wish to speak with you."

No answer.

Hiro laid his ear to the door. He heard no movement on the other side. Closing his eyes, he listened more carefully.

"What do you want?" Soro's voice came through the door, so close that he was clearly standing directly on the other side.

Hiro jumped back from the shoji and stepped on Father Mateo's foot. The Jesuit inhaled sharply.

"Who is it?" Soro demanded.

Hiro recovered his composure. "Surely you recognize my voice by now."

"The samurai. Is the foreigner with you? Have you caught the killer?"

"The abbot orders you to join the other priests in the meditation hall," Hiro said.

"For safety." Father Mateo frowned at Hiro.

The door did not open.

"While I appreciate his concern," Soro said, "my son and I prefer this room. Please convey our apologies to the abbot."

"We wish to speak with you," Hiro said. "Open the door."

"Are we not speaking together now?" the pilgrim asked.

"Open the door," Hiro said, "or I will break it down."

The door slid open just enough for half of Soro's face to appear in the opening. "Samurai or not, if you destroy temple property you will be the one who faces consequences."

For a moment, Hiro understood why Oda Nobunaga hated priests. "Perhaps. But you will face my sword right now."

Soro's gaze flickered to Hiro's waist. "You would draw it on holy ground? Against an unarmed pilgrim?"

Father Mateo intervened. "Please come to the meditation hall. Consider your son. Do it for him, if not yourself."

"It is for Ippen's sake that I refuse," Soro replied. "In this room I can keep him safe. In a large hall, full of men, a killer could slip a knife in his ribs without me knowing anything, until it was too late."

"This killer does not strike in crowded rooms," Hiro said.

"The fact he has not done so yet does not mean he will not," Soro insisted. "I refuse to play games of chance with Ippen's life."

Hiro admired Soro's courage, but also considered it out of character for a Buddhist priest. He decided to push the issue. "Perhaps you wish to remain alone so you can kill again."

"You think I killed these men?" The pilgrim's eyes blazed with sudden anger, but it disappeared almost instantly as his expression shifted from fury to humility. Behind the door, he bowed. "Forgive me, I have overstepped my place."

"Outbursts like that would justify your death," Hiro said. "However, I will show mercy, and forgive, if you and your son accompany us to the meditation hall."

"It appears I have no choice." Soro opened the door and gestured to the child, who stood in the far corner of the room. "Ippen, let's go."

The child hesitated, staring at the wooden cabinet.

"The abbot's ashes will be fine," Soro reassured the boy. "The killer does not care about the dead."

"But—" Ippen continued to stare at the cabinet.

"No." The word came out with an angry edge that Soro did not try to hide.

Ippen ducked his head, but not before Hiro saw the tears that filled his eyes. The child picked up a cloak that lay nearby on the floor and wrapped it around his shoulders. Holding the hem of his robe off the floor with both hands, he started forward.

"Have you a plan to catch the killer?" Soro asked as the child approached the door. "Or do you simply hope he gets bored and decides to leave?"

"Unless you're the killer, my plan does not concern you," Hiro said. "And if you are, you'll learn it soon enough."

Soro stared as if deciding whether or not to take offense. Sighing, he laid a hand on Ippen's shoulder and guided the child from the room.

Kenshin and Shokai had returned to the meditation hall before Hiro and Father Mateo, but Gensho had not. The physician and his student stood together near the entry, a short but significant distance from Nichiyo and Myokan. Doyu and Bussho knelt on the far side of the room, in front of the Buddhas. As usual, the former abbot's chin was resting on his chest, eyes closed as he breathed heavily in sleep.

Outside, the blizzard howled. The shutters rattled, and the rafters creaked. The freezing winds that chilled the entry every time the door slid open made the braziers struggle to keep the room a comfortable temperature. Even so, despite the chill, the air in the hall felt close and stale.

Soro approached Nichiyo, with Ippen trailing behind.

"You are now the abbot?" The pilgrim's question echoed through the silent room.

Nichiyo's eyes refocused slowly, as if pulled from unusually distant thoughts. "Soro-*san*. I see you agreed to join us."

"Clearly, I could not refuse your generous offer of sanctuary, especially when delivered by such a persuasive messenger." Anger coiled in Soro's words like a viper in the reeds.

Nichiyo seemed unaware. He pointed to the southwest corner of the room, beside the entry. "Until we find the killer, we must stay together in this hall . . . for safety." He tacked the final words on as an afterthought. "You and your son may sit over there. Do not approach within arm's length of any other priest or leave the hall without permission. If you wish to speak to anyone, speak from a distance."

"Do you think me a killer?" Soro asked.

"No one said that," Father Mateo intervened, "the abbot merely—"

"Wishes to accuse me of these crimes, which I did not commit." Soro's eyes flared, though his voice retained a deadly calm.

CHAPTER 29

Nichiyo crossed his arms. "As acting abbot of Myo-in, I have a duty to protect the priests and visitors beneath this roof."

"A duty, I note, you have failed thus far," Soro said.

Myokan moved to the abbot's side, gripping a bamboo staff. Soro pretended to ignore him, but subtly shifted his gaze and balance as the guardian approached.

The pilgrim did not fear a fight.

"Nichiyo-*san* has decided." Myokan spoke with authority. "Remaining in separate groups, but within this hall, will ensure that no one comes to harm."

"You cannot ensure my safety, or Ippen's," Soro said.

"Forgive my interference," Father Mateo offered, "but the plan seems wise to me. The killer will not strike where we can see him."

"With respect, I will not risk my life, or Ippen's, on assumptions."

"We need to remain together, but separate, for self-defense." Nichiyo's voice held an edge of desperation. "At least until we catch the killer."

Hiro noted the use of *we*, despite the fact that, thus far, Nichiyo had done nothing but order other people around.

"Shouldn't the guardian stand by the entrance, rather than guarding you alone?" Hiro spoke lightly to make the question appear more innocent.

Nichiyo flushed. Apparently, the abbot had not missed the implication of his cowardice. "I suppose. . . . Yes, I suppose he should. Myokan, please guard the entrance for us."

"Where is Gensho-*san*?" Father Mateo asked.

"In the kitchen, preparing the evening meal," Shokai answered from across the room.

Kenshin looked at his student and then at the rest of them. Unlike Shokai, he clearly had not been listening.

"They asked about Gensho-*san*," Shokai explained.

Soro and Ippen retreated to the corner Nichiyo suggested. Hiro beckoned for Father Mateo to follow him across the hall. He walked to the front of the room, as far as possible from the others.

"What's the plan?" Father Mateo whispered in Portuguese.

"It hasn't changed. Identify the next intended victim, and prevent the murder if we can."

"The killer may change his mind, with us all here together."

"That could happen," Hiro said. "Assassins generally refuse to attack in the open. However, he may attempt to separate his victim from the group."

"No one will leave the hall alone. Not now."

"The victim will not be alone," Hiro countered. "The killer will go with him."

"I pray he simply abandons the idea of killing altogether."

"He may." Hiro didn't believe it. "Unless his orders require him not to."

"If so, gathering everyone together was the worst thing we could do."

Hiro stared at Nichiyo. "Or the most efficient. Only time will tell."

Soro stood up quickly as Hiro and Father Mateo approached the corner where he knelt beside Ippen. "That's close enough."

Hiro stopped four steps from the pilgrim. After a pause, he took another step.

Soro's eyes narrowed. "I have nothing more to tell you."

"How many temples are there on Mount Kōya?" Hiro spoke softly to prevent his voice from carrying.

Confusion melted the suspicion from Soro's face. "Dozens? I don't know."

"Don't you live at a Shingon temple?" Hiro asked.

Soro shifted his gaze to Father Mateo, who had joined them. "Where is the center of your faith?"

"Rome or heaven, depending who you ask."

"And how many temples exist in Rome?"

Father Mateo smiled. "None. But how many churches? That, I do not know."

"Precisely," Soro said. "Knowing the number of temples on Kōya does not prove a priest's veracity any more than not knowing proves him false."

"That is not why I asked," Hiro lied. "With dozens of choices, why pick Myo-in?"

"They had room. With a storm blowing in, I did not want to risk the search for lodgings closer to Okunoin."

"You thought the others would be full this late in the year?" Hiro asked.

"When traveling with a child"—Soro nodded to Ippen—"a man cannot afford to disregard safety, as samurai might do."

Hiro let the insult pass.

Ippen stood up and bowed to the Jesuit. "Please, sir, how long must we stay here, in this hall?" The child transferred his gaze to Soro. "It is almost time for the evening prayers."

"We will say them here."

"But the ashes," Ippen said, more urgently.

"We do not need them," Soro said. "The jusanbutsu hear us everywhere."

"They may not know—"

"Enough!" Soro drew a breath and continued more calmly. "They will know."

Ippen looked doubtful but said no more.

"With respect," Soro said to Hiro, "you waste your time. I came to Kōya to inter the dead, not make more of them."

"Thank you for your cooperation." Father Mateo bowed.

Soro hesitated, but returned the gesture. "I do hope you find the killer quickly."

Myokan stood beside the door that led to the entry, bamboo staff in hand. He surveyed the room, relaxed but alert, with a surprising lack of tension in his face.

"I wondered when you would speak with me," he said as Hiro and the Jesuit approached.

"You could have spoken with us first, if you have information," Hiro countered.

"But I don't." Myokan's fingers tightened on the staff. "I can't even understand why anyone would want them dead."

Hiro could almost feel the abbot listening from the nearby corner. He gestured through the doorway toward the narrow entry. "May we speak privately? If you don't mind?"

Instead of answering, Myokan stepped through the door. Father Mateo followed, as did Hiro, who shut the door behind them.

"Have you something to tell me?" Myokan spoke in a hushed, almost conspiratorial tone.

"Actually," Hiro whispered back as he moved as far as possible from the door, "I hoped you might have something more to tell us, now that others cannot hear."

CHAPTER 30

Myokan shook his head in disappointment. "I would help you if I could, but I do not know who killed these priests, or why, or what he hoped to gain."

"Can you think of anything the victims had in common?" Hiro asked.

"All were senior priests of Myo-in." Myokan bit the inside of his lip. He furrowed his forehead, as if in thought. "None of them wanted Nichiyo-*san* to succeed Anan-*sama* as abbot."

"Anan seemed to respect Nichiyo," Hiro said.

Myokan shifted his gaze to the shoji that separated the entry from the hall beyond. "He did, but . . . there are rumors." He drew a breath as if to continue, but let it out again without speaking.

Hiro waited. To his relief, the Jesuit did also.

After a silence so long that Hiro doubted the guardian would continue, Myokan spoke, but so softly that they had to strain to hear him over the rattling shutters and the wailing wind. "I do not wish to spread untruths, but some of us—the other priests—believe that Nichiyo-*san* came to Myo-in to hide."

"From what?" Hiro asked.

The guardian shrugged. "We do not know. Something he did before he was a priest."

"And who believes this?"

Before Myokan could answer, the shoji that led to the meditation hall slid open. Nichiyo's worried face appeared. "Is something wrong?"

Hiro wondered whether the abbot had unusually prescient timing, or merely a habit of listening at doors.

"Not at all." Father Mateo walked toward Nichiyo. "Since we have time, would you be willing to tell me more about your Shingon ways?"

The abbot swelled with pride. "Of course. I know many of Kōbō Daishi's teachings by heart. I have studied the sutras and mandalas in detail. As a novice and a foreigner, your mind will grasp only the smallest fraction of the dharma, but I will do what I can to advance your limited understanding."

Given the dramatic change of topic, Hiro suspected Father Mateo had a plan. Without knowing more, however, he could only remain silent and trust the Jesuit to take the lead.

"Before he died, Anan-*sama* had begun to teach me about the . . . jusanbutsu?" Father Mateo paused as if uncertain of the pronunciation. "We had gotten as far as Fugen. I was hoping you could tell me more about him."

"A curious coincidence." Nichiyo's voice held a suspicious edge. "If the killer is choosing his victims to represent the jusanbutsu, the next one will be posed as Fugen."

"That is partly why I asked," the Jesuit admitted. "Perhaps if I knew more about your deities, I could prevent another death. However, I also have a genuine interest in your Shingon faith."

"Why? You want to destroy us," Myokan put in.

Father Mateo focused on Nichiyo. "I respect your wisdom and your ways. I wish to learn. Will you honor me by sharing what you know?"

"Of course I will teach you." Nichiyo gestured for the Jesuit to follow him into the meditation hall. "However, I do not think you need to worry about the killer any more. He would not dare attack us here, when we are all together."

Hiro disagreed, but said nothing. Small-minded men had large opinions that left no mental room for any ideas but their own.

Hiro and Father Mateo followed Nichiyo into an empty corner of the meditation hall. Myokan followed, watching the Jesuit carefully. Clearly, he remained suspicious of the foreigner's motives.

The abbot knelt beside a brazier that sent feeble rays of warmth into the room. He gestured for the others to do likewise. "Fugen is a bodhisattva. Do you understand what this term means?"

"Not well." Father Mateo knelt. "However, I do not wish to bore my translator—he was raised a Buddhist, though he cannot teach the tenets well."

"This is not his fault." Nichiyo's face grew smug. "One cannot expect a ronin to understand the complexities of dharma."

"Matsui-*san*," the Jesuit said, "perhaps you could continue talking with the priests while I sit here, and learn from Abbot Nichiyo?"

Hiro bowed as the plan became clear. Father Mateo would keep the abbot too distracted to eavesdrop, allowing Hiro to continue the investigation unobserved.

With Gensho still unavailable, Hiro knew exactly where—and with whom—to begin.

✦

Kenshin and Shokai rose as Hiro approached.

"May we help you?" Kenshin asked.

Ordinarily, Hiro would try to separate the student from the teacher. However, the information he hoped to obtain did not require privacy, and under the circumstances he doubted he could accomplish a fully private conversation anyway. "I wondered if you could tell me, do any of your fellow priests remind you of Fugen?"

Kenshin's eyebrows lowered thoughtfully. He looked past Hiro at the other priests. "Are you trying to guess the killer's next target?"

Hiro waited.

"We associate Fugen-*sama* with diligent recitation of the sutras and constant prayer." Kenshin spoke softly, as if thinking aloud.

"Any of the remaining senior priests, including Kenshin-*san*, could fill that role," Shokai declared. "In fact, I think Kenshin-*san* is the most like Fugen-*sama*."

The physician shook his head. "I consider myself more Yakushi than Fugen." After a pause, he added, "Yakushi-*sama* is the Buddha of medicine."

Hiro nodded. "I remember."

"Doyu-*sama* reminded me most of Fugen-*sama*, before his mind declined." Kenshin smiled kindly at the elderly priest, who now lay curled on the tatami like a sleeping child, head resting peacefully on his arm. "But now? I would have to say Gensho-*san*."

"He is not even qualified to teach," Shokai objected.

"Do not confuse power with diligence," Kenshin admonished the younger man, though his voice was gentle. "Gensho-*san* studies day and night. He never misses a ritual, and dedicates every waking moment to serving others. He agreed to help me pray for the shogun, and has done so without fail. As a humble man, he would deny it, but Gensho-*san* is most like Fugen-*sama*."

And he is out in the storm alone. Hiro's instincts jangled an alarm.

"With respect, I disagree." Shokai renewed his objection. "But if anyone tries to harm you, Kenshin-*san*, I will kill him first."

"While I appreciate your devotion, do not forget Kōbō Daishi's admonition: 'a man who holds a sword will feel the need to kill.' Remember: violence is not our way."

Shokai narrowed his eyes but did not argue.

Suppressing his concern for Gensho, Hiro asked one final question. "Do you know why Nichiyo-*san* decided to become a priest?"

A flicker of unusual curiosity lit Shokai's eyes.

Kenshin's face grew sad. "He does not like it spoken of."

"Killers do not like their actions talked of either," Hiro said.

"No, he—"

"*Ippen!*" Soro's voice rang out behind them, sharp with fear. "Where is my son?"

CHAPTER 31

Hiro turned to see the pilgrim standing near the exit.

"Ippen is gone." Panic raised the pitch of Soro's voice.

"Are you certain?" Nichiyo stood and turned to face him.

Father Mateo rose to his feet, as did Myokan. Hiro noted the guardian was sitting with the Jesuit, instead of standing guard at the entry door.

"He is not here!" Anger replaced fear as Soro turned on the abbot.

Hiro started across the room, with Kenshin and Shokai in his wake.

"Where could he have gone?" Myokan looked around, though the space had no hiding places large enough to conceal a child.

"You did not watch your son?" Nichiyo's voice held a hint of disapproval.

"We had begun the prayers for our abbot." Soro's voice caught halfway through. "I thought Ippen was also praying, silently."

"You didn't hear him stand and walk away?" Myokan asked.

Hiro agreed with the suspicion in the guardian's voice. Given his repeatedly voiced concerns for Ippen's safety, it seemed strange that Soro now had let the child disappear.

"Closed eyes see nothing," Soro said.

"That teaching refers to the mind, not physical vision," Myokan objected.

"Yet it speaks the truth of both." Soro turned to the door. "I'm going to find him."

155

Myokan hurried toward the exit, staff in hand.

"You don't know he left the building," Father Mateo said.

"He is not here." Soro gestured around the room. "And isn't— Step away." He directed the final words to Myokan, who blocked the exit.

"The child most likely went to the latrine," Nichiyo said. "He will return."

"He would not do that without telling me," Soro replied, "and I would not have let him leave alone."

"I agree with the abbot." Myokan nodded to Nichiyo. "You were praying. The child probably didn't want to interrupt."

"He would not have left during prayers—"

"Come now," Nichiyo replied, "can any man among us claim he never sneaked away from obligations as a boy?"

"Ippen would not." Soro narrowed his eyes at the abbot. "Where is your missing priest? The one called Gensho-*san*?"

"In the kitchen, preparing the evening meal," Kenshin said. "But—"

Soro took a step toward Myokan. "Clear the way."

The guardian shook his head. "The abbot said—"

The pilgrim's fist shot forward.

Myokan blocked with his staff as Soro's other hand flashed out like a striking snake. A snap like branches breaking echoed through the hall. Myokan gasped and dropped the staff, clutching his shattered wrist.

The bamboo weapon fell to the floor with a silent clatter.

Myokan bent forward, supporting his injured arm with the other hand.

Soro snatched the staff from the ground. Holding it horizontally, he hooked it under Myokan's chin, pulled the young man upright, and forced him back against the wall, pressing the staff against the guardian's throat.

Myokan choked. His face turned red.

Before Hiro could intervene, Soro lowered the staff and backed away. Myokan bent forward, coughing, and clutched his broken wrist again.

"I have no quarrel with any of you." Soro waved the staff in an arc. "But do not try to stop me. I am going to find my son."

"If you leave this room, neither Myo-in nor I bear any responsibility for your safety." Nichiyo raised a trembling hand. "If the killer murders you, we bear no guilt."

Soro left the hall, still carrying the bamboo staff.

"I'm going with him," Hiro said.

"And I with you," the Jesuit added.

"Don't be fool—" Nichiyo began, but they had already followed the pilgrim out the door.

Soro glanced back over his shoulder as Hiro and Father Mateo joined him in the entry. He already wore a pair of sandals and held not only the staff but a lantern that glowed with coals from the brazier by the door. He turned to face them. "I warned you. Do not interfere."

"We wish to help you find your son." Father Mateo selected a pair of temple sandals from the rack beside the door.

Hiro let the Jesuit's answer stand despite its partial truth. If Soro was innocent, they would indeed attempt to reunite him with his son. But if, as Hiro now suspected, the pilgrim was using the child to create a distraction, the only help Hiro planned to offer Soro was a personal audience with the kings of hell.

He slipped on a pair of sandals as Soro opened the door. To Hiro's dismay, the shoes were damp from melting snow. He tried not to wonder whose feet had worn them last.

Outside, the cold made Hiro completely forget his borrowed sandals. Wind blew through his robe as though it weren't even there. The swirling snow felt like a thousand tiny needles on his face. It pricked his eyes, making it hard to see.

His sandals crunched on the layer of frozen snow that coated the temple yard. Ducking his head and squinting to keep the snow out of his eyes, he followed Soro, with Father Mateo at his side.

The pilgrim headed for the wooden latrine on the east side of the yard. The choice suggested Ippen truly had disappeared, but Hiro remained alert.

They could be walking into an ambush—even if Soro was not the one who laid it.

The storm obscured the latrine until they stood directly in front of the narrow, wooden building. Soro raised his lantern, illuminating another that hung from a peg on the outer wall of the latrine. The lantern was dark and cold, blown out by the wind or—more likely—unlit since before the storm began.

No light shone out the building's slatted windows, suggesting the latrine was empty.

However, the door stood slightly ajar.

Hiro squinted at the opening as the blizzard lashed his face. No child he knew would willingly enter a dark latrine in a snowstorm. Especially not with a killer on the loose.

Soro pushed the door open and hurried inside, with Father Mateo on his heels. Hiro drew his wakizashi and followed, opting for the shorter sword because of the building's narrow shape. With several men inside, a sword fight would be challenging at best. Even so, he dared not draw the shuriken hidden in his sleeve. Only shinobi carried the lethal metal stars, and Hiro would not betray his identity until—and unless—he had no other choice.

Inside, the glow of Soro's lantern permeated the latrine. Oblong holes cut into the floor on either side of the entry gaped like accusing mouths, but they were far too narrow to conceal a child. The boxlike urinals beyond the waste holes would not hold a cat, and the stone washbasin near the door was empty, clean, and dry.

The scent of ammonia spiked the air, but even Hiro's sensitive nose picked up no hint of solid waste. The priests had cleaned the chamber recently and well.

"Ippen?" Soro's unnecessary question echoed dully in the narrow room.

Father Mateo ran a hand through his hair. "The boy's not here."

CHAPTER 32

Soro's eyes narrowed. "If I find him less than well, someone will die a most unpleasant death."

He pushed past them and out of the latrine.

Father Mateo began to follow, but Hiro laid a hand on the Jesuit's arm. "Stay close and alert." He switched to Portuguese. "That man moves like an assassin. If he's a spy, the child is too."

"But he's only a child—"

"A blade in a child's hand is no less lethal for its wielder's age." Hiro stared at the Jesuit. "We cannot assume that anyone is innocent. Not anymore."

Father Mateo frowned. "We're going to lose Soro in the storm."

"Unlikely," Hiro said. "Unless I miss my guess, he's headed for the kitchen."

"To kill Gensho?"

"One way or the other, yes."

Hiro stepped out of the latrine, ducking his head against the howling wind as he hurried south around the residence hall to the kitchen. He considered sending the Jesuit back to the meditation hall, but suspected Father Mateo would not go. More importantly, Hiro wasn't sure the hall was safe. He suspected Soro was an assassin, but not necessarily the one they were looking for.

By the time they reached the kitchen building, Hiro had almost lost his sense of direction in the blinding storm. He moved with unusual caution, sword in hand, and struggled not to strike out blindly against the shadows that tricked his eyes and mind. He felt palpable relief as the kitchen appeared through the whirling snow.

With Father Mateo next to him, Hiro threw open the door and stepped inside.

The smell of steaming rice made his stomach snarl. Too many hours had passed since his last meal. Shaking off that thought, he looked for Soro.

Melting snow and watery footprints left a trail across the eating area. The pilgrim's lantern sat at the edge of the tatami, casting speckled shadows over the mats and the earthen floor beyond.

Shards of pottery littered the ground around the stove. Nearby, Gensho lay on his back in a puddle of liquid and glistening vegetable fragments, arms held up to block his face. Soro straddled the larger man, pressing the bamboo staff against Gensho's neck. The cook's face was the vibrant mauve of a pickled plum, and he gasped for air.

"*Stop that!*" Father Mateo shouted. "Let him go."

Soro turned to look.

The instant the pilgrim's attention shifted, Gensho rolled to the side and broke his assailant's hold. Forcing the staff away, he regained his feet and grasped a wooden spoon that rested on the stove. He brandished the feeble weapon like a sword.

"I told you not to interfere!" Soro shook the staff at Gensho. "Where is Ippen?"

"Your son?" Gensho held the serving spoon between them as he backed away. "How would I know?"

"Liar!" Soro feinted. "Where is Ippen?"

"I don't know!" Gensho glanced at Hiro. "What's happening?"

"The boy is missing," Father Mateo said. "Soro, please—"

"I would never harm a child." Gensho gestured to the pot that simmered on the stove and then to the shattered ceramic vessel on the floor. "I've been here all afternoon. First I chopped the wood and filled the fuel boxes at the abbot's home and in the meditation hall. Since then, I've been here, cooking, as I was when you attacked me."

Hiro approached the edge of the seating area. He caught a whiff of vinegar on the air. Given the sodden slivers of vegetables littering the floor, the broken jar had once held *tsukemono*.

Hiro's stomach rumbled again. He regretted the loss of the pickles, despite the tension in the room.

"Where is my child?" Soro repeated.

Father Mateo stepped down from the platform. "Soro, please."

Hiro followed. "Put down the staff. I will not ask again."

Soro stared at the wakizashi in Hiro's hand as if considering his options.

"Be reasonable," Father Mateo said. "If someone took your son by force, he would have struggled or cried in alarm. You would have heard. We would have noticed."

Soro lowered the staff a fraction. "Why would he leave the hall at all? He had no reason—" He inhaled sharply. "No. . . ."

Soro raced across the floor, jumped onto the tatami, seized the lantern, and fled the room without stopping to close the door behind him.

"Go back to the meditation hall," Hiro told Gensho as he sheathed his sword. "You are not safe alone."

"As soon as the rice is ready."

"Do not wait. Go now, if you want to live."

Hiro doubted the priest would heed his advice, but the burly cook would make a poor Fugen, so under the circumstances following Soro seemed the better choice. The pilgrim had already disappeared into the snow, but Hiro had put the pieces together at the same time Soro had, and knew where the man had gone.

Hiro and Father Mateo ran through the snow to the residence hall. They rounded the corner to the guest rooms just as Soro's shout rent the air.

"Ippen!" The pilgrim stood in the open doorway to his guest room.

Hiro and the Jesuit reached the room a moment later.

Ippen knelt on the floor, arms wrapped tightly around the wooden box that held the abbot's ashes. Tears ran down the child's pale cheeks, glittering in the light from Soro's lantern.

"I had to," Ippen pleaded. "Someone had to say the prayers. She—"

"I explained this!" Fury warred with fear in Soro's voice as he set the staff and lantern on the table. "You do not need the ashes in the room to say the prayers!"

He fell to his knees and wrapped the child in an embrace. "That urn holds only ashes. Nothing more. The soul is gone."

The child said something indistinct, the words dissolved in sobs and muted by the fabric of Soro's robe.

"He is alive." Father Mateo sounded on the verge of tears. He made the sign of the cross. "Praise God."

Hiro felt no such emotion. "Tell me, who is truly in the urn?"

"Our abbot," Soro said. "As I already told you."

"Now *you* lie." Hiro rested a hand on the hilt of his katana. "No child risks death to pray for an abbot, and Shingon priests don't fight like shinobi. Who are you, and what is your business here?"

Soro opened his mouth.

"Before you answer," Hiro warned, "if you lie to me again, I kill the child."

"Hiro!" Father Mateo exclaimed.

Ippen gasped and clutched the box.

Soro rose, retrieving the staff from the table as he did so. He turned to face Hiro, eyes deadly and face impassive.

"You know the penalty for lying to samurai," Hiro said. "It is my right."

"We came to Kōya for a burial." Soro spoke softly. "That is no lie."

"Nor is it the entire truth. Explain yourself, and quickly, or explain to the kings of hell."

Ippen sobbed and clutched the ashes tighter.

"Who hired you?" Hiro persisted. "What's your purpose here?"

"I am a pilgrim." Soro glanced at the sword. "If you don't believe that, you must kill me."

Ippen made a strangled noise, halfway between terror and a sob.

"Consider the child," Father Mateo urged in Portuguese.

Soro glanced at the Jesuit. "What's he saying?"

"Not your business," Hiro growled. "You have one minute, and one choice. Reveal your clan, and purpose here, or I will kill the child."

CHAPTER 33

"Hiro!" Father Mateo exclaimed.

Soro stepped backward, shielding Ippen. "You'll have to kill me first."

"I can live with that," Hiro said.

"But I cannot," Father Mateo objected. "You—"

"His time is up." Hiro drew his katana.

Soro shifted the staff to his right hand. With his left, he pushed Ippen to the floor.

The box popped free and fell to the tatami with a thump.

Ippen shrieked and lunged after it.

"Don't do this." Soro dropped into a fighting crouch.

Hiro raised the sword but did not advance.

"Wait." Soro lowered the staff to the table. "I will tell you what you want to know. But close the door." He glanced into the hallway. "I do not want the other priests to hear."

Hiro nodded to Father Mateo. "Shut the door and stand beside it." He stared at Soro. "If you make a sudden move, or try to attack, I will kill you—and your child—while the foreigner runs to the meditation hall and reveals you as the killer."

"I'm not leaving you here to kill a child," Father Mateo said in Portuguese.

"You need to trust me," Hiro replied in kind. "If this goes badly, you must run."

Hiro heard the door slide closed behind him, and took the sound for the Jesuit's consent.

"Who are you, truly?" he asked Soro. "Why did you come to Myo-in?"

Ippen stood up, holding the box. "To bury my mother. Please don't kill my uncle too."

Soro's shoulders dropped a fraction. Though barely noticeable, the reaction made Hiro suspect the child had told the truth.

"You are his uncle?" Father Mateo asked.

Soro sighed. "My sister died several weeks ago, unexpectedly, and Ippen has no other family."

"Why make up a story about an abbot?" Father Mateo asked. "Why not simply tell the truth?"

"Because," Hiro said, "it might have drawn attention to the fact that Ippen is a girl."

The child's eyes flew wide with terror.

Soro exhaled slowly. "How long have you known?"

"Until now, I mostly just suspected," Hiro admitted, "but it fits the facts. You would not leave the child alone, and did not want her in the meditation hall. She didn't know the morning service, or that prayers can be said for the dead without the ashes present. Finally, her robes don't fit, and she raises the hem from the floor like a woman wearing a long kimono. Boys don't do that."

Soro glanced at the child. "I hadn't noticed it."

"The question remains," Hiro continued, "who are you?"

"I told you who I am."

Hiro shook his head. "No Shingon priest would violate the taboo against women on Mount Kōya."

"Technically, she is not yet a woman," Soro said.

"A priest would have left her at the nyonindo," Hiro persisted. "You took pains to hide her identity. I suspect you hide a secret of your own behind those pilgrim robes."

"I could not leave her behind," Soro said. "She has no other family. If something happened . . ."

"Iga or Koga?" Hiro asked.

Soro's forehead wrinkled. "What?"

"Your clan. Iga or Koga ryu?"

"Y-you are mistaken," Soro stammered. "I have never been to Iga. Or to Koga, for that matter."

"No?" Hiro asked. "That's strange. I thought I heard the shadow of Iga in your speech."

"I don't know why. I've never been there."

A shoji rattled in the hall outside. Soro picked up his staff and bent his knees, prepared to fight.

"Matsui-*san*!" a voice yelled. "Are you here? We need your help!"

"That's Shokai!" Father Mateo slid the door open and looked into the hall. "Shokai-*san*? What has happened?"

The floorboards in the hallway creaked as soft footsteps approached. Hiro moved sideways, giving himself a view of the door without losing sight of Soro.

Snowflakes spotted Shokai's shaven head and packed the folds of his dark robe. His nose and cheeks were flushed, and the scars on his face had turned stark purple.

"Come quickly." Panic tinged his voice. "Doyu-*sama* is dead!"

"Do—the former abbot?" Father Mateo asked.

At the same time, Hiro said, "What happened?"

"We thought he was sleeping." Shokai sounded choked. "We thought . . . Gensho-*san* returned, with rice. We tried to wake him. He was dead."

"You tried to wake Doyu-*sama*," Father Mateo clarified.

"We thought he was sleeping," Shokai repeated. "Please, you must come quickly."

Hiro suspected a trap.

Soro laid a hand on Ippen's shoulder. "My son and I will remain here until the storm has passed."

"It is not safe—" Shokai began.

"You think the meditation hall is safer?" Soro asked. "Another priest is dead!"

"The abbot—"

Father Mateo intervened. "Perhaps I can offer a solution. Soro will join the rest of us in the meditation hall, while the children—Ippen and Bussho—can stay with the women in the abbot's hall."

Hiro admired the Jesuit's plan. Not only did it prevent the girl's return to the meditation hall, but it placed the children in the safest possible location. He did not trust Hatsuko, but doubted the samurai woman would kill a child in front of Ana and the nun. No spy worth the name would risk exposure in that way, especially without a sword or a clear retreat.

"The house is defiled," Shokai objected.

"And unsafe," Soro added, but with less certainty.

"On the contrary," Father Mateo said, "one of the women at the nyonindo is samurai, and trained in the arts of war. She agreed to guard the women, and will defend the children also."

Unless she kills them, Hiro thought, though even he considered that unlikely enough to take the risk. Moreover, he believed he could catch the killer before the children became a target.

"She's an *onna-bugeisha*?" Soro asked. "I suppose, since Ippen is not ordained, exposure to the women would not harm him."

"I believe you said the same of Bussho—that he is not yet ordained." Father Mateo spoke pointedly to Shokai. "Though, of course, the abbot will decide."

Hiro expected the younger priest to argue, but Shokai merely nodded. "It would keep him safe. I will ask the abbot."

Ippen clutched the box more tightly. "I want to stay here, with . . . the ashes."

"I have decided," Soro said. "No argument."

Ippen bit her lip. Her nose grew red.

The fear in her eyes sent an unexpected stab of sympathy through Hiro. "Do you like cats?"

She looked up. "Cats?"

"The foreigner brought his cat to the temple." Hiro gestured to Father Mateo. "He left it with the women, in the abbot's hall."

"D-does it bite?" Ippen sniffled, but her eyes were dry.

"Only spiders," Hiro said.

"Your cat should not do that here." The child spoke with unusual gravity. "Temple spiders could be someone's relative, reborn in a lesser state."

"Perhaps you could keep an eye on the cat for us," Hiro suggested, "until the storm abates."

Ippen nodded. "I'll make sure it does not eat the spiders."

CHAPTER 34

The entire group returned to the meditation hall. As they struggled together through the storm, Hiro wondered whether Soro's willingness to leave Ippen with Hatsuko indicated concern for the child or a dangerous—and suspicious—trust for the samurai woman. Unable to decide without more information, he made a mental note to pay careful attention when they left the children at the abbot's home.

Myokan met the group in the entry, broken wrist now bandaged and secured with a sling around his neck. He seemed relieved to see Hiro, though his eyes narrowed slightly when Father Mateo came through the door, and his gaze lingered on the staff in Soro's hands. The pilgrim did not return it, nor did the guardian demand it back. With his injury, he couldn't really use it anyway.

The two men stared at one another.

Slowly, Soro leaned the staff against the wall beside the sandal rack. "I'll leave this here, for now."

Myokan nodded. "Did you hear what happened?"

"You think I'd forget to tell them?" Shokai scowled as he knocked the snow from his shoulders and placed his sandals on the rack.

"We have not moved Doyu-*sama*," Myokan told Hiro. "You can see him as he lay."

Faint sobbing sounds came through the door from the meditation room.

"Is that Bussho?" Father Mateo asked. "He's in there with the body?"

169

"He refused to leave," Myokan replied.

"We have come to take him to the abbot's residence, with Ippen." Father Mateo gestured to the child at Soro's side.

"After we examine Doyu-*sama*," Hiro added.

"Ippen does not need to see . . ." Soro nodded toward the open doorway.

"Of course not," Father Mateo agreed. "You can both wait here. We won't be long."

Hiro deposited his sandals on the shelf beside the door, marking their position to ensure he took the same ones later, and then hurried into the meditation room.

Doyu's body lay on its side, curled up like a child. His head had fallen backward off his arm. His cheek rested gently against his shoulder, with the back of his head against the floor. His eyes were closed, his face relaxed.

Nichiyo and Gensho turned as Hiro and Father Mateo entered the room. Kenshin stood beside Bussho, bent over as if speaking to the boy.

The physician straightened. "You found them quickly."

"They were in the pilgrim's room," Shokai answered from the doorway.

Father Mateo paused beside Nichiyo. "What happened?"

"This death seems unlike the others," the abbot said. "He was not posed."

Hiro knelt beside the corpse. The body showed no visible signs of blood or trauma. Dark robes could hide blood, but the cloth did not look wet and the tatami had no spots or stains.

"I tried to wake him up to eat." Gensho gestured to a pot of rice and a stack of bowls in the center of the room. "When I touched his shoulder, his head rolled off his arm. I knew at once . . ."

"I thought he was just tired from the headache," Bussho sobbed.

"He complained of a headache?" Hiro asked.

Bussho sniffed, then nodded. He wiped his tears with the heel of his hand. "For the last two days."

"Two days?" Hiro asked. "Did he have headaches often?"

"Not that I remember." Bussho shook his head.

"He mentioned the headache to me yesterday," Kenshin said. "I examined him, but saw no injuries other than the bruises on his shoulders from the fall. I gave him a dose of willow tea in the afternoon, and a stronger one last night, before he went to sleep."

"He slept through the night." Bussho sniffled. "But said it hurt again this morning."

Hiro looked over his shoulder at Nichiyo. "You said he fell from the temple roof three days ago."

"He did, and I examined him afterward," Kenshin said. "He had some tenderness, and minor bruising, but no other injuries. The headache did not start that day."

"Maybe not," Hiro said, "but I suspect it was connected."

"How?" the physician asked, dismayed. "His head was not bruised or swollen. I would have seen it."

"A blow to the head can cause internal bleeding." Hiro bent to examine the back of Doyu's skull. As Kenshin said, it looked unharmed. "Sometimes it heals on its own, but if the bleeding is severe, and does not stop, eventually it kills."

"He had no symptoms," Nichiyo protested, "aside from the headache."

"He seemed disoriented earlier," Hiro said, "and drowsy."

"He did keep falling asleep in the morning service." Bussho's lips trembled. "And afterward, in here. I thought he was just sleepy." Tears streamed down his cheeks again. "This is my fault!"

"It is not your fault." Kenshin laid a reassuring hand on Bussho's shoulder. "It is mine. I failed to recognize his injury."

Hiro agreed with this assessment, especially since willow tea increased the risk of bleeding. However, he kept this information to himself. It would only make the physician feel worse, and would not help Bussho.

"Are you certain he was not poisoned?" Father Mateo murmured in Portuguese.

Hiro nodded.

"What did he say?" the abbot asked.

Hiro stood. "We should take the children out."

Father Mateo gestured toward the door. "We are taking the pilgrim's child, Ippen, to stay with the women in the abbot's hall, where the samurai woman can keep him safe until—until the storm has passed."

"No!" Bussho flung himself, face-first, on Doyu's robe. "Don't make me leave him."

"Bussho," Kenshin said gently, "Doyu-*sama* is not here. What remains is only an empty vessel."

"You wish to entrust his safety to a *woman*?" Nichiyo asked.

"To a samurai," Father Mateo corrected. "And since no Shingon priest would willingly enter a woman's presence, she will know that anyone who tries intends them harm."

The abbot frowned, but Kenshin spoke first. "It would remove him from this scene. . . ."

Bussho raised his head. "I cannot stay with women. It is forbidden."

"You are not ordained," Kenshin replied. "We all spent time with women before becoming priests. It will cause no lasting harm. More importantly, the samurai woman can keep you safe."

"Do I have to?" The boy turned pleading eyes on Nichiyo.

The abbot stroked his chin.

"It will keep him safe," Kenshin repeated.

A rumble of thunder echoed in the distance.

"I am the abbot." Nichiyo patted his chest with his hand. "I make the decisions."

Gensho made a derisive noise. "Then decide to keep the children safe."

"I am concerned for all of us," Nichiyo said. "Not just the children."

"Confess, right now!" Shokai demanded.

Nichiyo jumped. Everyone stared.

"Who are you speaking to?" Kenshin asked.

"The killer. He must be here." Shokai turned to the doorway and raised his voice. "The killer must confess and face the judgment he deserves!"

Hiro stared at the arrogant young priest, wondering whether the outburst was prompted by fear or an attempt to hide his guilt.

An awkward silence fell.

"While you wait for that to happen," Father Mateo said, "may we take the children to the abbot's house?"

Hiro stared. He might have expected such a comment from himself, but not from the Jesuit.

"Yes," Nichiyo said. "I have decided. Bussho, go with them."

The boy stood up obediently, jaw clenched against his tears. He bowed and followed Father Mateo from the room.

Hiro paused in front of Shokai long enough to say, "Do let me know if the killer confesses while we're gone."

CHAPTER 35

As he followed the others through the snow to the abbot's hall, Hiro cupped his hands over his mouth. He blew into them, trying to keep his fingers warm. The cold seemed deeper and more biting than winter storms in Iga, the isolation more complete. He stomped his chilly feet. With all the back-and-forth, and the thin temple sandals, his tabi had no time to dry before he soaked them in the snow again.

Despite the persistent feeling that something—or someone—was watching them through the storm, he paused outside the abbot's door to knock and announce their arrival. He did not trust Hatsuko, but, killer or no, he did believe she would attack any man who entered unannounced.

The door slid open. A gasp of warm air emerged but dissipated almost before Hiro's mind had fully registered its presence.

Hatsuko stood in the doorway, staff in hand. After staring at Hiro and the others for a moment, she withdrew and cleared the entry. "Come inside."

Ana and the nun stood up as Hiro and the others filed into the room, which suddenly felt too small to hold them all. The scent of incense had faded slightly, though its sweetly stale scent still permeated the chilly air, as if the ghosts of the abbot's prayers refused to leave the familiar space.

"Would you like some tea? Or rice? We have enough to share." The nun gestured to the kettle hanging above the fire and a covered pot resting nearby. Three empty bowls sat stacked beside the pot. They glistened slightly, suggesting a recent washing.

Behind them, Hatsuko shut the door and slid the bolt back into place. "What's going on?"

"We hoped you would watch the children." Father Mateo gestured to Ippen and Bussho.

Hatsuko frowned. "Another man has died."

The Jesuit nodded.

"Hm." Ana glared at Hiro. "I suppose you're involved in this somehow."

"This time it was not murder," Father Mateo said.

"He simply died," Hiro added.

"Seems to happen frequently, when you're around," the housekeeper retorted.

"Please," the Jesuit asked, "will you protect the children?"

"Of course we will," the nun declared. "They are welcome here with us."

Ippen spotted Gato sleeping near the fire. After slipping off her too-large temple sandals by the door, she hurried forward.

Gato opened her eyes and raised her head as the child approached. Her whiskers twitched. Ippen knelt beside the cat and extended a hand. Gato considered the offering for only a moment before butting her head against the child's fingers.

Ippen's face lit up. "It likes me!"

"Don't let anyone in here," Hiro said, "except for Father Mateo and me."

"And him, I suppose." Hatsuko nodded at Soro. "And anyone else who needs a favor?"

"That is not what I said." Hiro wondered why he felt the compulsion to argue with the samurai woman. "We pose no threat."

"That's not what you said the last time," she retorted before he could even decide how to warn her about Soro.

Her words echoed through Hiro's head in Neko's voice. His throat constricted as if clutched by ghostly hands.

Hatsuko's expression darkened. "It was a joke." She nodded toward the children. "Do not worry. I will keep them safe."

Father Mateo knelt beside Bussho, who stood at the door as if unwilling to join the others by the fire. "I am sorry about Doyu-*sama*."

The boy nodded but did not speak.

"Do not be ashamed to cry. We all feel sadness when a loved one dies." The Jesuit raised a hand, but closed and lowered it again as if realizing his touch would not be welcome.

Bussho drew a deep, slow breath and let it out again slowly. "Kōbō Daishi said he cried when bidding farewell to those he loved. I did not understand before. I thought detachment from the world meant losing sorrow also. But I understand him now." A single tear ran down his cheek. He wiped it away with the palm of his hand and looked at Hiro. "I hope you find the person who murdered Anan-*sama* and Ringa-*san* and Jorin-*san*. It is wrong to wish for someone's death. However, I want this person to face the jusanbutsu before he takes another life, or injures his own soul any further. If you find him . . ."

"I will find him," Hiro promised. *And unlike you, I have no problem wishing for his death.*

"Doyu-*sama* has died?" The elderly nun lowered her face. When she raised it again, her eyes were red, but dry. "Do not feel sorrow for him, child. His soul is free, like the birds that wing across the sky."

"You knew Doyu-*sama*?" Bussho asked.

The nun beckoned for the boy to join her by the fire. "We came to this mountain together, as children. I have not seen him since that day, but I know he grew into an honorable man, a wise leader who led this temple well and cared for it deeply. Regrettably, I also heard of his decline."

Bussho approached and knelt beside her. "How?"

She smiled. "We hear many things at the nyonindo."

"What if Doyu-*sama* cannot give a proper account of himself to the jusanbutsu?" Bussho's voice cracked. "He could barely remember his name. What if he can't remember his life and deeds?"

"Did not Kōbō Daishi teach that when the universe disappears, all sentient beings become enlightened, and everything passes into nirvana?" She paused.

Bussho nodded.

"Doyu-*sama*'s universe disappeared years ago," the nun explained. "As his memory faded, his attachment to this world slipped away until only enlightenment remained. Had he not become like a child?"

A spark of hope appeared in Bussho's eyes. "You think they will show him mercy?"

"Jizō-*sama* would not allow otherwise."

The flicker of a smile raised the edges of Bussho's lips. Their trembling stilled.

Hiro approved of the woman's words, even if he did not share her faith in benevolent gods or Buddhas. The state of Doyu's soul no longer mattered to anyone but Doyu.

For the living, comfort was more important than a truth that could not be known.

Hiro noted the pinched expression on Father Mateo's face. He could tell the Jesuit struggled, torn between the desire to talk about his god and the knowledge that his foreign religion's view of the afterlife could offer no reassurance to a Buddhist.

Not for the first time, Hiro wondered how the gods of different religions—if they existed—negotiated the fates of the dead. He pictured them arguing over souls like merchants haggling over bags of rice.

Thunder crashed, close enough to make the building shake.

Hiro glanced at the ceiling and reminded himself that he didn't believe in signs.

Hatsuko drew close and lowered her voice. "I need a blade."

Not a chance. Aloud he said, "You have a staff."

She narrowed her eyes. "Why don't you trust me?"

"The better question is, why should I trust you?"

She stared at him for a moment. "I have introduced myself, but I do not think I caught your name and clan."

He bowed just deeply enough to avoid insulting her. "I am Matsui Hiro, from Totomi Province." He normally used the name with his real province of origin—Iga—but decided not to risk it, given Oda Nobunaga's hatred for the Iga ryu.

Understanding transformed Hatsuko's face. "You distrust me because your lord supports the Ashikaga, while Daimyō Azai allies himself with Oda. Don't deny it."

Hiro hadn't planned to. People who jumped to their own inaccurate conclusions saved him the trouble of creating plausible lies.

"Perhaps," she continued, "we could agree to put our politics aside and focus on the greater threat? If it makes you feel better, I promise to hate you again as soon as safety grants me the luxury of unfounded prejudices."

Hiro raised an eyebrow and did not answer.

She heaved an exasperated sigh. "Would you truly rather cling to distant loyalties than save the lives of people in this room?"

"Distant?" Unexpected anger bloomed in Hiro's chest as he realized he could not read the woman well enough to know if she deceived him. "Your daimyō married Oda Nobunaga's sister."

"Daimyō Azai refused my sword and my oath," she spat. "I am loyal to myself alone."

"Persuasive words, if true."

"You distrust me because I am a woman."

Hiro caught a trace of disappointment in her voice. "That has nothing—"

Father Mateo intervened in Portuguese. "Stop arguing and give her a sword."

"So she can turn it back on me?" Hiro replied in the Jesuit's language.

"Give her a short one. You'll have longer reach."

"That is not funny." Hiro watched Hatsuko from the corner of his eye. She did not seem to understand Portuguese, though Hiro knew how easily such ignorance could be feigned. "And arming her is out of the question."

Soro produced a sheathed dagger from beneath his robe and offered it to the samurai woman. "Defend my son."

Father Mateo opened his mouth as if to correct the pilgrim's error, but shut it quickly, apparently remembering that not everyone knew the truth about Ippen. Hiro agreed with the omission. For the moment, it caused less trouble to go along with Soro's story.

Hatsuko bowed and accepted the weapon with both hands. "I will. I swear it on my life."

Straightening, she drew the dagger and examined the blade. It flashed in the firelight, sharp and lethal.

Hatsuko returned the dagger to its sheath with an approving nod. "It is not a sword, but it will do."

CHAPTER 36

Hiro followed Father Mateo and Soro across the yard to the meditation hall, with Hatsuko's words repeating in his mind. *You distrust me because I am a woman. . . .*

He snorted angrily against the storm, stopped in his tracks, and watched the swirling snow. He wondered how Neko would have stopped this murderer.

I would kill him.

Hiro startled and looked around.

Father Mateo and Soro had disappeared into the blizzard. He stood alone in the temple yard, surrounded by whipping winds and whirling snow.

He was alone, and yet her voice had seemed so real.

He shook his head and continued walking. Neko was dead. The dead did not speak, or rise, or offer advice from beyond the grave. The idea had come from his own mind, even if he thought it in Neko's voice.

That said, it was precisely what she would have done—and what he had to do as well.

As soon as he returned to the meditation hall, he would examine Doyu's corpse again. He hoped to find evidence of murder. Without it, he could not be certain the killer would let Doyu count as Fugen, which meant Hiro could not now determine the next target with any accuracy.

Despite his loathing of assumptions, he felt confident the killer planned to use Father Mateo as Jizō. The pieces fit too well. He could simply protect the Jesuit until the proper time, but Hiro wanted to stop the killer now. As a trained assassin, Hiro was the hunter, not the hunted. It angered him that the murderer had killed three priests—or possibly four—with Hiro no closer to solving the crimes.

It ruffled his pride.

As he stomped the snow from his temple sandals outside the door to the meditation hall, he realized he needed a plan to save the Jesuit and stop the killer from completing his grisly council of the dead.

Hiro left his sandals at the end of the rack and hurried into the meditation room, which now was almost empty. Father Mateo stood talking with Myokan and Nichiyo, while Soro stood alone by the brazier in the corner of the room. As the pilgrim extended his hands toward the coals, Hiro felt a flash of suspicion. Soro seemed unusually relaxed for a man, whether uncle or father, who had just left a beloved child in a stranger's care.

That thought vanished, replaced by another. "Where is the body?"

"Doyu-*sama*?" Nichiyo asked. "Kenshin-*san* and Shokai took him to the annex."

"And Gensho-*san* is in the latrine," Myokan added.

"Do we need to examine the body again?" Father Mateo asked.

Hiro weighed the potential danger of going back into the storm against the value of evidence they might still find on Doyu's corpse. "I think we do."

"Why?" Nichiyo sounded suspicious. "You said he died of natural causes."

"Bleeding in the skull is hardly natural," Hiro countered, "and although I find it likely that the injury resulted from his recent fall, I'd like to rule out murder absolutely. Wouldn't you?"

The abbot's face turned red. "Of course. I simply thought . . . that is, you said . . ."

"Make them wait until Gensho-*san* returns," Myokan said. "We still have only their word that they wish to help us, and most of the Kirishitans wish us harm."

Hiro ignored the accusation.

However, the Jesuit did not.

"Do you truly think I am a killer?" Father Mateo approached the guardian, who glanced at the entry as if wishing for his staff.

"I heard the foreigners talking in Kyoto." Myokan squared his shoulders. "You are one of them."

"That does not make me a murderer," the Jesuit said, "any more than it makes you guilty if we learn another Buddhist killed these men."

Myokan drew back.

"No man bears responsibility for the choices another man makes." Father Mateo raised the cross that hung around his neck. "Some men do evil in the name of God, but, on my honor, I am not among them."

The outer door of the meditation hall rattled open. Heavy footsteps sounded in the entry, and a moment later, Gensho joined them in the room. He rubbed his hands together as he started toward the brazier, but paused uncertainly when he saw Soro by the fire.

The pilgrim beckoned. "Warm your hands."

Gensho nodded thanks and approached the brazier, but stood on the opposite side.

Hiro remembered the dagger Soro produced from beneath his robe. He had not asked about it at the time, but the weapon was yet another piece of evidence against the pilgrim's story. Many traveling priests did carry staves or knives for self-defense, but this particular pilgrim seemed significantly more than he claimed to be.

"Time to go," Hiro told Father Mateo.

"I still don't understand why you need to examine him again," Nichiyo said.

"We did not truly examine him before," Hiro replied. "I made deductions based on superficial information. Do you have a reason for objecting to a full examination?"

"He was the abbot."

"So was Anan," Hiro countered.

"Yes, but Anan-*sama* was murdered."

"And only examination will tell us if Doyu was as well."

"Wait!" Nichiyo gasped as Hiro headed for the door. "We should stay together. What if the killer attacks while you are gone?"

"Surely three of you can overpower a single man." Hiro glanced at each of them in turn. "No matter which of you begins the trouble."

Soro did not react, though Gensho and Myokan both nodded. The abbot drew his hands to his chest and looked at the others nervously.

"Stay in separate parts of the room, as you suggested earlier," Father Mateo told Nichiyo. "It may help."

Nichiyo frowned, but moved away from Myokan.

Hiro beckoned for the Jesuit to follow. "We will return as soon as possible."

CHAPTER 37

Aswirl of snowflakes followed Hiro and Father Mateo through the door and into the hondō annex. The fresh, cold air diluted the peppery smell of incense, but only until the door slid closed. However, this time Hiro didn't mind the odor quite as much. As between its cloying sweetness and the stench of decaying flesh, he preferred the incense any day, and though cold would help delay the bodies' putrefaction, the holy smoke would further extend the time when Hiro's sensitive nose began to smell death's presence in the room.

The bodies lay in a row with their heads toward the altar and feet toward the door, with sufficient space between them for a priest or mourner to kneel at their sides. Like the others, Doyu now wore a purple robe emblazoned with the crest of Myo-in. His corpse lay between Ringa and Anan, with Jorin on Anan's other side.

Kenshin knelt by Doyu's head, while Shokai knelt beside his feet. They chanted in unison, Kenshin speaking the words from memory while, as before, Shokai read from a book.

Father Mateo leaned toward Hiro and whispered, "Why do they use Sanskrit, rather than Japanese?"

Hiro brushed snow from his robe. "Tradition, I suppose."

As he waited for the prayer to end, he watched the flecks of snow melt into the tatami floor.

Kenshin stood and turned to face the door. "Has something happened?"

"Nothing new," Hiro said. "We came for a closer look at the body."

"To identify the cause of death," Father Mateo added.

"We saw no new injuries when we changed his robe." Kenshin gestured to the corpse. "But you may examine him further, if you wish."

Father Mateo stared at the line of bodies. "Do you lay the dead in order of seniority?"

"Ringa-*san* was not the most important." Shokai pursed his lips in disapproval.

"We merely placed Doyu-*sama* beside the man who succeeded him as abbot," Kenshin said. "We believed he would prefer to lie between Anan-*sama* and the temple guardian."

Hiro suspected Doyu would have preferred to stay alive. Instead of saying so, he approached the corpse.

As before, he saw no visible wounds or bruises. He knelt beside the body and raised Doyu's eyelids one at a time. The dead man's pupils were large and dark, the whites of his eyes unblemished.

Hiro unfastened the ties of the dead man's robe.

"Is that necessary?" Unexpectedly, the question came from Father Mateo.

"It is if we want to learn what killed him."

The Jesuit gestured to Kenshin. "They saw no unusual injuries. Do we truly need to disturb the dead?"

"The dead don't care." Hiro opened the dead man's robe, exposing the body, which was naked except for a clean white loincloth wrapped around the dead man's groin and upper thighs. Doyu's ribs were visible beneath his liver-spotted skin. His chest looked sunken, but from age, not injury.

Hiro did not touch the loincloth. A man who suffered injury there would not have died in silence. "I would like to see his back."

Kenshin knelt on the opposite side of the body as Hiro removed the dead man's right arm from his robe. With Kenshin's help, he rolled the body away, exposing Doyu's back.

Colorful bruises marked the former abbot's shoulders. Their black-and-purple centers faded to a sickly but vibrant green around the edges.

"He was beaten," Father Mateo gasped.

"Not recently, if at all." Hiro indicated the greenish band around the outside of the bruises. "This color takes several days to develop. Most likely, these came from his recent fall."

"I saw no such injuries when I examined him, right after the accident," Kenshin said.

"Deep bruises may take time to show," Hiro replied. "Perhaps you examined him too early."

Kenshin looked unconvinced, but did not argue.

"Someone said he hit his head." Father Mateo frowned. "Why doesn't he have bruises there, or on his neck?"

"He would have struck the ground right here." Hiro indicated the largest bruises on the abbot's shoulders. "If his head impacted the ground a moment later, he might have only bled inside the skull. He has no bruises on his neck because it never struck the ground."

Hiro nodded to Kenshin, and they returned the body to its back. Hiro slipped Doyu's arm into the sleeve and closed the robe.

"You see? Nothing," Shokai said. "He died of natural causes."

"He did not." Hiro retied the robe and stood. "However, it does appear he died because of the recent fall, and not from murder."

"No chance of poison?" Father Mateo asked.

"Even subtle poisons leave some sign." Hiro gestured to Doyu's face. "Discoloration of the nose and ears, or foam around the mouth. I see no indication he was poisoned."

"I regret not keeping a closer eye on him," Kenshin said.

"Watching him was Bussho's job, not yours," Shokai put in. "If anyone failed him—"

"Bussho bears no responsibility for Doyu-*sama*'s death." Kenshin spoke with unusual force. "Do not repeat, or even imply, such a thing again."

Shokai crossed his arms.

Kenshin sighed. "We should return to the meditation hall. Nichiyo-*san* will worry."

"Speaking of the abbot," Hiro said. "I'm told you were here when he came to Myo-in."

Kenshin looked at the bodies on the floor. "As of now, I am the only living priest who was, since Gensho-*san* was in Shikoku on a pilgrimage at the time." He looked up. "Why do you ask?"

"Do you know why he became a priest?"

"You heard the rumors." Kenshin gave Shokai a sidelong look. The younger man blushed and looked away. "That story is not mine to tell."

"And yet, Nichiyo-*san* won't tell it either," Hiro said.

"Have you asked him?"

"Not directly," Father Mateo admitted.

"I doubt his past will help you find the murderer you seek," the physician said. "But if you wish to know about a man, you should ask him personally."

"And if he lies?" Hiro asked.

"Have you a reason to believe he will?" Kenshin paused. "Perception varies according to the mind. When the mind is polluted, people and objects seem tainted. With respect, your opinion of Nichiyo-*san* may spring more from your own illusions than from his true nature."

"With similar respect," Hiro countered, "you seem unusually calm about the fact that, unless we stop the killer, everyone in this temple is going to die."

"Everyone becomes a corpse in time," Kenshin replied. "Kōbō Daishi taught that understanding this helps us to rid ourselves of false ideals. As it happens, it prevents false fears as well."

"The threat is hardly false," Hiro said.

"Perhaps, but I do not fear death. Suffering exists in this world, not in what lies beyond."

"Except for those condemned to hell," Shokai added.

Kenshin smiled. "Which I do not plan to be."

CHAPTER 38

As the four men fought back through the storm to the meditation hall, Hiro reviewed what he knew about the killings. Seven suspects remained: the surviving priests of Myo-in, Soro, and Hatsuko. He felt fairly confident that Soro was shinobi, but less certain about the alleged pilgrim's reasons for coming to Myo-in. The story about the child and her mother sounded plausible, particularly due to Ippen's gender. Assassins did use children as distractions on occasion, but Hiro saw no reason to use a girl on Kōya. Whoever planned the mission would have known to send a boy instead.

Hatsuko's involvement also seemed less likely. Hiro did not trust her, but if she was involved, she must be working with someone else. She could not know the temple, or its priests, in enough detail to carry out the murders personally.

Setting them aside for the moment, Hiro considered the surviving priests of Myo-in. His stomach clenched with more than cold as he realized someone he had spoken with in the last two hours was planning Father Mateo's death.

Four years ago, he'd sworn an oath to keep the Jesuit alive after an unknown client of the Iga ryu paid a hefty sum to ensure the foreign priest's protection. Hattori Hanzō assigned Hiro to the task, though neither Hiro nor the priest had ever learned the client's identity or his reasons for providing Father Mateo with a bodyguard. At first, Hiro had considered the assignment merely that—another mission for the Iga ryu, if less desirable than most. The client's motives did not matter. He had performed less savory tasks with far less explanation.

Now, four years later, it wasn't the oath, or the fact that he was honor bound to take his own life if Father Mateo died, that made Hiro's blood run colder than the ice that stung his face and swirled in the stormy wind.

He had not saved his older brother, Ichiro, who died on a failed mission before Hiro was old enough to shave. He had not saved his lover, Neko, from her bloody fate. The thought that if he failed again his closest friend would pay the price was almost more than Hiro's mind could bear.

He squinted at Father Mateo, who walked ahead of him through the snow. This foreign man, with his strange faith, was more than a mission, his survival more than just a matter of preserving the honor of the Iga ryu. Despite the differences between them, Hiro had grown to understand the Jesuit in ways he did not even understand the surviving brother who shared his blood—and he realized, with striking force, that he would gladly kill every living soul at Myo-in before he let Father Mateo come to harm.

The rage that burned inside his chest since Neko's death condensed into a focused burn. He had played the killer's game too long.

It was time for Hiro to take control.

Myokan met the snow-covered group in the narrow, wood-floored entry of the meditation hall. "Did you learn what killed Doyu-*sama*?" he asked.

Kenshin set his slippers on the rack. "We found no evidence of murder."

Myokan shifted his gaze to Hiro, who nodded agreement.

After leaving his borrowed sandals on the end of the rack beside Father Mateo's, Hiro followed the Jesuit and the other priests into the meditation room.

"How are you going to stop the killer?" Nichiyo demanded as Hiro appeared. "You are a warrior! You must save us!"

Hiro slowly turned to face the abbot. "I do not recall swearing an oath to keep you safe."

"You gave your word that you would catch the killer." Nichiyo's eyes were wide, his pupils dilated. "At this rate, we will all be dead before you have an answer."

"In which case, you will get your answer from the kings of hell."

Nichiyo gasped and covered his mouth with his hand as Hiro stalked away.

Father Mateo caught up as he reached the far front corner of the room, to the right of the Buddhas. Hiro stood with his back to the room and scowled at the carvings' enigmatic wooden smiles.

Normally, Hiro preferred to position himself where he could see approaching threats, but at the moment, he doubted he could look Nichiyo in the face without doing something he might—or, worse, might not—regret. Sooner, rather than later, he needed to ask the abbot about his past, but at the moment he would rather not have the pasty-faced coward in his field of view.

"You did not have to insult him," Father Mateo chided softly. "The man is frightened."

"That is not my problem," Hiro growled, avoiding the Jesuit's gaze.

He considered the Buddhas. Once again, he had the feeling he had forgotten something important about the triptych's meaning. His irritation grew as it continued to elude him.

"What is your problem?" Father Mateo shifted the conversation to Portuguese. "Is this about these murders, or is it Ne—"

"I told you not to say her name," Hiro snapped. "And this has nothing to do with her. I simply want to stop this killer, as you should too, unless you want to die."

"The physician spoke the truth, in the annex. Every man must die."

"Not if I can prevent it. I do not want your death on my conscience." His voice almost broke on the final word.

The Jesuit's expression wavered between compassion and sorrow. "Neko's death was not your fault. And, if it happens, mine will not be either."

Hiro clenched his jaw so hard he thought his teeth might crack. He would not talk about Neko. Not here. Not now. Perhaps not ever.

Even as he had the thought, he realized, with great surprise, that if he did choose to speak of Neko, Father Mateo was the only one he would trust to hear the words. Somehow, this foreign stranger had become his brother, in spirit if not in blood.

Still, this was not the time for introspection.

He changed the subject, but continued to speak in Portuguese, avoiding words that might alert anyone else to the topic they discussed. "I think the killer will consider the most recent death as one of the thirteen intended victims, even though it was not a murder." He counted the reasons off on his fingers. "The . . . dead man . . . served as abbot of this temple, so he had wisdom, and his declining mental state made him as innocent as a child. Given those characteristics, I think it likely the killer will now move on to the next of the thirteen deities."

"Which means you think that now, he comes for me." Father Mateo's face grew grim. "I agree. It's time to force the killer's hand."

"What do you mean?"

"We lay a trap, with me as bait."

"Unacceptable," Hiro said.

"Because you swore an oath?"

Hiro crossed his arms. "Because I will not let you die."

"I'm counting on it." Father Mateo smiled. "That's why it's called a trap."

"I will not let you risk yourself."

The Jesuit's smile faded. "I am at risk already, if your theory is correct. We might as well control the situation. I am not afraid—"

"You should be."

"I trust you to stop him." Father Mateo paused. "And if you cannot, my soul is ready to meet my Lord."

"Mine is not."

"You do not have to kill yourself," the Jesuit said. "I will write a letter, releasing you from your oath and commanding you to live."

"That is not what I meant." Hiro looked at the floor, because he could not say the words while looking his friend in the face. "I am unwilling for you to die."

"I don't intend to." The smile returned to Father Mateo's voice. "I made a plan to help us catch the killer."

"*You* made a plan?" Hiro stared at the priest.

Father Mateo frowned. "You're not the only man in Japan who's capable of doing that, you know."

The priest outlined his plan in whispered Portuguese. Hiro listened in growing disbelief. Despite a few minor flaws, the tactics seemed surprisingly sound.

"You're certain about this?" Hiro asked when the Jesuit finished. "In the past, you refused to use your god, or your religion, as a ruse."

"My need to worship is no ruse," Father Mateo said. "Today is the holy day of the week—the Lord's Day—and I wish to celebrate communion with my evening prayers. That ritual requires special implements and time to perform. More importantly, I cannot do it in this room."

"If you're certain." Hiro loathed the thought of placing Father Mateo in danger, but the priest would not be safe as long as the killer stalked the halls of Myo-in. At least this plan controlled the risk—in some ways, better than their previous attempts to capture killers.

Together they worked out the last details, correcting the problems until, at last, Hiro said, "I don't like putting you in danger, but this might just work."

Father Mateo nodded. "Let's get started."

CHAPTER 39

Father Mateo crossed the hall to Nichiyo. The abbot watched him warily, gaze shifting between the approaching Jesuit and Hiro, who followed a few steps behind, as befitted a ronin serving a foreign master.

Nichiyo rose as they approached.

Father Mateo bowed. "If you please, I would like to ask another question—about becoming a Shingon priest."

"You wish to accept our way?" Nichiyo's eyes lit up. "It will require study, of course, but—"

"Forgive me," Father Mateo said. "For now, I simply wish to learn the process. Could you tell me how and why you decided to become a priest?"

Nichiyo's cheeks turned purple. He would not meet the Jesuit's gaze. "I do not think . . ."

"It would mean a great deal to me." Father Mateo persisted as if unaware that, by Japanese custom, Nichiyo's unfinished sentence constituted a polite refusal.

The abbot smiled uncomfortably. "If you insist. . . ."

Once again, the Jesuit feigned ignorance. He clasped his hands. "Thank you! So, what brought you to Myo-in?"

"It is a private matter." Nichiyo paused. "Perhaps we should speak in the entry, where others cannot overhear."

"May my translator join us?" Father Mateo gestured to Hiro. "In case I do not understand the subtleties of your story?"

The abbot nodded. "If the killer tries to attack, I would prefer we had his sword."

They moved to the entry. Nichiyo shut the door, sequestering them in the tiny space. He stepped away, but continued to shift his feet and glance at the shoji, clearly nervous.

"Is your reason for coming to Myo-in a secret?" Father Mateo prompted.

"I prefer not to discuss it," Nichiyo admitted. "But . . . I know there are rumors, and I do not want you thinking I'm the killer."

"Rumors?" Father Mateo's surprise seemed remarkably genuine.

Nichiyo nodded, casting yet another glance at the door. "Some of the younger priests. They would not understand. Perhaps you will not either."

"I have no authority to judge you," Father Mateo said. "Only God can judge a man."

"I agree." Nichiyo straightened. His nervousness fell away. "And I did only what I had to do. I had no choice."

"I'm certain that's true," the Jesuit encouraged.

"I come from a farming family," Nichiyo said. "My father had three sons. I am the oldest and the smartest of the three."

"The oldest, and yet your father sent you to a temple?" Hiro found that strange.

Nichiyo's cheeks turned brilliant red. "My mother sent me, after my father and brothers died." He hesitated over the words.

Hiro suspected the deaths were not entirely accidental.

"My family's land lies near the sea. The year before I came here, a tsunami flooded our fields with ocean water. The rice plants died. We had no money, and no food, except a little bit my parents saved. My father refused to eat. He scavenged the countryside for anything edible, and gave his share to my brothers and me. It wasn't enough, but it kept us alive, at least for a while. That winter, my father grew sick. He died, and my younger brothers died as well.

"In the spring, my mother declared my survival a miracle. She shaved her head and became a nun, and sent me here, to Kōya, to become a priest. She said this way I would always have enough to eat and shelter from winter's storms."

"Forgive me," Father Mateo said, "but I fail to see why that would create rumors."

Nichiyo shrugged as if he did not know, either.

"Because that's not the entire story," Hiro said.

"Of course it is." Nichiyo gripped his robe. "They died of illness and starvation. My mother and I survived, by Buddha's grace."

"If that were true, you would not hesitate to tell the story," Hiro said. "You would take pride in the miracle of your survival, as you do in your knowledge and your status within the temple. Yet you hide it as if ashamed."

"I have no reason to be ashamed." Nichiyo raised his chin, but his cheeks flushed darker.

"Your survival was no miracle." Hiro paused. "Did you steal your brothers' share of the food by yourself, or did your mother help you?"

"I did not steal!" Nichiyo drew back.

"If you say so." Hiro let his voice register disbelief.

"Stealing involves taking something that does not belong to you," Nichiyo said. "I deserved to live. I was the smart one. My father's heir! They did not have enough food to save us all. My father knew it—that's why he gave his food away. He knew. I knew it also. There was only enough for one of us to live."

"And your mother?" Hiro asked.

"She did not know. She believed the Buddha intervened to save my life."

"But you know better," Hiro said.

Nichiyo looked down at the wooden floor. "I sneaked into the storeroom when the others were asleep, and ate. They never knew. But it was not stealing. It was mine, by right—especially after my father died. I was the heir."

"What happened to your lands?" Hiro asked.

"My mother gave it all to the Shingon temple near the village, the one where she became a nun."

"Why send you all the way to Kōya?" Father Mateo asked.

"To show her gratitude for my survival." After a pause, Nichiyo added, "I did not mind. Even though the food was mine, by right . . . I did not want her to learn the truth. She believed in the miracle so strongly."

And would have loathed you if she ever learned the truth of what you'd done, Hiro thought.

"I have told you the truth, because I am not a killer," Nichiyo said. "I only did what I must to survive. Do not waste time believing I'm the killer. You must find him and stop him before he kills us all."

"We intend to," Hiro said.

Nichiyo nodded in approval. "It's cold out here. Let's go back to the other room, where it's warmer."

He opened the shoji and stepped up into the meditation hall. Hiro and Father Mateo followed a few steps behind.

"If you please," Father Mateo called after the abbot, "I would like to request a favor."

CHAPTER 40

Hiro noted with approval that the Jesuit spoke loudly enough for everyone else in the room to hear him, but not so loudly as to make the volume seem deliberate.

"A favor?" Nichiyo turned back.

"I wish to request permission to leave the meditation hall for an hour or two this evening, on my own, to conduct my evening prayers in a more appropriate place."

Nichiyo raised his chin, and his chest puffed out slightly at the Jesuit's deferential tone. "I fear that would be difficult to manage."

Wind moaned through the eaves like a restless ghost, followed by a roll of thunder.

Father Mateo ignored the polite refusal. "I can use the guest room where I slept last night. I simply need a private place."

"Perhaps you did not hear me. With a killer on the loose, and your translator our only fully capable defender, it would be inconvenient for you to leave. . . ." Nichiyo trailed off as if expecting Father Mateo to withdraw the impossible request.

"I also need a candle and some juice or wine, if you have some to offer," the Jesuit said.

Nichiyo's eyebrows drew together. "You can say your prayers here. None of us will interfere."

"Regrettably, I cannot say my prayers in a room that holds an idol." Father Mateo gestured to the Buddha statues. "My faith does not permit it."

"Every part of Myo-in is consecrated to our Shingon faith." Nichiyo smiled politely. "One room is precisely the same as another."

197

"With respect, I disagree." Father Mateo spoke softly but firmly. "God requires me to conduct my rituals in solitude and in a proper space. I had hoped to obtain your permission, as a sign of respect for your authority. However, I cannot accept your refusal."

Nichiyo's smile vanished like a fallen leaf in a howling storm. "Then why did you bother to ask at all?"

Father Mateo bowed. "As I said, I respect your authority."

"You do not, if you would act against my word."

"On the contrary," Father Mateo said. "I respect you deeply, but I place no man before my duty to God. Surely, as a priest, you understand this."

"Forgive me." Kenshin approached, with Shokai at his side. "Is something wrong?"

"The foreigner wishes to leave the safety of the hall to pray in his guest room, alone."

"My translator will stand guard outside the door." Father Mateo gestured to Hiro, who took the cue to step up and join the group.

"Let him risk his life, if he wishes. What business is that of ours?" Shokai's comment drew another disapproving look from Kenshin.

Nichiyo's cheeks flushed red. "If he dies, his church might demand reparations, or invade Mount Kōya to avenge him!"

"My church does not avenge martyrs," Father Mateo began.

Nichiyo turned to Hiro. "Can you guarantee his people will not blame us if he dies?"

"I am only a translator," Hiro said.

"You are samurai."

"I am ronin." Hiro lowered his gaze and voice. "I speak for no one but myself."

"I take responsibility for whatever happens," Father Mateo said, "but I must pray, and you cannot stop me from leaving the hall."

"Cannot?" Nichiyo stepped back, cheeks darkening to an angry purple. "Myokan!"

The guardian started forward, but Hiro considered him no threat. The young priest's broken arm still hung in a sling across his chest, and his good hand held no weapon.

Even so, Hiro stepped between the guardian and Father Mateo. "Do you know what the foreign god does to men who try to prevent his priests from worshipping him?"

Myokan gave Nichiyo a sidelong look as Hiro continued, "He strikes them with lightning and rains fire from the sky to burn their temples to the ground."

A well-timed crack of thunder split the air and shook the hall.

Nichiyo and Kenshin jumped. Father Mateo raised his wide-eyed face to the ceiling. For an instant, Hiro wondered if the foreign god was listening after all—but the moment passed as quickly as it came.

"If something happens to the foreigner," Hiro told Nichiyo, "his people will say his god was punishing him for a lack of faith—perhaps because he stayed in a Buddhist temple."

"You see?" Myokan put in. "They do not like us. They want us dead."

"Nothing in my faith prohibits me from visiting Buddhist temples." Father Mateo sounded offended. "Moreover, I do not hate you, and I do not want to destroy this lovely temple."

"So you say," Myokan retorted.

Nichiyo spoke over the guardian. "Why, then, do you disrespect me?"

"You disrespect me also," the Jesuit said, but without anger.

Nichiyo's gaze shifted to Hiro. "If I let him go, will you stay here and defend us?"

"I can—" Myokan began, but the abbot spoke over him.

"You are injured. I want his sword. With him defending us, the killer will not dare attack." He paused. "Matsui-*san*, do you agree?"

Hiro's dislike of Nichiyo sharpened further. The abbot did not care about Father Mateo's safety—or the Jesuit's prayers—he merely feared the loss of the samurai's sword.

Or else he wanted to ensure the potential victim left the hall alone.

Nichiyo's face grew shrewd. "Surely he does not need you to translate when he speaks to his foreign god."

"Strange," Hiro said. "Until now, you insisted we leave the hall in pairs or not at all. Yet now you expect him to go alone. Is it really my sword you care about, or are you sacrificing him to save your own cowardly life a little longer?"

"I-I . . ." Nichiyo looked around as if for support, but no one spoke in his defense. His gaze fell on Father Mateo. "If I let him go with you, will you ask your god to keep us safe?"

"We do not need his foreign god!" Myokan hissed.

Father Mateo ignored the comment. "I will pray for the safety of this temple and every priest within its walls, and God will hear me."

"I am not responsible for your safety," Nichiyo said. "You take this on yourself."

"The decision is mine," Father Mateo acknowledged. "I absolve you of any guilt."

"Then you may go," the abbot spoke grudgingly. "But hurry back."

"May I ask an additional favor?" Father Mateo ignored Nichiyo's scowl. "Could I borrow a candle, and some wine or sake, if you have it? My ritual requires consecrated bread and wine."

"Candles, yes, but we do not drink alcohol on Kōya." Nichiyo paused, frowning. "Although . . . at one point we had *umeshu*, to serve the daimyō when they visit. . . ."

"We have several sealed bottles," Kenshin said. "I keep them locked away with the medicinal supplies, to keep them safe. That said, this request is most unusual. Anan-*sama* instructed us not to—"

"I am the abbot now." Nichiyo turned to Father Mateo. "You may have the umeshu. Kenshin will bring it to you when the time for your ritual arrives. Until then, it must remain in storage. Alcohol is not permitted in the meditation hall."

"With respect," Kenshin began, "I think—"

"I have decided," Nichiyo declared.

An awkward silence fell, but Gensho broke it quickly. "Would you like the candle now?"

CHAPTER 41

Gensho retrieved a small candle from a cabinet at the back of the hall and offered it to Father Mateo, who tucked the small taper into the pouch at his waist. After thanking the cook, Hiro and the Jesuit returned to their place at the front of the room.

"You don't have to do this." Hiro spoke in Portuguese, and softly.

"The plan?" Father Mateo replied in kind. "If we don't, the killer will murder someone else instead. Regardless of why he's doing this—and I still suspect a religious madman, not a trained assassin—he will kill again tonight."

"Perhaps, but maybe not."

"You promised not to lie to me." Father Mateo's voice held a reprimand.

"It's not a lie." *Not entirely.*

"Nor entirely true."

Hiro stared, disconcerted as usual by the Jesuit's uncanny—and no longer entirely rare—ability to guess his thoughts.

"I appreciate your concern," Father Mateo continued, "but I will take the risk. Jesus sacrificed himself on my behalf, but I cannot allow a mortal man to do the same."

Fear twisted Hiro's stomach, the sensation both unfamiliar and unpleasant.

"What I wonder . . ." Father Mateo turned to look at the other priests, most of whom appeared to be meditating. "How will the killer explain his departure from the hall? They will notice when he leaves."

"He will claim he needs to use the latrine." Hiro glanced at Soro. "Or claim to be checking on his son."

201

"Even so, when I'm discovered dead—"

"That will not happen." Hiro spoke more sharply than intended.

His tone drew a curious glance from Kenshin, who knelt beside Shokai on the opposite side of the hall.

"But, from the murderer's perspective," Father Mateo said. "How does he plan to avoid suspicion?"

Hiro considered what he would do in the killer's place. "He likely plans to kill us both and claim he caught me murdering you—"

"Forcing you to take the blame for the previous murders also." Father Mateo paused. "They might believe that, since the killings began right after we arrived."

"That story would also make the last few priests more vulnerable, because they would believe the danger past."

Father Mateo exhaled heavily. "I confess, I didn't expect you to let me do this. Normally, you try to keep me out of danger."

"Normally, you get into it anyway." Hiro forced a smile, to make it appear as if they spoke about something pleasant. "At least this way, I choose the terms on which we fight."

Father Mateo's smile was genuine. "You said 'we.'"

"What?"

"You included me." The Jesuit paused. "Thank you for that."

"I could hardly set this trap without you," Hiro said. "And don't forget, it might not work. The killer might not take the bait."

"I think he will."

Hiro sighed. "Regrettably, I think so too."

When evening came, Father Mateo stood up and straightened his kimono. "Time to go."

Nichiyo rose as Hiro and the Jesuit approached. "Then you insist on doing this?"

"I have a duty to God."

"Pardon my interruption." Kenshin had followed them across the hall. "Nichiyo-*san*, about the umeshu—"

"Why do you question my authority?" The abbot crossed his arms.

Kenshin bowed. "With apologies, I merely wished to remind you that we must retrieve it."

Nichiyo lowered his arms. "Oh. Yes." He glanced at the Jesuit. "You will conduct the ritual in your guest room?"

Father Mateo nodded. "After we go with Kenshin-*san* to get the . . . *ume-shu*?"

"An alcoholic drink," Kenshin explained, "like wine, but made from stone fruit. It has helpful medicinal properties, though of course we do not partake of it ourselves. Shokai will accompany me to the storehouse, and we will bring the flask to you together. That way, I won't need to return to the meditation hall alone while you conduct your ritual."

And I won't need to worry about you being alone with the umeshu, Hiro thought with approval.

"Thank you for your generosity." Father Mateo bowed to Nichiyo and started toward the door.

Shokai was waiting in the entry, holding a pair of lanterns. He extended one to Father Mateo. "To light your way."

The Jesuit accepted the unexpected offering with a grateful bow.

Hiro slipped on a pair of soggy temple sandals and followed Father Mateo into the storm.

Darkness had fallen. Sounds were muffled by the falling snow, which swirled dizzily through the lantern's tiny sphere of light and disappeared again the moment it passed beyond the lantern's reach.

Kenshin and Shokai set off in a different direction, angling off across the yard. Hiro watched their lantern bob away for a moment and then hurried along behind Father Mateo.

Hiro shuddered as the door slid shut behind them. Although the hall blocked out the storm, it felt no warmer than the air outside. The silent darkness and the chill reminded Hiro of a tomb.

Father Mateo shivered and raised the lantern. "No b-braziers."

"Risk of fire."

"Waste of fuel, too," the Jesuit said, teeth chattering, as he started down the hall. "Nobody's here."

The lantern cast a flickering light along the walls and illuminated the Jesuit's breath, which emerged from his mouth in tiny clouds, like the ghosts of thoughts unsaid.

Inside the guest room, Father Mateo used the lantern's coals to coax a fire in the brazier. He added wood from the bucket on the floor. Slowly, the flames took hold and the room grew brighter, if not warm.

The Jesuit examined the bucket. "At least we can warm the room for a while. Hopefully, we won't be here all night."

"If we are, it means the killer chose a different victim." Hiro almost hoped he would, and that he would choose Nichiyo, despite the abbot's utter lack of resemblance to the selfless Jizō.

The Jesuit shivered.

"Are you frightened, or just cold?"

"Nervous, perhaps." The Jesuit rubbed his scarred hands together and held them toward the tiny fire. "Not frightened. I came to Japan prepared to die whenever the Lord requires it. I hope he will not expect my life tonight, but even if he does, I commend myself into his hands."

My hands will be the ones that save you, Hiro thought. "Where do you plan to say your prayers?"

Father Mateo surveyed the room. "Have you a preference?"

Hiro gestured to the floor on the opposite side of the room from the entrance. "If you kneel here, near the veranda, I will see the killer coming. We'll leave the door open, so he thinks you are alone."

"Won't he see you also?"

"No." Hiro opened the paper-paneled shoji that separated the guest room from the enclosed veranda. Heavy, wooden shutters walled off the outer edge of the narrow porch. They rattled as a blizzard wind surged by.

The Jesuit crossed the room to join him and exhaled sharply, wrapping his arms around himself for warmth. "It's even colder here."

"The outer shutters give no insulation," Hiro said, "and the brazier's heat won't reach the veranda with the shoji closed." He stepped through the doorway onto the porch and slid the paneled door shut behind him.

Father Mateo's shadow danced on the paper panels, backlit by the fire in the brazier near the door. The Jesuit's shadow raised its hands in a questioning gesture. His voice was slightly muted by the shoji. "The killer won't see you, but you won't see him either, when he comes."

Hiro opened the door, withdrew a shuriken from the hidden pocket in his sleeve, and used one of the weapon's metal points to poke a tiny hole in the paper panel near the shoji's wooden frame. Withdrawing the metal star, he carefully smoothed the edges of the hole away from the opening, creating a tiny but effective peephole.

"Now I can see him coming." Hiro slipped the shuriken back into his sleeve, stepped onto the veranda, and closed the door. He put his eye to the peephole. "Can you see me watching?"

"No. I can barely see the opening, even though I know it's there."

"Which the killer won't." Hiro opened the shoji again and pointed to the floor directly in front of it. "Let's put the table here. You can kneel facing it with your back to the door."

Hiro moved the low wooden table across the room while Father Mateo unpacked his Bible, a candleholder, and a thin leather package that held a handful of small, flat crackers.

"Are those *senbei*?" Hiro asked.

"Not quite communion bread," the priest admitted, "but, once consecrated, they suffice."

Hiro examined the crackers. "They look like regular *senbei*."

"As they are until the epiclesis, when by God's grace they change." The Jesuit smiled. "Though how, and exactly what happens, remains a mystery."

"It's all a mystery to me."

"If that is true, you understand Christianity far better than you think."

As the Jesuit spoke, the door to the hall slid open.

Hiro drew his sword.

CHAPTER 42

Kenshin entered the room, one hand concealed in his kimono. Shokai stood in the hall behind him, carrying a lantern.

"We mean no harm!" The physician withdrew his hand, revealing a small ceramic flask with a stopper in the top. A seal covered the stopper, protecting the bottle's contents against the air.

Kenshin extended the bottle, offering it to the Jesuit with both hands. "We brought your umeshu."

Father Mateo accepted it with a bow. "Thank you. And we apologize for startling you."

Hiro sheathed his sword, but said nothing.

Kenshin eyed the table near the veranda door. "I don't suppose . . . That is, does your ritual permit observers? I would like to see a Kirishitan rite."

Father Mateo's eyes grew sad. "Regrettably . . ."

"Please forgive my presumption." Kenshin raised his hands apologetically, though Hiro noted the flash of relief on Shokai's face. "I did not wish to interfere."

"I would like to show you. . . ." Father Mateo struggled, clearly torn between the plan and his desire to share his faith. "Perhaps another time?"

"I do not wish to inconvenience you," Kenshin said.

"Truly, I would like to show you." Father Mateo paused. "But this particular ritual—"

"I understand. You cannot be disturbed. We will not keep you any longer." Kenshin bowed and left the room, closing the door behind him.

"Give me that." Hiro extended a hand for the bottle.

Father Mateo clutched it. "Why? What's wrong?"

"It might be poisoned."

The Jesuit handed the bottle over quickly, as if it might grow teeth and bite. He rubbed his hands on his robe.

The bottle held minute traces of dust, though it looked as if someone, most likely Kenshin, had wiped it clean before bringing it to the room. Hiro carried the bottle to the brazier, where the light was best, and examined the seal more closely.

The seal across the stopper was unbroken, with no cracks or punctures. Hiro pressed his thumb against it, hard, but it left no impression.

He handed the bottle back to the Jesuit. "It's safe."

"How do you know?" Father Mateo accepted the wine, but held it gingerly.

"The seal has cured, which means it set at least two days ago—before the killings started. Given the dust on the bottle, it's likely far older than that. Either way, you can use it."

"Dust?" The Jesuit examined the bottle. "I don't see any."

"Someone cleaned it off, but traces remain in the corners of the seal."

Father Mateo set the umeshu and a single teacup on the table alongside his Bible and the *senbei*. With a sudden movement, as if remembering something he'd forgotten, the Jesuit pulled the candle from his pouch and set it in the holder. "Now I'm ready."

"Then begin." Hiro stepped over the table and onto the veranda. After sliding the shoji closed, he placed his eye to the peephole and watched the Jesuit approach the table.

"Open the hallway door enough for someone to see that you're alone," Hiro whispered. "If you hear anyone approaching, stop your prayers and face the door."

"Won't that dissuade the killer from approaching?" Father Mateo whispered.

"Not if he believes you are alone."

Father Mateo crossed the room and opened the sliding door. He peered through the opening as if expecting someone to burst through and attack.

He faced the shoji. "Is this wide enough?"

Hiro didn't answer.

The Jesuit considered the door for a moment longer before returning to the table. He knelt before it and lit the candle.

"How do you think he'll try to kill me?" Father Mateo whispered in Portuguese, head bowed as if in prayer. "What method will he choose to create Jizō?"

"No clue," Hiro whispered softly, "but I'm prepared for anything."

He dearly hoped the words were true.

Although he could not see the surface of the makeshift altar through the peephole, Hiro heard the Bible open and a crackling sound as Father Mateo broke the seal on the umeshu.

The Jesuit coughed. "Wow. That's strong."

"Did you drink it already?" Hiro whispered. He didn't consider umeshu all that strong, but the Jesuit drank no alcohol, aside from rituals like this one, so naturally Father Mateo's thoughts on the matter would be skewed.

"It smells like it could peel the lacquer off a tea tray. Japanese people like this?"

"I don't."

"I don't blame you."

Liquid gurgled faintly as Father Mateo poured a serving of umeshu into the teacup. The Jesuit bowed his head in prayer.

In the hall, a floorboard squeaked.

Father Mateo's head jerked up.

Hiro retrieved the shuriken from his sleeve. His heartbeat quickened. Slowing his breathing, he shifted the metal star to his left hand, leaving his right one empty to open the shoji and draw his wakizashi.

The door to the hallway opened further.

Soro stepped inside.

Father Mateo turned and rose. Panic flashed through Hiro's chest as the Jesuit's body blocked his view. Despite the urge to burst through the shoji and intercept Soro, Hiro forced himself to wait.

"What are you doing here?" Father Mateo asked.

"I needed to use the latrine."

Footsteps pattered on the tatami as Soro advanced into the room. Hiro twisted sideways, but to no avail. He could not see.

And could not risk it.

Hiro threw the shoji open, pushed the Jesuit aside, and leaped across the table. He felt the heat of the candle on the sole of his foot and hoped his robe would not catch fire. As he landed, he drew his sword and raised it high, prepared to strike. His left hand gripped the shuriken more tightly, points protruding between his fingers like tiny daggers.

"This is not the latrine."

A dagger appeared in Soro's hand. "Nor a *dōjō*, though it seems you wish to spar."

"You have one minute to explain why I should let you live," Hiro said. "And be persuasive. This time, you won't get a second chance."

Soro lowered his dagger but kept it ready. "I came to help you."

"Help us?" Father Mateo asked.

Soro kept his gaze on Hiro. "To capture the killer. Don't deny that's what you hope to do, assuming he's foolish enough to fall for an obvious trap like this."

"Never underestimate the power of a fool to act in character," Hiro said. "However, we don't need your help."

"I could hide back there, with you." Soro nodded to the shoji. "A pair of blades is better than just one."

"That will not be necessary."

Soro shifted his weight to a more neutral position, but did not sheathe the dagger.

"Leave us." Hiro nodded to the hall. "Before you force me to take an action you regret."

"You will not kill me." Soro raised the dagger.

Hiro did not wait for the attack. With a leap, he closed the distance and slashed his sword at the pilgrim's neck.

Soro spun away with the grace of a master. Hiro's blade passed harmlessly through empty air. Soro dropped and swung his dagger in

an arc toward Hiro's knees. When Hiro jumped away, the pilgrim followed, attacking with a silent speed that spoke of more than temple
training.

Hiro glanced at Father Mateo, who had pressed his back to the
wall and moved along it toward the door.

"Stay here!" Hiro swung the wakizashi wildly, hoping to make the
pilgrim back away. As Soro did, Hiro spun into a defensive position in
front of the Jesuit.

"I know what you are, shinobi," Hiro said. "Your style betrays you."

Soro gestured with his dagger. "The shuriken does the same for
you, my brother."

CHAPTER 43

Hiro scowled. "I have two brothers. One is dead, and you are not the other."

"I am not your enemy, either," Soro said. "We do not need to fight."

"Then drop your weapon, kneel, and surrender."

"If I do, will you assure my safety, and Ippen's also?" Soro asked.

"Ippen, yes." Hiro gestured with his wakizashi. "You, I make no promises. Who are you really?"

"Just a pilgrim, passing through."

"Wrong answer." Hiro feinted.

Soro dodged. "We seem to have reached an impasse."

"Not really." Hiro blocked the door, but kept himself in position to defend the Jesuit as well. "If you escape, I will go directly to the abbot's hall and kill the child."

"You wouldn't." Soro nodded to Father Mateo. "Your foreign master won't allow it."

"Are you willing to bet your daughter's life on the quality of my obedience?" Hiro raised an eyebrow.

"My niece," Soro corrected.

"If you say so." Hiro's voice revealed his disbelief. "In either case, she dies."

"You wouldn't dare."

Father Mateo cleared his throat. "Regrettably, I do believe he would."

Soro stared at the Jesuit for several seconds. "You win." He bowed his head. "I surrender."

He bent his knees as if to kneel, but launched himself forward, arms extended, dagger aiming straight for Hiro's stomach.

211

Hiro barely leaped aside in time. He swung his left fist downward, striking Soro's hand with the points of the shuriken. Soro grunted. The dagger fell to the floor, and Hiro kicked it into the corner. He backhanded Soro across the face, driving the other man to his knees.

Before the pilgrim could recover, Hiro pressed the point of his wakizashi against the side of Soro's neck, beneath his chin.

"Do you feel that?" Hiro hissed. "If you so much as sneeze, your life is over."

Soro clenched his jaw.

Father Mateo looked shocked, but to Hiro's relief the Jesuit held his tongue. He shifted his attention back to Soro. "Who sent you to Myo-in? Who did you come to kill?"

The pilgrim did not answer.

Hiro's fury rose. "If you don't tell me what I want to know, I will kill first you and then Ippen—but she will not die quickly. Trust me, she will tell me everything she knows before her heart stops beating."

Soro spoke through gritted teeth. "The girl knows nothing."

"We will see. Or you can save her life by telling me the truth."

He was faintly aware of Father Mateo's plea for mercy, but the Jesuit's voice seemed far away, muffled by the pounding of angry blood in Hiro's ears.

"I did not come as an assassin," Soro gasped. "I swear it."

"Liar!" Hatred burned in Hiro's chest, overwhelming every impulse but the desire to destroy. His throat felt tight. His fingers itched to drive the sword through Soro's neck, to feel the delicate flesh give way and watch his enemy's life bleed out in a crimson river on the floor.

But first, he would make the assassin talk—no matter what he had to do to force the truth through Soro's stubborn lips.

"We serve the same master," the pilgrim whispered. "I belong to the Iga ryu—as you do."

"Prove it," Hiro said, "with something more than empty words."

"I cannot." Soro paused. "Ringa was the only other Iga shinobi at Myo-in, and he can no longer vouch for my identity. Hattori Hanzō is not here to claim me—"

"You think those names will save you?" Hiro asked. "Everyone knows the leader of the Iga ryu."

"But Ringa," Father Mateo said.

"He could have learned that from the man—or woman—who sent him here."

"Woman?" Soro twisted his head a fraction, as if trying to see Hiro's face. "Do you mean Hatsuko? She's involved in this?"

"You tell me. You handed her your blade." He glanced at the dagger in the corner—a perfect match to the one the pilgrim gave Hatsuko earlier in the day.

Soro followed Hiro's gaze. "I carry two. As for Hatsuko, I met her a couple of days ago, on the journey up the mountain. She's a pilgrim, or she claimed to be."

"A popular story, apparently."

"I swear, on Ippen's life, I never met the woman before two days ago." Soro paused. "As a sign of good faith—you're right. Ippen is my daughter. Let me up so we can talk."

"If you attempt to rise, I'll kill you."

"Hiro!" Father Mateo switched to Portuguese. "He is your clansman."

"He's a liar." Hiro did not release his grip on the sword or switch to Portuguese. "I do not recognize his name or face."

"Ippen's mother—my wife—did not die of illness," Soro said. "We lived in one of Iga's smaller villages, in the mountains. She was there, with Ippen, when Oda's samurai attacked. She sent our daughter into the forest, but did not manage to escape herself. After the samurai burned the village, Ippen took refuge in a nearby temple. The priests disguised her as a boy. I found her there when I returned and learned what Oda's men had done."

"Why would Oda Nobunaga burn your village?" Hiro demanded, though he knew the answer.

"Because he hates the Iga ryu, and Koga also. He wants to destroy us, to ensure we cannot prevent him from becoming shogun."

"You denied your connection to Iga's shadows." Hiro's anger smoldered. "What makes you believe you can reclaim it now?"

"Would you have revealed yourself to me?"

"I did, when I asked the question."

"Fair enough," Soro said. "Although, in truth, there was no need. I know who you are, Hattori Hiro. You resemble Hanzō-*sama* far too closely to be anyone but his infamous cousin. I did not reveal myself before because it would have placed our lives, and Ippen's, at even greater risk."

A silent voice in Hiro's head broke through his rage, reminding him that only a man familiar with Hattori Hanzō's face would know how strongly the cousins resembled one another, and that Hanzō's enemies did not live long enough to tell the tale.

Even so, he was not ready to relent. "What changed your mind?"

"The killings. At this point, I fear we will only survive if we work together. That is why I armed Hatsuko, and why I'm risking Hanzō-*sama*'s wrath to reveal myself to you."

"Get up." Hiro withdrew his blade from Soro's neck, but kept the wakizashi poised to kill at a moment's notice. "Return to the meditation hall. You are not wanted here."

"But I can help you." Soro stood and smoothed the wrinkles from his robe.

"You attacked me," Hiro said.

"You attacked me first." Soro looked at his dagger. "I merely tried to defend myself. Now that we recognize one another, we can work together."

"I already have someone to help me." Hiro gestured to Father Mateo. "Additionally, the killer will not attack unless he thinks his victim is alone."

"He already knows you're not in the meditation hall either," Soro said.

"All the more reason for you to return."

Soro sighed. "I don't suppose you'll let me take my dagger."

"If you are who you claim to be, you have another weapon hidden somewhere." Hiro gestured to the door. "Go now, before I change my mind."

Soro started to leave but paused in the doorway. "If you don't return to the hall by dawn, I will come back to help."

"Do not bother," Hiro said. "If we're not back by morning, we are dead."

CHAPTER 44

After Soro disappeared down the darkened hall, Father Mateo said, "He could have helped us."

"Or killed us, if his story was a lie." Hiro retrieved Soro's dagger and stepped over the low wooden table. Once more he slid the shoji closed, concealing himself from view.

He hid the dagger in his sleeve, put his eye to the peephole, and saw Father Mateo approach the table.

The Jesuit's kimono rustled as he knelt. Paper fluttered softly as he turned his Bible to the proper page.

The room fell silent. Outside, the wind moaned past, rattling the wooden shutters at Hiro's back. Although they were well constructed, the blizzard pushed small puffs of air between the shutter seams, sending occasional frigid drafts down Hiro's back and across his feet. His tabi—and the toes beneath—were damp and cold from melted snow.

"*In nomine Patris, et Filii, et Spiritus Sancti. Gloria in excelsis Deo . . .*" Father Mateo intoned in fluid Latin.

Hiro could only imagine how long and hard the Jesuit must have studied to learn so many languages with fluency. He remembered the endless hours he spent learning Portuguese, and the years his brother, Kazu, slaved to perfect the various Japanese dialects and regional accents. Most Japanese people thought their native tongue the most difficult in the world, but Hiro suspected every language had its stumbling blocks.

"*Et erit in novissimis diebus . . .*" The Jesuit's voice continued to rise and fall in rhythmic prayer.

Hiro didn't understand a single word. As the minutes passed and no one else arrived, Hiro wondered if the killer might select a different victim for Jizō. He doubted it, but also had to admit his belief that Father Mateo was the next intended victim was a bit of an assumption. Based on facts, of course, but not absolute knowledge.

That said, he did feel certain the next victim would be posed as Jizō. Whether the killer was working for Oda Nobunaga or—as Father Mateo suspected—had only a madman's reasons for posing his victims as the jusanbutsu, it seemed clear the murders would not stop until thirteen corpses lay lined up in the hondō annex.

With Father Mateo's chanting, the howling wind, and occasional rumbles of thunder as background music, Hiro pondered, yet again, the suspects and the evidence against them.

He struck Soro off the list. The man was a liar, but all shinobi lied, and Hanzō would not send a spy to assassinate Ringa at the same time he sent Hiro with a message and assignment for the priest.

He distrusted Hatsuko, but no one sent a female spy to assassinate priests on a mountain that banned women. If she worked for Oda, or anyone else, she was a messenger at best.

Eliminating them as suspects meant the killer lived at Myo-in.

Hiro considered the possible motivations for the crime. Despite occasional statements to the contrary, he believed that understanding the killer's motivation helped. In this case, it might identify which victim or victims the killer truly wanted dead and which of them—if any—were decoys, meant to disguise the real crime.

Unfortunately, none of the usual motives for murder fit these killings. In Hiro's experience, people killed for one of three reasons: power, love, or money. Shingon priests forswore all three.

At least, they were supposed to.

Nichiyo clearly gained from Anan's death. If the other victims would have objected to the coward becoming abbot, their deaths made sense as well, though Hiro wasn't certain Nichiyo possessed the courage for such a dangerous gamble. Still, the drive for power motivated men to take surprising risks.

Regrettably, Doyu's death did not make sense in the context of Nichiyo's hopes to become the abbot of Myo-in. The ancient priest had barely comprehended Anan's death. He would not have objected to Nichiyo becoming abbot, and if he had, nobody would have listened.

Finally, Hiro doubted Nichiyo would go to the trouble of positioning corpses as the jusanbutsu. The acting abbot struck Hiro as selfish, but not particularly creative.

The problem was, the bodies' positions didn't make sense in any other context either. Clearly, they meant something to the killer. In fact, the poses were likely the key to the murderer's identity, but Hiro could not conceive of any reason a man would pose his victims as the deities who judged the dead. An unbeliever would not care, and a true practitioner of Shingon Buddhism would not wish to offend the kings of hell—

Hiro's blood ran cold as the killer's identity, and motive, fell into place.

A moment later, he gasped aloud.

The killer did not need to sneak away from the hall to kill Father Mateo.

He had already done the fatal deed.

"*Stop!*" Hiro threw himself forward through the shoji.

Paper panels ripped as Hiro crashed through the lattice. The wooden frame splintered, impaling his arm and scratching his face. His shin barked painfully against the table, knocking both the candle and the Bible to the floor. The flask tipped over and rolled away.

Father Mateo cried out in alarm. The teacup flew from his hand and spilled a rooster tail of umeshu across the tatami.

Hiro landed on the Jesuit, knocking him flat. His elbow sank into the Jesuit's stomach.

Father Mateo grunted in pain.

Hiro rolled to the side and regained his feet.

The Jesuit lay on the floor, eyes wide. "You're on fire!"

Small flames licked at the hem of Hiro's gray kimono.

Father Mateo laid hold of the cushion underneath him, pulled it free, and beat at the flames on Hiro's robe.

The fire went out in moments, though the scent of ruined silk remained.

The candle lay on the floor nearby. A coil of smoke rose from the wick, though fortunately the fire had gone out after igniting Hiro's clothes.

Father Mateo smacked the candle with the pillow.

"You can stop," Hiro said. "The fire's gone."

"Are you injured?"

"No." Hiro pointed to the teacup, lying empty on the floor. The bottle of umeshu rested on its side nearby. Wine dribbled from its mouth into a puddle that also held the fragments of crushed-up leaves. "Did you drink it?"

Father Mateo's forehead wrinkled at the fear in Hiro's voice. "The umeshu?"

"*Did you drink it?*"

"Not yet, no. I hadn't reached that point in the— What's wrong?"

Hiro collapsed to a kneeling position. He exhaled shakily, hands on his thighs and head tipped forward. Slowly, he drew a breath and raised his head.

"The umeshu is poisoned."

CHAPTER 45

"Poisoned?" Father Mateo stared at the bottle. "But you said . . ."

"I erred." The words came out with surprising ease, given Hiro's hatred for mistakes. He leaned over and examined the fragments of slender leaves that had spilled from the bottle along with the umeshu. "These leaves are yew."

"But yew is poisonous." Father Mateo grasped the cross that hung around his neck.

"Precisely." Hiro stood up, his strength renewed by the realization that the Jesuit had not drunk the poison. "Its presence confirms the killer's identity."

"How?" The Jesuit followed Hiro to the door. "And when did you figure out—"

"No time. I'll tell you at the meditation hall."

Myokan peered cautiously into the entry as Hiro and Father Mateo returned to the meditation hall. His mouth fell open. "You came back."

"You expected otherwise?" Hiro set his temple sandals on the rack.

"N-no. Of course not." Myokan backed away to clear the door as Hiro and the Jesuit entered the meditation room.

Despite the hour, the braziers in the hall burned brightly, filling the room with light. The priests remained in separate corners: Soro to the right of the entry, Nichiyo in the corner to the left. On the far end of the hall, Gensho lay on the tatami with his arm beneath his head. His snores rang through the room. A short distance away, Kenshin and Shokai knelt together in front of the Buddha statues.

Hiro's gaze lingered on the Buddhas. While standing on the guest room veranda, he had also finally understood what the images triggered in his mind. He wished he had remembered sooner—the realization might have saved some trouble.

Soro took a step forward. "No one has left the room since I returned. Has something happened? Ippen . . . ?"

"Nothing has happened to the child," Hiro said. "We returned because we know who murdered Ringa-*san* and the other priests."

"You caught the killer?" Nichiyo's shrill question pierced the air.

"Not yet, but we know his name." Hiro gestured to the sleeping priest. "Wake Gensho-*san*."

"He's responsible?" Nichiyo asked with disgust. "Myokan, bind him so he can't escape."

The guardian glanced at his broken arm, but started across the room. Hiro wondered how the slender, injured priest intended to subdue the burly Gensho.

As Myokan approached, the muscular cook woke up. He jumped to his feet and backed away from the guardian. "What's going on?"

"How could you?" Myokan demanded.

"Do not harm him," Father Mateo said. "Let us explain."

"What's going on here?" Gensho repeated.

"I knew he did it," Nichiyo said. "His jealousy turned to hatred, once he realized he would never advance beyond his current, lowly station."

"As it happens," Hiro said. "This killer did not act from jealous motives. In fact, he seems to think his actions selfless."

"Impossible!" Myokan declared. "Murder is not a selfless act."

"It is for a person who believes the dead are freed from the burdens of worldly sorrow, and who plans to surrender his own life as soon as he completes his grisly task." Hiro turned to Kenshin. "You suggested the dead can escape both judgment and rebirth, if their souls are worthy?"

"Not just can, they do. They join the Buddha nature in what he"—Kenshin gestured to Father Mateo—"refers to as heaven."

"I don't understand." Gensho moved toward Hiro, giving Myokan a wide and careful berth. "You think the killer wanted to help his victims escape the suffering of the world? But why?"

"No Shingon priest would take a life deliberately." Myokan pointed at Soro. "But perhaps that one is not a priest."

"Watch your words," the pilgrim said. "I have not murdered anyone."

Not here, at least, Hiro thought. "I, too, struggled to understand the killer's motive, until I realized what he stood to gain."

"No one gains from the deaths of the innocent," Myokan declared.

"He did." Gensho pointed at Nichiyo. "He used their deaths to seize the abbot's place."

"How dare you!" Nichiyo took a threatening step toward the larger man. "I think you murdered them yourself, hoping whoever became the abbot would let you advance, despite your previous failures."

"I no longer care about advancement in this world," Gensho said. "As you would know, if you cared for us as Anan-*sama* did."

"Enough squabbling!" Soro interrupted. "Let Matsui-*san* explain."

In the silence that followed, all eyes turned to Hiro.

"Men customarily kill for one of three reasons: power, love, or money," Hiro said. "At first I thought, as you do, that the killer wanted power. However, as the killings continued, I could not reconcile that motive with the chosen victims or the way he posed their bodies."

"Surely he did not kill for money," Nichiyo said. "Myo-in has no significant worldly treasures."

Hiro nodded. "Leaving only love."

"But women are forbidden," Shokai protested. "How—"

"There are other forms of love," Hiro said, "and love—or, more specifically, the grief that follows the loss of love—can drive a man insane. He will believe, and do, all kinds of things a normal man would not."

He turned to Kenshin. "Like murdering priests to atone for a dead man's sins."

"What?" Father Mateo blinked. "*Kenshin* killed them?"

Gensho's mouth fell open.

"He would not do that." Shokai shook his head.

"He would, and did, to help his childhood friend, the former shogun, Ashikaga Yoshiteru," Hiro said.

A flicker of concern crossed Kenshin's face as he stared at the Jesuit. "You did not drink the umeshu?" He shifted his gaze to Hiro. "If you stopped him, you will ruin everything!"

"I do not understand," Nichiyo said. "What is happening?"

Hiro laid a hand on the hilt of his katana. "You're going to need a new physician."

"Kenshin-*sama* is not the killer," Shokai declared. "He would not do this. Tell them!" He shot Kenshin a pleading look, but the physician didn't seem to notice.

"He lost his mind, from grief, when the shogun died," Hiro explained.

"I am not a madman!" Sparks of anger flared in Kenshin's eyes. "You do not understand. This is the only way to save the shogun!"

CHAPTER 46

"We have no shogun," Nichiyo said. "Ashikaga Yoshiteru died last summer, and the emperor has not yet appointed anyone to take his place."

"My father brought me to Myo-in to pray for Yoshiteru." Kenshin's eyes unfocused, as if looking backward into memory. "For many years, I allowed my selfishness and anger to keep me from that duty. I did not pray as I should have, but instead beseeched the Buddha to help me leave this temple and return to Kyoto as a warrior.

"Anan-*sama* warned me of Kōbō Daishi's saying that a man who holds a sword will always feel the urge to kill. He said, unless I put such thoughts behind me, I would never reach enlightenment. But I was foolish. I resented the loss of the life I thought I wanted—the life I wrongfully believed that I deserved. Also, I missed my friend so much.

"Eventually, I accepted my life and my purpose. I embraced my duty and prayed for my friend's success. But still, he died. I did not pray enough. I did not save him. This was my fault, and now I must correct it—I must save his soul from hell."

"How could the shogun's death be your fault?" Gensho asked. "You haven't left Mount Kōya in decades."

"Nonetheless, it is my fault." Kenshin's eyes refocused. "Even after I embraced my duty to pray for the shogun's safety, I hid evil in my heart. I resented that Yoshiteru never called me back to Kyoto. I was angry that he left me here, to live and die in a tiny mountain temple. I was jealous and hurt. He forgot me. He rejected me. He turned his back on our oath of brotherhood.

"But when the news of his death reached Kōya, I was terrified. I knew the kings of hell would judge him harshly, because I failed him in my prayers. They would condemn his soul. He would suffer forever, all because of me."

"The fate of the shogun's soul does not depend on you," Father Mateo said.

Kenshin continued as if he had not heard the Jesuit. "I prayed, day and night, for the shogun's soul. I begged the jusanbutsu to release his spirit from further suffering. Every morning and every night, I hoped and waited for a sign that the Buddhas heard my prayers, and yet I knew, deep in my heart, that I had failed. My soul held too much suffering. I could not move the kings of hell."

Father Mateo began to speak, but Hiro silenced the Jesuit with a look.

"Because my soul was marred," Kenshin declared, "I sought the help of others—priests so similar to the jusanbutsu that the deities would have to listen to their pleas. I asked these men to help me pray for the shogun's soul."

"And then you killed them?" Shokai frowned. "You asked me to help you pray. Did you intend to kill me also?"

Kenshin did not pause. "The more we prayed, the more I realized that prayers alone were not enough. I grew desperate. I prayed for guidance, for a sign." He extended his hands to Father Mateo. "Then you arrived, in answer to my prayers. You showed me what to do."

"Me?" the Jesuit stepped backward.

"Buddha sent you," Kenshin said. "To show me that the prayers of the living were not powerful enough to save the dead—I must do more. You explained how your Jesus, an innocent man, had to die to save his people. Now, he stands beside the throne of your foreign god and intervenes on behalf of the dead, to ensure your god shows mercy. When I heard you speak, I realized . . . I needed to send emissaries to the jusanbutsu, priests who could serve as intermediaries for the shogun, like your Jesus does for dead Kirishitans."

Father Mateo clutched his cross. "That isn't how it works at all."

"It is! You told me so! And, like your Jesus, I made sure my emissaries' deaths were undeserved, so they would bear no fault. I posed them, so the kings of hell would recognize which man I sent to each. I sent them in order, starting with Ringa, who so resembled Fudō Myō-ō that it became his nickname. That very night, I set the stakes in the yard, and hid in the darkness waiting for him to check the gates before he slept. I stuck a dagger in his back, between his ribs, until he fell." Kenshin's expression darkened as he looked at Father Mateo. "But you broke the cycle when you did not drink the umeshu."

Shokai rounded on Kenshin. "What do you mean? The umeshu was sealed."

"I added crushed yew leaves the night he arrived, and then resealed it. I did it right after I talked with the foreign priest and realized what I had to do. It needed time to steep, so the yew could infiltrate the alcohol. He told me that his ritual required wine, and I suspected whoever had become the abbot by that time would offer to let him use our umeshu."

"You planned this out in such detail that quickly?" Shokai sounded horrified.

"I had to act quickly," Kenshin said, "before the storm passed over and the visitors escaped."

"I am curious," Hiro said. "Who had you asked to pray to Jizō before we came to Myo-in?"

"No one." Kenshin spoke as though this should have been obvious. "Jizō did not need persuading. He does not condemn the dead. He speaks on their behalf."

"Then why attempt to kill the foreign priest?"

"Once he showed me what I had to do, that part was obvious." Kenshin gestured to Father Mateo. "He calls himself *Jizō-ito*—and his faith requires him to pray for other people's souls."

"I am a *Jesuit*," Father Mateo corrected, "and I pray to the creator god, the Lord Almighty, not to Buddha."

"You agreed to pray for the shogun," Kenshin said. "You promised, on the night you came."

"Yes, but . . ." Father Mateo trailed off as if unwilling to argue and uncertain his words would make a difference anyway.

"You promised!" Kenshin's voice cracked. "Don't you understand? We have to save the shogun! We must die and intercede." He pointed at Father Mateo. "You showed me what must be done!"

"I did not!" Father Mateo ran both hands through his hair, which stood up in unruly clumps. "You misinterpreted everything I told you. God abhors human sacrifice, and murder is forbidden."

"In our doctrine also," Nichiyo put in.

"The shogun's soul will never rest unless we can persuade the jusan-butsu to spare his spirit," Kenshin said. "The foreigners' god will listen to intercessors. The Buddhas will listen also, and show mercy."

"You killed Anan-*sama*. . . ." Gensho shook his head in disbelief, as if just realizing what had happened.

"He died willingly," Kenshin said. "He saw me coming, and he did not fight."

"How did it happen?" Hiro asked.

"I waited around the corner while Shokai delivered his morning tray," Kenshin explained. "When I entered the room, he asked why I had come. I put my hands around his neck, but gently, and told him what he had to do. After that, I pushed him to the floor and covered his mouth with a cushion until he died."

"He did not struggle or cry out?" Nichiyo asked.

"He struggled a little, but then he went limp, as if he agreed." Kenshin held his hands in front of him, palms up. He stared at them as he spoke. "He died so easily. He did not suffer."

Hiro doubted the physician understood the mechanics of suffocation. No one who did would call it an easy death.

"Killing him was easier than I expected. His life went out so quickly that he must have given it willingly. He agreed about what must be done."

"Anan-*sama* was old, and weak." Gensho's hands balled into fists. "He did not have the strength to fight!"

"What about Jorin?" Hiro asked. "Did he agree to die as well?"

Kenshin lowered his hands. He blinked as if confused. "He came to the annex to pray for the dead at precisely the moment he needed to. I knew he would. That's why I brought the cat to the hondō. Buddha sent Jorin there to die, just like your foreign god sent Jesus to the city where they killed him."

"No, that's not what happened." Horror twisted Father Mateo's features. "Christ was god, as well as man. His death was a completely different kind of sacrifice. . . . He chose to die."

"You told me people nailed him to a cross," Kenshin said evenly. "That does not sound like suicide—and gods cannot die like men do."

"Jesus was unique, both god and man." The Jesuit struggled to explain. "His death was selfless . . . but at any moment, he could have stopped it, if he changed his mind."

"Your victims did not have that choice," Hiro put in.

"That's not the point!" Father Mateo rounded on Kenshin. "You defile the sacrifice of God with your comparisons. What you have done is murder—wicked, despicable murder—and nothing more."

CHAPTER 47

Hiro stared, mouth open, momentarily at a loss for words.

Father Mateo ran both hands through his hair again. His curls stood up like a halo of tiny dark brown flames. He turned to Hiro, eyes so full of pain and anger that, for a moment, the Jesuit looked exactly like Fudō Myō-ō.

Father Mateo clasped his hands and raised his face to the ceiling as tears filled his eyes. His lips moved in a silent, desperate prayer: "*Lord, forgive me. I have failed.*"

"When did you murder Jorin?" Shokai asked. "You weren't alone. We were together the entire morning. . . ."

Kenshin nodded at the recognition on the young priest's face. "Except for the time you spent in the goma hall, writing the prayers for Ringa-*san* and Anan-*sama*. I sent you there, remember?"

"What would you have done if I returned too quickly?"

Kenshin shrugged. "It does not matter. You did not return. The Buddha shielded you from harm, as I knew he would."

Hiro let that pass, for the moment. "Did you murder Doyu?"

"No," Kenshin admitted. "Fugen intervened and took Doyu-*sama*, to save Bussho."

"You would have killed a child?" Father Mateo sounded as if he could scarcely believe it.

"After Yoshiteru's death, Bussho alone came forward and volunteered to help me pray for his spirit," Kenshin said. "Every day since then, he recites the sutras for many hours without rest. No one in the temple was a closer match for Fugen, but when Doyu-*sama* died at precisely the moment the next sacrifice was due, I knew that Fugen must have taken Doyu-*sama*'s life to spare Bussho."

"Bodhisattvas do not murder people!" Nichiyo declared.

Hiro ignored the outburst. "And after Doyu-*sama*, you planned to kill the foreign priest."

"For Jizō." Kenshin nodded. "I had poisoned the wine, and replaced the seal, the night you arrived at Myo-in."

"How did you know he would conduct the communion ritual?" Hiro asked. "What if he did not need the wine?"

"I knew he would. He told me about the wine and the ritual the night we talked. He explained he did this every week, on his holy day—which is today. I merely had to wait."

"But you objected to giving him the umeshu," Nichiyo protested. "You said—"

The hint of a smile appeared on Kenshin's face. "If I seemed too eager, he might have suspected something. They were trying to stop the murders. I could not risk"—his smile disappeared—"but you ruined it! You did not drink the umeshu, and now I have no one to send Jizō."

"I don't even believe in Jizō!" Father Mateo exclaimed. "Whatever made you think I would speak to a Buddha on your behalf?"

"On the shogun's behalf," Kenshin corrected. "Jizō hears you, whether or not you believe in him. He exists to save souls in need of rescue. You came to Japan to save the souls of Japanese people—you told me so. Jizō will always listen to a man who shares his purpose so completely."

"Jizō does not exist!" Father Mateo struggled to regain control. When he spoke, his voice was calm. "There is only one God, the Lord Almighty, who made the heavens, the earth, and everything in them."

"And he can help you ask Jizō to save the shogun's soul," Kenshin replied.

"It does not work that way!" Father Mateo threw his hands into the air.

"Do not bother," Hiro said in Portuguese. "You can't convince a man who is not sane."

"What do we do with him?" Soro nodded toward Kenshin, who had finally gone silent.

"He must answer for his crimes." Nichiyo glanced at Hiro as if for confirmation.

"But how?" Soro asked. "What punishment will you impose?"

Kenshin straightened. "I will take my own life to atone for my actions. I never planned to survive this anyway. After the foreigner, and Shokai, went to see the jusanbutsu, I planned to poison the rest of you at dawn, and to consume the last of it myself, to petition Yakushi-*sama*."

"You planned to kill me." Shokai exhaled heavily. "I trusted you!"

"As I trust you with the enormous task of petitioning Miroku-*sama*, Buddha of the future," Kenshin said. "My beloved student. You are the future of Myo-in. . . ."

"Not if you kill me." Shokai clenched his fist.

"I have failed Lord Ashikaga," Kenshin said. "He was my friend, my brother. But my selfishness has cost him dearly. Now, we all must make amends." He grasped his side and grunted.

Father Mateo took a step forward. "Is something wrong? Did you take the poison already?"

"I have earned my fate." The physician winced.

"What's happening?" Nichiyo asked. "Is he going to die?"

"One way or another," Hiro said.

Father Mateo took another step toward the physician. "Let us help you."

"Help him?" Shokai drew back. "He deserves to die."

"But not to suffer," Father Mateo said. "Not even he deserves that fate." He spoke to Kenshin. "It's too late for the men you killed, but not for you. Let me tell you the real truth about God. I cannot save your life, but maybe, if you listen well, your soul can still be saved."

"Have you lost your sanity as well?" Hiro demanded in Portuguese. "He is a killer. He deserves his fate."

"No man deserves to burn in hell," the Jesuit replied in kind.

Hiro began to disagree, but Kenshin spoke. "What of Shogun Ashikaga? Can your god save him as well?"

Father Mateo grasped his cross again, as if for strength. "I am sorry. Once a man is dead, it is too late."

Kenshin gripped his side again. "Then I will go to see the jusan-butsu, as I planned."

Nichiyo took a tentative step forward. "Kenshin-*san*, you must not spend your last few minutes speaking bitterness. Sit down and meditate while you still can."

"Meditate?" Shokai repeated. "Surely you don't intend to let him die in here."

"He will defile the hall," Myokan agreed.

"Then we will cleanse it." Nichiyo straightened and faced the other priests. "A man does not earn merit by withholding mercy or refusing aid to a dying man who repents of his wrongdoings."

Hiro stared at the abbot, shocked by the sudden transformation. For the first time, Nichiyo was acting like a leader, rather than a craven weakling.

"He has not repented." Myokan scowled. "He only regrets that he failed to kill us all."

"He made innocent people suffer," Shokai added. "He deserves to suffer too."

Hiro felt the tension rise. Despite Shingon's pursuit of peace, the priests seemed on the verge of violence.

"Wait." Nichiyo raised his hands. "Please listen. Kōbō Daishi taught that even people who do wicked things are not purely, or even mostly, evil. 'Men who perform evil acts will aspire to follow a moral path when they feel a sense of community.'"

"How can you quote Kōbō Daishi in his defense?" Shokai demanded. "He took advantage of our community to commit his evil acts. He deserves to be cast out into the snow."

"Enlightened men do not seek vengeance," Nichiyo insisted. "If we cause his death, we will bear the shame for the rest of our lives. Show mercy. Let him die in peace."

Kenshin tucked his hand into his robe, as if from stomach pains, but metal glinted underneath the cloth.

"Get back!" Hiro pushed Father Mateo away, but not before Kenshin's hand lashed out, revealing the dagger he concealed underneath his robe.

The Jesuit staggered backward, tripped, and fell.

Cloth ripped. Shokai cried out in pain.

Instead of attacking the Jesuit, Kenshin had lunged for his student, slashing Shokai's robe and side.

Foregoing his sword, Hiro punched the physician in the face. Kenshin's nose shattered with a crunch that Hiro felt as much as heard. As he withdrew his fist, he slammed the other one down on Kenshin's wrist, knocking the blade from the physician's hand. The dagger bounced off the floor and rolled away.

Kenshin collapsed with a startled cry. He raised his hands to cover his ruined nose.

Blood ran through his fingers, vivid red, and traced a pair of rivers down his arms. It dripped from his elbows and streaked his robe. Droplets spattered the tatami floor.

"How badly are you hurt?" Hiro spoke to Shokai, but kept his gaze on Kenshin. Injured men were as dangerous as wounded bears.

"I will recover," Shokai said.

Kenshin lowered his bloody hands.

Hiro pointed to the physician. "He's not poisoned. He hoped you would relax your guard so he could try to finish what he started."

Without warning, Kenshin launched himself at Hiro, bloody hands extended. He said something, but the words were lost in a spray of blood.

In a single, fluid motion, Hiro drew his wakizashi and slit the physician's neck from ear to ear.

CHAPTER 48

Hot blood geysered from Kenshin's neck. It sprayed Hiro's face and spattered across his robe. He inhaled its ferrous scent. The odor reminded him of Neko's death and stoked his rage.

Hiro grabbed the chest of the physician's robe and pulled him close, thrusting the wakizashi into Kenshin's stomach and then twisting the blade as he forced it upward. The physician's eyes went wide with shock. His breath escaped in a gasp that became a gurgle as the wakizashi punctured first his lung and then his heart.

The light flowed out of Kenshin's eyes. As the spirit departed, Hiro pushed the body away and withdrew his sword. The corpse collapsed, this time in a lifeless heap from which Kenshin would never rise.

Blood ran from the wounds and pooled beneath him on the floor.

Hiro turned to Nichiyo.

The abbot's hands flew up. He backed away, tripping over his heels and nearly falling in his haste.

Gensho approached and offered Hiro a scrap of cloth. "To clean your sword."

He accepted the offering and began to wipe the blood from the wakizashi. He took his time, cleaning the hilt and guard as well as the blade.

As he finished cleaning the sword, Hiro realized the room was silent, and had been so since Kenshin's death.

Slowly, he surveyed the hall.

Father Mateo stood beside him, head cast down and face a mask of grief. His eyes were closed. His lips moved, though no sound emerged.

Myokan had backed away to stand beside the abbot. Both men stared at Kenshin's corpse, though Myokan's stony gaze revealed far less than Nichiyo's teary eyes and quivering lips. Gensho crossed his arms and frowned at the body. Soro stood beside him, holding Kenshin's blade.

Only Shokai had moved away. He knelt in the corner, bandaging his side.

The wakizashi would require additional cleaning, but Hiro had done as much as he could for the moment. He slipped the blade into its sheath and allowed Gensho to take the bloody cloth.

"May I ask . . . ?" Nichiyo spoke haltingly. "Could you . . . ? That is . . . how did you figure out that Kenshin-*san* was responsible?"

Father Mateo opened his eyes and raised his head to hear the answer.

Hiro thought before he spoke, sorting the parts of the story he could tell from the ones his oaths to Iga required him to conceal. "When Ringa died, we did not know more deaths would follow. Anan-*sama* thought the killer targeted the guardian in order to threaten Myo-in. At the time, that theory seemed plausible."

"In fact, Anan-*sama*'s death appeared to confirm it," Father Mateo added.

"Making you the primary suspect." Hiro gestured to Nichiyo.

The abbot paled. "I would never . . ."

"Jorin's death fit that pattern also," Hiro continued, "since a man who wished to become the abbot would also wish to eliminate those who might oppose him."

"I am not a killer!" Nichiyo's cheeks flushed red. "I have learned . . ." He trailed off as if still unwilling to admit his past to the other priests.

"However," Hiro said, "Jorin's murder also revealed the larger pattern—"

"That the murderer was selecting victims who mirrored the jusan-butsu," Father Mateo finished.

Hiro nodded. "Which, in turn, suggested this was more than a power struggle over temple leadership."

"Because, if he killed all thirteen victims, no one would be left alive," Myokan said.

"Precisely." Hiro paused. From here, he had to choose his words with care, and construct a lie the priests would accept in place of his original belief that Oda Nobunaga had tried to destroy the temple to eliminate shinobi agents. As usual, he opted for a lie that held a grain of truth. "At that point, I suspected the killer wanted to destroy the temple."

"Why would anyone want to destroy our temple?" Nichiyo sounded hurt.

"The shogun's death has left the samurai clans in conflict," Hiro said. "At least three daimyō claim the shogunate. The clans are on the brink of war. With so much tension in the land, someone might believe that Kōya's temples have the power to influence the emperor's decision."

"As samurai, you might believe that," Nichiyo replied, "but Myo-in is small. We have no influence outside Mount Kōya."

"Even so," Hiro said, "I thought the deaths might have been caused by a samurai hoping to purge the temple of priests who supported his enemies."

"I would have suspected spies," Myokan put in. "Once, in Kyoto, I heard that shinobi dress as priests and hide in temples to avoid detection."

Nichiyo made a dismissive noise. "That's samurai nonsense. We have no shinobi at Myo-in."

"None of our priests, anyway." Shokai glanced at Soro.

"I suspected the pilgrim also," Hiro said. "But he, too, seemed unlikely."

"He could not have matched the dead to the jusanbutsu," Myokan agreed. "He does not know us well enough."

"What made you realize that it was Kenshin-*san*?" Gensho asked. "Of all of us, he seemed the most unlikely."

"Many times, the most unlikely suspect is the guilty one, but as it happens"—Hiro gestured to the Buddha triptych at the far end of the hall—"they, and his love for the shogun, revealed the truth."

"The Buddhas spoke to you?" Gensho sounded dubious.

"No, but the killer posed his victims as the jusanbutsu, indicating a deep attachment to them. In fact, when Doyu-*sama* died, Kenshin-*san* and Shokai laid him with the other victims—not beside Jorin, as most people would have done, but between Ringa and Anan."

"Kenshin-*san* put him there," Shokai confirmed. "To show respect, because Doyu-*sama* had been the abbot."

"That may be what he told you," Hiro said, "but that positioning created a Shaka Triad"—he gestured to the Buddhas again—"Anan as the historical Buddha, flanked by Jorin as Monju on one side and by Doyu, as Fugen, on the other."

"That is the way those deities are normally displayed," Nichiyo acknowledged, "but how did that reveal Kenshin-*san*'s guilt?"

"It didn't, at the time. In fact, I didn't even recognize the significance of that positioning until I realized Kenshin was the killer. The arrangement meant that Kenshin was thinking of the victims in terms of the Buddhas their corpses represented, rather than the men they were in life." Hiro shook his head. "Had I recognized it earlier, I would have known that either Kenshin or Shokai must be the killer."

"However," Father Mateo said, "by the time of Doyu-*sama*'s death, we knew—or at least suspected—that the killer planned to use me as Jizō." The Jesuit's voice was soft, but Hiro felt relieved that Father Mateo had recovered enough to join the conversation. "So we set a trap."

CHAPTER 49

"I still don't understand what made you realize the umeshu was poisoned," Shokai said. "The seal was intact."

"We didn't know," Father Mateo admitted. "At least, I didn't know. I almost drank it."

"The seal fooled me too, at first," Hiro said, "but I realized, just in time, that we were not the only ones to set a trap."

"What, exactly, did you realize?" Nichiyo asked. "What told you it was Kenshin-*san*?"

"His prayers." Hiro nodded to Father Mateo, who seemed startled by the answer. "It occurred to me that no genuine priest would deliberately insult his gods, and since every suspect who remained was a real priest, that meant the killer somehow thought his actions would be pleasing to the Buddhas."

"Murder pleases no one," Nichiyo declared, "except the murderer."

"Precisely," Hiro said, "and yet, the killer somehow thought the Buddhas would accept what he had done. Only one man among you had a cause that fit, and then, only if he was suffering a serious delusion."

"But still . . . why Kenshin-*san*? He cared so much for everyone."

"Including the shogun," Hiro agreed, "and that is what gave him away. I told you before, men kill for three reasons. Once I eliminated power and money, only love remained. And when I tried to connect dead bodies posed as Buddhas with any kind of love—"

"You realized Kenshin-*san* was trying to save the shogun," Father Mateo finished. "I have to admit, I don't believe I would have seen the connection on my own."

"I wouldn't have." Shokai bowed to Hiro, holding the position for several seconds to convey his deep sincerity. "I apologize for doubting you, and thank you for saving my life."

Hiro glanced at Father Mateo and suppressed a shudder. He had come too close to failing his friend. The memory of Neko's lifeless body sprang to mind, but in his thoughts her face transformed, and it was not her corpse, but that of the Jesuit, he saw.

His throat closed off as panic choked him like a rope around his neck.

Years of training kept his face a mask, but on the inside, Hiro struggled for control.

His own words echoed in his head: *The grief that follows the loss of love can drive a man insane. He will believe, and do, all kinds of things a normal man would not.*

In that instant, he realized Neko's death had almost cost him Father Mateo's life as well. Grief had made him ignore the facts and see Oda's men in every shadow. Father Mateo had tried to warn him—more than once—but the loss of Neko had made him blind.

He still loved her, and missed her, and would mourn her, but Hiro could not hold his grief so closely any longer. Regardless of the role he played in her death, he could not change the past. His sorrow and rage would not bring her back, and the single-minded pursuit of vengeance would only cause more death and suffering.

This revelation did not diminish Hiro's desire to avenge her, or his decision to do so if and when the opportunity arose. That said, the living had to live for something other than the dead, and Hiro was still very much alive.

Suddenly, he realized everyone was staring at him, and that Father Mateo wore an expression of unusual concern.

"Did I miss something?"

The Jesuit gestured to Nichiyo. "The abbot asked if we would inform the women that the killer has been stopped."

"Of course." Hiro turned to Soro. "Would you like to come with us?"

The pilgrim nodded. "With the danger past, Ippen should stay with me."

"A priest?" Hatsuko repeated when Hiro and Father Mateo finished explaining what had happened, omitting the gorier details due to the presence of Ippen and Bussho. "It was not an assassin after all?"

Father Mateo shook his head. "Merely a man consumed by grief."

"Then I don't need this anymore." Hatsuko drew the dagger from her obi and returned it to Soro with a bow. "Thank you for entrusting it to me."

He accepted it with a bow of his own. "Thank you for watching over my son."

Hatsuko held Soro's gaze just long enough to make Hiro suspect she knew the truth about the child's gender. "Gladly."

"Thank you also." Soro bowed to Hiro and then to Father Mateo. "I will pray for the success of your pilgrimage."

"I will pray for you as well." The Jesuit returned the bow.

Hiro let Father Mateo's words speak for them both, but bowed as Soro and Ippen left the abbot's home.

"Pardon me," Bussho said as the door slid shut behind the pilgrims. "When Doyu-*sama* died, was he in pain?"

Father Mateo gave Hiro a warning look, but the shinobi did not have to lie. "He had no pain. He simply fell asleep and did not wake."

The child looked unconvinced. "But he told me he was hurting."

"Do you hurt when you are sleeping?" Hiro asked.

"No." Big tears welled up in Bussho's eyes. "I miss him, but it makes me glad to know he was not hurting when he died. I will pray for his spirit faithfully, night and day."

Hiro knelt to face the boy. "Remember him, but not to the exclusion of the living. Breathing people make better companions than the dead."

Bussho nodded. "'The fallen blossom returns not to the bough, but others grow to take its place.' I will remember." He bowed. "Please excuse me. I must check with Abbot Nichiyo, and ask what chores and studies he would like me to perform today."

As the door shut behind him, Father Mateo murmured in Portuguese, "Anan-*sama* was right—he's not a normal child."

"Before you go," Hatsuko said. "You thought I was involved in the murders, didn't you? Because samurai women are devious?"

Despite its accusatory nature, the question did not sound entirely hostile.

Hiro gambled on a bold and honest answer. "Why do you wish to start an argument no man can win?"

"What do you mean?" she asked.

"Precisely what I said. If I admit that I considered you a suspect, you'll resent me for misjudging you. If I did not suspect you, you'll resent me for misjudging not just you, but every woman. Thus, you start an argument no man can win. I ask you . . . why?"

She watched him, expression unreadable.

Awkward silence filled the room.

Then, unexpectedly, Hatsuko laughed.

Father Mateo joined in politely, but Hiro waited for her answer.

"No samurai in Ōmi would have dared to call that question out," she said at last. "I withdraw my former statement. You are not a common samurai."

"While I appreciate the compliment, you have not answered my question."

The smile that followed began in her eyes and illuminated her entire face. "The fact that you suspected me reveals that you respect me as samurai—as your equal. Many men would not. I merely asked the question to find out what you would say."

"And now you know." To Hiro's surprise, he was not entirely repulsed by the flirtation in her tone. This was neither the time nor the place to indulge such interests—a fact she clearly knew as well as he did. Even so, it startled him to realize the heart that Neko's loss had wounded still held the capacity to heal.

Hatsuko bowed. "I hope we will meet again one day, in more appropriate circumstances. If you find yourself in Ōmi, please call on the Endō. My clan, and I, will welcome you as friends."

At least, until you learn the truth about us. Hiro bowed. "We appreciate your generous invitation."

"Remember it," she said, "because I do not make it idly."

"Where will you go when the storm is over?" Father Mateo asked.

"To continue my pilgrimage." Hatsuko bent and picked up Gato, who was twining around her ankles. The cat settled into her arms with a happy purr. "I leave for Shikoku as soon as the weather clears."

"This is a difficult time of year to undertake that pilgrimage," Hiro said.

She shrugged. "Nothing worth doing in life is simple."

Hiro nodded. "True, indeed."

CHAPTER 50

That night as he prepared for sleep in the room he shared with the Jesuit, Hiro realized the wind had died. An eerie silence filled the room. He stared at the ceiling and listened to the stillness.

Father Mateo noticed. "Is something wrong?"

"I think the storm has passed."

Before the Jesuit could reply, someone knocked outside the door.

"May I enter?" It was Soro's voice.

When Hiro gave permission, the shoji opened.

Soro entered, closed the door, and bowed. "I came to thank you for sparing Ippen, and for keeping our secrets."

"You thanked us already," Hiro said. "By the way, I think Hatsuko knows."

"I suspect it also," Soro agreed, "but it does not matter. The storm is clearing. By the day after tomorrow, or the next day at the latest, we'll be gone."

"Where will you go?" the Jesuit asked.

"Are you by any chance returning to Iga?" Soro looked hopeful. "I have a message for Hanzō-*sama*. Normally, Ringa would have passed it on, but I don't know the messengers he used."

Hiro considered the list of names he carried in his memory, and the warning those men and women would not receive unless he, too, returned to the ryu—or took the mission on himself.

He made the decision instantly. "Regrettably, we cannot help. Our path does not return to Iga."

Soro nodded thoughtfully. "Then I will take the message there myself."

"What of Ippen?" Father Mateo asked. "Will she go with you?"

"Of course. A priest with an acolyte attracts no more attention than a pilgrim traveling alone." Soro bowed again. "Safe travels, wherever your path may lead."

He opened the door, stepped into the hall, and slid the shoji closed behind him. The floorboards squeaked beneath his feet as he returned to the room next door.

Father Mateo's face collapsed into a sorrow deep enough that Hiro felt it too.

"Where *do* we go from here? These deaths"—he ran a hand through his hair—"they weigh upon my soul."

"What happened here was not your fault."

Father Mateo's eyes grew red. "I should have held my tongue, when he asked about Jesus. I should have known he would not understand. But I never thought . . . it never even occurred to me . . ." He ran his hands through his hair again, lowered them to his lap, and stared at them sadly.

"Mateo!" Hiro snapped.

The Jesuit looked up quickly.

"Were you lying when you told me I was not to blame for Neko's death?"

"Of course not."

"Because we are not merely friends, but brothers," Hiro said, "and brothers do not lie to one another."

After giving the words a moment to sink in, he continued, "You told me, after Neko died, that no man is responsible for the choices of another. I realize now, you were correct. The words are true even when the choices in question hurt the ones we love. You are not responsible for Kenshin's choices. These deaths were not your fault."

"But—"

Hiro didn't let him finish. "However, we now have a choice of our own to make: there are more lives that we can save."

"More lives? What do you mean?"

"Hattori Hanzō needs someone to warn the Iga agents stationed on the travel road that runs along the coast to Edo. With Ringa dead, the duty falls to us."

"Hanzō ordered us to go to the Portuguese settlement at Yokoseura," the priest objected.

"Which we never planned to do anyway," Hiro said, "and now that I realize striking Oda Nobunaga directly would be suicide—"

Relief washed over the Jesuit's face. "I cannot tell you how glad I am to hear that."

"I also realize we can avenge Neko, and prevent unnecessary deaths, by depriving Oda of his targets on the coastal road."

Father Mateo examined his scarred hands. "Saving others will not atone for my actions here. But still, we cannot change the past." He raised his head abruptly. "What will we do about Ana and Gato?"

"Take them with us." Hiro raised an eyebrow. "Unless you want to tell Ana that she has to stay behind."

"Won't her presence make us seem suspicious?"

Hiro slipped into the humble voice he used when playing the role of ronin translator. "My master wishes to see Edo, but refuses to travel without his housekeeper and his beloved cat." He sighed. "These foreigners are strange indeed."

Father Mateo laughed. "That might just work."

"It's a dangerous mission, especially with the daimyō threatening war. I would not blame you if you'd rather wait for me in Yokoseura."

"Brothers do not abandon one another." Father Mateo extended his right hand. "Not now, not ever."

Hiro stared at the Jesuit's hand, confused.

"Never mind." The priest lay down on his futon and covered himself with a quilt. "Let's get some rest. I think we're going to need it."

CAST OF CHARACTERS

(IN ALPHABETICAL ORDER)

Where present, Japanese characters' surnames precede their given names, in the Japanese style. Western surnames follow the characters' given names, in accordance with Western conventions.

Ana – Father Mateo's housekeeper

Anan – the abbot of Myo-in, a Shingon Buddhist temple on Mount Kōya

Bussho – an eight-year-old Buddhist acolyte who lives at Myo-in

Doyu – the former abbot of Myo-in

Endō Hatsuko – a samurai woman from Ōmi Province

Father Mateo Ávila de Santos – a Christian priest from Portugal

Gato – Hiro's cat

Gensho – a Shingon Buddhist priest who lives and studies at Myo-in

Hattori Hanzō* – one of Japan's most famous ninja commanders, and leader of the Iga ryu; born Hattori Masanari, also known as "Devil Hanzō"

Hattori Hiro – a shinobi (ninja) assassin from the Iga ryu, hired by an anonymous benefactor to guard Father Mateo; at times, he uses the alias Matsui Hiro

Ippen – a child

Jorin – a Shingon Buddhist priest specializing in the study of Buddhist laws who lives and studies at Myo-in

Kenshin – a Shingon Buddhist priest and the temple physician of Myo-in

Matsunaga Hisahide* – a samurai warlord who seized Kyoto in June 1565

Myokan – Ringa's student, a teenaged Shingon Buddhist priest who lives at Myo-in

Nichiyo – a Shingon Buddhist priest who lives and studies at Myo-in, on Mount Kōya

Oda Nobunaga* – a samurai warlord who wanted to become the shogun and rule Japan

Ringa – an Iga ninja spy, living undercover as a Shingon Buddhist priest and the temple guardian of Myo-in

Shokai – Kenshin's student, a teenaged Shingon Buddhist priest who lives at Myo-in

Soro – a Buddhist pilgrim visiting Myo-in

* Designates a character who, though fictionally represented, is based upon a historical figure. (All other characters are entirely fictitious.)

JUSANBUTSU

These following thirteen deities (incarnations of the Buddha and bodhisattvas) are among the most important in Shingon practice. "Bosatsu" indicates a bodhisattva, whereas "Nyorai" is a Japanese honorific term for Buddha (or others in the highest ranks of the Buddhist pantheon).

In addition to judging and guiding the spirits of the dead, the jusanbutsu assist and guide the living into the realm of enlightenment. Invocations are made to the jusanbutsu on behalf of the dead on the following days (measured from the date of death):

Fudō Myō-ō (seventh day)
Shaka Nyorai (fourteenth day)
Monju Bosatsu (twenty-first day)
Fugen Bosatsu (twenty-eighth day)
Jizō Bosatsu (thirty-fifth day)
Miroku Bosatsu/Maitreya (forty-second day)
Yakushi Nyorai (forty-ninth day)
Kannon Bosatsu (hundredth day)
Seishi Bosatsu (one year)
Amida Nyorai (two years)
Ashuku Nyorai (six years)
Dainichi Nyorai (twelve years)
Kokuzo Bosatsu (thirty-two years)

GLOSSARY OF JAPANESE TERMS

A

ajari (Sanskrit: ācārya): a Shingon priest who has completed additional study and training beyond ordination, and is authorized to act as a teacher to other Shingon practitioners

B

bodhisattva: a being who has achieved enlightenment and earned the right to enter nirvana, but delays doing so out of compassion in order to help save other suffering beings
Bosatsu: the Japanese transliteration of "bodhisattva"

D

daimyō: a samurai lord, usually the ruler of a province and/or the head of a samurai clan
dōjō: a training hall for martial arts, originally adjunct to or located within a temple

F

Fudō Myō-ō (Sanskrit: Acala): a wrathful but compassionate Buddhist deity, highly venerated among followers of the Shingon sect in Japan
Fugen Bosatsu: a Buddhist deity who symbolizes universal beauty and compassion; he is often considered the counterpart to the wisdom of Monju Bosatsu

futon: a thin padded mattress, small and pliable enough to be folded and stored out of sight during the day

G

goma: the ritual of consecrated fire; an important Shingon Buddhist ceremony performed to help destroy negative thoughts and desires, as well as to offer prayers and requests for blessings

gomadofu: sesame tofu

H

hakama: loose, pleated pants worn over kimono or beneath a tunic or surcoat

hondō: literally, "main hall"; the building in a Buddhist temple where the most important images and objects of worship are enshrined

I

irori: a traditional sunken hearth and fireplace used for heating and cooking in Japanese homes

itadakimasu: literally, "I humbly receive"; a traditional Japanese blessing or expression of thanks before a meal

J

Jizō: also Jizō Bosatsu; one of Japan's most popular *bodhisattvas*, sometimes called "the excuse Buddha" for his great compassion and desire to save all sentient beings

K

kami: the Japanese word for "god" or "divine spirit"; used to describe the gods of Japan's indigenous Shintō faith, the spirits inhabiting natural objects, and certain natural forces of divine origin

katana: the longer of the two swords worn by a samurai (the shorter one is the wakizashi)

kimono: literally, "a thing to wear"; a full-length wraparound robe traditionally worn by Japanese people of all ages and genders

Kirishitan: the Japanese term for "Christian," specifically used to refer to the Roman Catholic priests who came to Japan during the sixteenth and seventeenth centuries

M

Miroku: also Miroku Bosatsu/Maitreya; the "Buddha of the future," who many Buddhists believe will come to save the world at the end of days

miso: a traditional Japanese food paste made from fermented soybeans (or, sometimes, rice or barley)

mon: a traditional Japanese family crest; the symbol of a samurai clan

Monju: also Monju Bosatsu; a Buddhist deity who dispenses wisdom, corrects people's ignorance and delusions, and delivers joy to people by dispensing knowledge

N

nyonindo: the "women's hall" on Mount Kōya where women stayed to pray and meditate during the feudal era, when women were not allowed on the summit of the sacred mountain

Nyorai: a highly respectful Japanese honorific term used to refer to the historical Buddha, one of his incarnations, or those occupying the four highest ranks of the Japanese Buddhist pantheon

O

obi: a wide sash wrapped around the waist to hold a kimono closed; worn by people of all ages and genders

onna-bugeisha: a warrior woman; another term for a female samurai warrior

R

ronin: a masterless samurai

ryu: literally, "school"; shinobi clans used this term as a combination identifier and association name (Hiro is a member of the Iga ryu)

S

sake: also "saké"; an alcoholic beverage made from fermented rice

-sama: a suffix used to show even higher respect than *-san*

samurai: a member of the medieval Japanese nobility, the warrior caste that formed the highest-ranking social class

-san: a suffix used to show respect

Shaka: also Shaka Nyorai; another name for Prince Gauthama Siddhartha, the historical Buddha and the founder of the Buddhist faith

shinobi: literally, "shadowed person"; *shinobi* is the Japanese pronunciation of the word that many Westerners pronounce "ninja," which is based on a Chinese pronunciation of the written characters

shogun: the military dictator and commander who acted as de facto ruler of medieval Japan

shogunate: a name for the shogun's government and/or the compound where the shogun lived

shoji: a sliding door, usually consisting of a wooden frame with oiled paper panels

shuriken: an easily concealed, palm-sized weapon made of metal and often shaped like a cross or star, which shinobi used for throwing or as a handheld weapon in close combat

T

tabi: traditional Japanese socks, which have a separation between the big toe and the other toes, allowing them to be worn with sandals

taikō: a Japanese drum

tanto: a fixed-blade dagger with a single- or double-edged blade measuring six to twelve inches (15–30 cm) in length

tatami: a traditional Japanese mat-style floor covering made in standard sizes, with the length measuring exactly twice its width; tatami usually contained a straw core covered with grass or rushes

tokonoma: a decorative alcove or recessed space set into the wall of a Japanese room; the tokonoma typically held a piece of art, a flower arrangement, or a hanging scroll

tsukemono: literally, "pickled things"; a general term for the pickled vegetables that typically accompany a traditional Japanese meal

U
ume: a Japanese stone fruit (*Prunus mume*) related to both apricots and plums
umeboshi: pickled, salted plums—a Japanese delicacy
umeshu: a traditional Japanese liqueur, or wine, made from fermented ume fruit

W
wakizashi: the shorter of the two swords worn by a samurai (the longer one is the katana)

For additional cultural information, expanded definitions, and author's notes, visit http://www.susanspann.com

ACKNOWLEDGMENTS

I t takes a village to raise a story, as well as a child, and I would be gravely remiss if I did not thank the many people who helped to make this book a reality.

First and foremost: thank you (yes, *you*) for choosing this book and for spending some of your valuable time with Hiro, Father Mateo, and me. I am grateful for the gift of your precious hours.

To Agatha Christie, who wrote the stories that taught me to love mystery as a child. *Trial on Mount Kōya* is my love letter to one of my favorites: her classic *And Then There Were None*.

Thanks to my agent, Sandra Bond, for believing in my books— and in me. Thank you for your sage advice, your editing skills, and your efforts that always go above and beyond the call of duty. You are the best friend and business partner an author could ever hope to have.

Thanks to Dan Mayer, my talented editor, for giving Hiro and Father Mateo the chance to continue their adventures, and for giving me the direction I need to make each novel stronger than it would be if I had to do this on my own. Someday, I hope to toast the books with you in Tokyo.

Thank you to Jill Maxick, Jeff Curry, Nicole Sommer-Lecht, Lisa Michalski, Hanna Etu, and everyone else at Seventh Street Books who contributed to making this book a reality. Each and every one of you is truly special, and I am fortunate to work with such a talented, supportive group of people.

Thank you to the many priests, historians, docents, and volunteers on Mount Kōya and elsewhere in Japan who took the time to share their knowledge and answer my many questions, not only for this book but for each of the Hiro Hattori novels. I hope I have done your culture and your faith the honor and justice they deserve. *Domo arigatō gozaimasu*, and if I have made any errors, I humbly apologize.

Heather, Kerry, Corinne, Julianne, Rae, and Laura—I love you all, and will always be grateful for your constant help, support, and reinforcement. To the Rocky Mountain Fiction Writers' organization and all of its members: you are magic; you are gold; you are my herd. I wish I had space to mention all of my other friends by name, but since I don't, please know, I love you and could not do this—or anything else—without you.

To Michael and Christopher: thank you for helping me keep my dreams in the air and my butt in the chair. And to my family: Paula, Spencer, Robert, Lola, Spencer (III), Gene, Marcie, Bob, Anna, and Matteo—words alone are not enough to thank you for all you are and do.

If you're still reading, thank you again for sticking with me—and this book—to the end. If you like this novel, or any other, I hope you'll consider telling a friend. Your praise and your recommendation are the greatest rewards an author can receive.

ABOUT THE AUTHOR

Susan Spann is the 2015 Rocky Mountain Fiction Writers' Writer of the Year, and the author of five previous novels in the Hiro Hattori / Shinobi Mystery series: *Claws of the Cat*, *Blade of the Samurai*, *Flask of the Drunken Master*, *The Ninja's Daughter*, and *Betrayal at Iga*. She has a degree in Asian studies from Tufts University and a lifelong love of Japanese history and culture. When not writing, she enjoys hiking, photography, and traveling in Japan.